The Journey of Johnny Vincent

By Troy Henriksen

For information, or to order additional copies, please contact:

Beacon Publishing Group
P.O. Box 41573 Charleston, S.C. 29423
800.817.8480| beaconpublishinggroup.com

Publisher's catalog available by request.

ISBN-13: 978-1-949472-37-0

ISBN-10: 1-949472-29-5

Published in 2021. New York, NY 10001.

First Edition. Printed in the USA.

Cover Art by Troy Henriksen

The Journey of
Johnny Vincent

Dedicated to Jim Morrison and Sabine Baby Angel Love. Special thanks to Nick M and Cassie.

Table of Contents

Chapter 1
Good Morning, Good Morning

Johnny Vincent sat on the edge of his unmade bed strumming his folk guitar. He was relentlessly trying to write a song inspired from the 1950s macabre hit song "I Put A Spell On You" by Screaming Jay Hawkins. He replaced the seductive "I put a spell on you" chorus, with his chorus "The world has gone bad, the world has gone bad." He sang it over and over again. He kept his eyes fixed on the corner of the ceiling, as if the song was hiding there. Clicking his teeth together keeping time, he could feel the presence of a new song. The chorus had appeared but the bridge and verses were still hiding. He had the mood, tempo, tone, and idea like a dirty charcoal sketch.

He wanted a song that reconciled himself with the injustice and hardship of life. Relying heavily on instinct and intuition to guide him, he had faith it would be a good one. The ingredients had been brewing in his subconscious for a long time. He wanted something more than a simple pop song, but it may have been out of his reach. Johnny understood the need to push the limits, and perhaps he was too hard on himself. He was still finding his way as a young artist. He needed to be patient, and available for the magic cathartic hour the song would make its way into his dimension. He knew the song was with him and eventually would snag it. Sometimes, on rare and unexpected occasions, a song could fall like an apple from a tree. This was not one of those occasions.

Johnny had been writing songs since the age of eight. Now at 32, he figured he had written around a 100. Some were shitty, some were very good, and a few were legitimate hits that he was proud of. For him, a hit song was when it all came together perfectly—the words, the idea, and melody. He carried a notepad and pen with him, collecting phrases, rhymes, and ideas that could be used. He had a collection of unfinished songs to borrow from, like a junkyard of old cars and parts. What he had learned was that the idea of a song was most important, and usually with a good idea, the song fell into place. He believed songs existed in another realm and the writer just needed the key to that dimension. He often thought songs were gifts from angels.

At times, his loyalty to his muse could be too intrusive and demanding, such as the time he was helping his friend Richard move a couch down three flights of stairs. Richard was an intelligent guy who knew everything there was to know when it came to music. But Richard always needed help of some kind, money, a ride, a cosigner, a storage space, etc. It was never ending. While balancing the couch on the railing of the third floor hallway, Johnny was flashed with the idea and chorus to a catchy pop song. He abandoned the couch and left it hanging. He ran home to his guitar to finish the song. The song was "What Are Good Friends For" and was about his relationship with Richard. The song cost him his friendship. That's the way it is when you tell your problems to a song writer.

The way Johnny saw it was, people, places and things, come and go but songs live on forever. His songs also talked about politics, nuclear war, racism, love and death. Johnny was proud of his songs, even his lousy ones. He felt material success was right around the corner. His next song had to be a hit; his self-worth depended on it.

Johnny wasn't very tall, but tall enough at 5'8. If he wore boots, he got the height he wished he had. He was seen as a loner but never got lonely, thanks to his songs. He rolled his own cigarettes, didn't care for drugs, enjoyed mushrooms once and awhile but preferred the occasional cold beer. A kind soul who would never hurt anyone. People often mistook him for being shy, in which he wasn't, he was just quiet. His mom often said he'd make a good cowboy from a western movie, with a peaceful smile, light brown hair with brown eyes and was usually unshaven. He ate leftover bagels and sandwiches thrown out from the local cafes and made an effort recently to eat more so he didn't get too skinny.

He didn't have a girlfriend and didn't think he'd have one anytime soon. He assumed he didn't meet the checklist of what the local Boston girls looked for in a man his age: a house, a car and a secure job. He dressed himself from the Salvation Army and combined different odd vintage shirts, jackets, and pants. This blend of mix-and-match gave him his own unique style. Deep down, he often felt like something was wrong with himself, he never felt good enough, and his teeth-chattering habit gave him the appearance of always being cold. He chased writing songs, looking for that magic song that would make life full, complete and perfect. It was always just out of reach and right before him.

When he was a teenager and in his early twenties, he played in bands, but never felt cool enough nor did he know how to structure a song. The bands never lasted and he remained a solo act. Over time, he became an intuitive player, or 'wild', as some would say. To make money he did odd jobs, working as a gardener, a carpenter's helper, moving furniture and didn't really like any of these jobs. The only job he ever cherished was working at Flippies Used Records, a place he felt at home at but Flippies went out of business. He never finished high school because of his dyslexia, and school felt like a waste of time, or worse, a punishment. These days, he felt like it was time to hit the road and his time in Boston was coming to an end. He knew this in his heart, but he wasn't sure where to go.

Johnny lived in a 12x14 foot room on the top floor of a third-story triple-decker house in South Boston. It was warm, clean, and empty with hardwood floors. The room had drawn orange shades on one window that diffused the light. The orange curtains created a sunset effect that he cherished. It brought back his earliest memories of form and light. On the wall was a small Mexican 8x10 inch painting on tin, of a man on a horse with a noose around his neck about to be executed. A strange little painting he bought at a yard sale.

The emptiness of the room provided good acoustics, making it perfect for songwriting. When he sang his songs, they echoed throughout the house, even when he tried to be quiet they still could be heard. The house was owned by Dotty K, a retired newspaper editor and speed reader. Dotty spent her days sitting on the main floor of the house at a makeshift coffee bar that extended from her apartment to the hallway. There she drank coffee, smoked cigarettes, and finished a book a day. Dotty was always ready for conversation at any moment. Her last tenant, a carpenter, made this configuration coffee bar for her. Now it was impossible to leave the building without passing her as the make-shift coffee bar was also at the bottom of the house stairs.

Dotty had made a deal with Johnny that if he had a 20 minute coffee break with her each day, she'd reduce his rent, making his room very affordable. He agreed to the deal, as it allowed him to pursue his passion of songwriting. There were no other tenants, just him and Dotty. She knew and enjoyed all his songs. Living is simple and easy when you don't need much.

Sandra Simpson, Johnny's mother, was an old hippy with long gray hair and false teeth. You knew she had false teeth because she wiggled and adjusted them while she talked. When she was young, her tall clumsy, lanky manner was cute and forgivable but at 60, it was plain annoying. She had lost her teeth from an eating disorder, neglect and no dentist visits. Sandra wore too much clothing. She dressed in layers of wool sweaters, cotton shirts, silk scarves, jewelry and buttons that said things like "Keep On Truckin" and "Fuck The Government". You could hear Sandra coming as her jewelry and buttons jangled when she walked. She had constant back pain and was addicted to painkillers, jigsaw puzzles, magical thinking, and cigarettes.

Born in 1950 in Southern California, she was an only child. Her father, Alvin Simpson, was of Swedish descent and worked as an investment banker. Her mother, Mary was of Irish descent and worked as an English teacher. By all accounts, she had a normal childhood. When she was 18, she moved to Hollywood to follow her dreams of becoming an actress, like her favorite movie star Lauren Bacall. During her time there she landed a couple of small parts in a few B movies made for the drive inn, modeled for a tool company calendar and eventually became a go-go dancer. Once her beauty ran out, she became a nurses aid and worked as a caregiver.

Johnny never knew his father and often fell into a depression when he thought about his illegitimacy too much. As a child he would often ask strangers, "Have you seen my father? If you do, tell him I'm looking for him." His mother never told him who his father was, she'd always say he was away working and not to worry. In Johnny's mind, his father was a truck driver or someone who was on the road a lot or worked on an oil rig or in a coal mine. Either way, his mysterious father didn't have time for a family.

Johnny and his mother lived in the same city but across town. She lived with and married an abusive alcoholic Vietnam War Veteran named Stanley Marlon. She had hooked up with Stanley when Johnny was 10 and was still with him. Stanley was a big man of 6'4 with a bald head and beer belly. Stanley also had old, faded tattoos, a rubbery face that looked like someone had put a cigar out on it and was usually drunk.

Johnny's mom and Stanley had a child together, a girl named Candy. Candy was 21 with red hair and freckles and had the posture of a ballet dancer; she'd studied ballet for 10 years but never made it to being a fulltime ballerina. Candy was often in-and-out of rehab because of her substance abuse problems. She also had a baby girl, Priscilla, with her junky boyfriend, Pete. Pete was a likable Irish Catholic boy who sometimes went too far trying to score drugs and was usually in trouble for shoplifting and petty crimes, which was how he supported his and Candy's drug habits. None really understood what Candy saw in him.

Knowing his mother and sister struggled with addictive behaviors, Johnny kept a close watch on his own habits. He didn't want to become an addict too.

Johnny had been up since eight A.M. trying to write the song he had in his head, "The World Has

Gone Bad" and now it was almost noon. He knew he'd better stop so his back wouldn't be sore for his gig tonight at Billy Bob's Bar. He never turned down a gig and had been performing live concerts since he was 16. He had seen child prodigies master the guitar at age 12, they would pass through town playing gigs with great guitarists. Johnny wasn't one of them, he had to work for every note he produced, and most times he felt he made no progress.

For the last 10 years he had been busking on the streets and in the subways in Boston. For the most part he didn't mind playing on the street but it could get tiresome at times, especially in the winter or the cops giving him a hard time. He did his best not to perform cover songs and overcome his stage fright. It was never easy for him to play, he usually got nervous. He also didn't think he was that good of a guitar player or singer, but he was good enough. And even if some thought his style appeared weak, he knew his expression was sincere and honest. The fact that his songs were original set him apart from the rest of the musicians. And no matter what people thought, at least he could say it was his own music, and he knew deep down he was going somewhere, he just hadn't figured out where that somewhere was yet. Johnny put his guitar in its case and started to get ready for his gig. He'd finish his new song later.

Chapter 2
Billy Bob's Bar

Billy Bob's Bar used to be an Irish pub, and before that it was a sports bar, now it was a mix of the two. Located on Mass Ave across from the Charles River going into Cambridge, situated between a bank and ice cream parlor. Billy's had a good sound system making it a desirable place to play. Not much thought had gone into the artwork on the brick walls, old photos of Hollywood movie stars centered around an American flag. The new wooden floors had been waxed to shine and Johnny thought whoever cleaned them did a good job. The stage was three feet off the ground with enough room for three people and a good view of the bar. At full capacity the bar could hold around 200 people and Johnny expected it to be half that tonight. For Johnny this was a good audience, normally he played for small venues of 20 to 50 people. The most people he had ever played for was 1,500 at a summer folk festival.

Billy's Bar had its regular crowd, basic Bostonians who were all diehard loyal fans of either the Bruins hockey team, the Red Sox baseball team, the Celtics basketball team, and the New England Patriots football team. Bostonians are fanatical in their devotion for their teams and have a heavy New England accent when they speak. The accent dropped the R from their speech. Parking the cars sounded like 'pahking the cahs'. Johnny didn't really have the Boston accent, he'd kept the west coast accent, which emphasized the Rs. This always made Johnny somewhat suspect of being an outsider, and to top it off, Johnny didn't really care for sports. He had seen the Red Sox play at Fenway Park but had no interest in the game, however he was in awe of being united with 50,000 people. The grandeur of the Fenway Park was fascinating; it's the oldest ballpark in the country. If Johnny went to a game and it wasn't often, it was to sit in the bleachers, marvel at the lights, green field and organ music that cheered the fans on.

Billy Bar was owned by Billy, a retired policeman, who looked like any ordinary 65 year-old Irish Catholic man, who could pass for an accountant. Billy was 5'10, medium build, alert and sportive. He had reading glasses hanging around his neck, and when he put them on and looked up at you from over the top of them, his ordinariness disappeared. You got the feeling that he'd probably planted a weapon or two. There was an aura to him that gave the impression he felt immune to the law, and the last person you'd want to mess with.

To bring more business to the bar, Billy started now hosting live music events. This was the second time Johnny played there, and he was nervous. Billy had worked out a deal with Johnny where he would play for two hours, and get a free dinner of fish and chips, three drinks, and $50. This worked for Johnny as he needs three gigs a week to survive as a singer-songwriter.

He was happy with the gig at Billy Bob's Bar but he didn't like playing cover songs, he only played them to survive. Outside of open mic nights where original music was appreciated, Johnny knew it was commonly understood that you have to perform cover songs, unless your own songs were so good that they'd take off right away. Even the best of songs had to mature and age like a good wine, they needed to be road worn, played and played and sung to gain the power needed to take wings and fly. Building your own audience was vital for this to happen, and Johnny was still struggling. Last week he played some Chuck Berry, Beatles, and Van Morrison covers. To make the show more fun he slipped in one of his original songs every third song or so. Tonight he wanted to try his new song, "A Lot Like You". The song was about immigration and racism, and poked fun at the polarization taking part in the world today. Johnny felt good about this new song and had high hopes for it. He was convinced it would be a huge seller if he had the right connections in the music business. He took every gig seriously, no matter if it was a hundred people or three, you never knew who could be in the audience.

Johnny finished his fish and chips and drank down the rest of his beer. Burped, licked his lips, wiped his face with a napkin, grabbed his guitar, and approached the stage. A group of six people sat at the table in front of the stage, three guys and three girls. They were all in their early 40s and worked for the city as civil servants. Johnny wouldn't call them rude, but they weren't the type of people he'd hang out with. They were the type people he'd never felt comfortable around. They followed the rules, they did as they were told, they wouldn't think twice of locking you up if ordered. These were the type of people who did well in school, furthered their education, and had rigid parents. They were the quiet and obedient types, which could be dangerous.

It was now nine P.M. and Johnny had agreed to play until 11 P.M. On his setlist for tonight, he included his own song "No More Room To Be Weird ". He purposely chose it for the ordinary people in front of him, he knew ordinary people made the best Nazis. Earlier in the day, Johnny had changed the strings on his 1969 Gibson J200 folk guitar. The new strings gave the guitar a full, rich and crisp sound, making it a pleasure to play. For a good luck mojo, Johnny used a Pink Floyd guitar pick and flowered guitar strap, a Christmas gift from Candy. He wore his usual performance attire: a white tuxedo jacket, jeans, and loafers. He had bought the tuxedo jacket at the Salvation Army; it's been his favorite jacket since and he wears it all the time. Johnny has 25 songs on his setlist tonight, and a note that read 'be calm and cool like Neil Young', even though he didn't really like Neil, but he admired his confidence on stage.

Johnny took to the stage, feeling cool, calm, and smooth as he delivered each song with elegance. He wasn't nervous anymore, and this excited him. Everyone appeared to be having a good evening as they ate, drank and laughed. He noticed most of the people listened to him and clapped after each song, except the table of civil servants; they didn't acknowledge him at all and talked while he played. Normally this would have been ok, but since they were so close to the stage, it annoyed Johnny. Around the fifth cover song, Johnny decided it was time for one of his originals.

"I would like to thank everyone for coming out tonight. Please remember to tip the bartenders and servers. Thank you, Billy, for having me, I really appreciate it. My name is Johnny Vincent. I have

CDs for sale if anyone is interested. Here's a new song I wrote called "A lot Like You," He said into the microphone and started to play a simple G chord and his teeth started clicking to the beat, he began to sing...

I am watching an uprising, it's live on TV
Should not be surprising people in misery
We all want a second chance a better tomorrow
Maybe we can dance get money to borrow

I am just like you oh no no I am not like you
Oh yeah I am just like you

We all have our hope and dreams and desire
To find a wife a kid and one day to retire
To hang out with best friends laugh at jokes told
Go home to someone special to hold

I am just like you oh no no, I am not like you
Oh yeah yeah I am just like you

You may be from Canada Australia Brazil too
Hawaii Africa USA or the zoo, I am just like you
Now I'm afraid of the dark, you'll never see me cry
I go jogging in the park I don't know why

But that ain't true no no no I am not like you

The Journey of Johnny Vincent

Yeah yeah yeah I am just like you

You maybe be a Muslim, Catholic or a Jew
I'm not like you, yeah yeah yeah I'm just like you

No no no I am not like you
Yeah yeah yeah I'm just like you

"That was a song I wrote about racism and the immigration problem, I hope you liked it," He told the crowd. There was no answer and hardly anyone clapped, but more noticeable was the group of civil workers who didn't stop talking.

"Play something we know!" shouted a woman at the civil servant table.

"Yeah!" said the guy across from her.

"Hotel California!" yelled another woman at the same table.

Johnny looked over at Billy, who gave him the evil eye, motioning to do another cover song. What the fuck, I just played five cover songs, I do one original and they get on my case, He thought. He took a deep breath, dismissed the negative thoughts, and strummed a few chords and decided to give them what they wanted. He started playing...

On a dark desert highway cool wind in my hair
The smell of colitas rising up in the air

Up ahead in the distance I saw a shimmering light
My head grew heavy my sight grew dim
I had to stop for the night

There she stood in the doorway
I heard the mission bell
I was thinking to myself this could be heaven or hell
Then she lit up a candle and showed me the way
There were voices down the corridor I heard them
say

Welcome to the Hotel California...

As the song hit the chorus, a handful of people started
singing and clapping. Johnny couldn't go on with it
anymore. He bursted out in anger and started yelling
at the people at the front table as his teeth continue to
chatter, "Fuck you, people, you all suck! I'm out of
here!" Johnny kicked the mic over, causing the PA
to create a rumbling of booming feedback. "I can't
take another minute of this," he said, shaking as he
walked off stage. Johnny left through the side door
and went out onto the street into the warm late
summer air.

"Oh shit," he murmured to himself walking along
the side of the building. "Why, why did I do that? Oh
fuck, fuck, fuck." With his chattering, he realized
he'd ruined another gig because of his temper on

stage. He stopped and went back inside to see if he could save the gig. He saw Billy and approached him, ready to apologize.

"Get your shit and get out of here now and never come back," demanded Billy.

"But but, please, I am sorry," begged Johnny.

"No," said Billy, "get out now."

The six civil servants at the table looked on in surprise. They couldn't understand why Johnny had become so enraged and stormed off. Johnny got his guitar and approached the people at the table.

"I'm sorry, I need to sing my songs. I'm trying to create new music and you people are so empty and meaningless, glib and just dumb. Goodnight," Johnny told them as he was leaving.

"Out!" yelled Billy.

As Johnny was leaving, a cute girl wearing old jeans, who looked like Liza Minelli with short black hair approached him.

"That was great!" she said to him.

"Great?" Johnny gasped.

"It was so raw and real. I thought it was a performance, like part of your act."

"No, I'm afraid it wasn't an act. I was really upset," Johnny sighed.

"I can understand. Your song "A Lot Like You" was good. I don't want to hear songs that are 20 years old."

"Gee, thank you. That's really nice of you to say so." This excited Johnny and gave justice to the evening, here was his chance. "You wanna join me for a drink somewhere else?"

"No, next time. I'm with my girlfriend tonight."

"Girlfriend?" Said Johnny hiding the disappointment.

"Yes, she's sitting over there," she said, pointing to her girlfriend.

"Ok, thanks for the nice words, see you around," He said.

Johnny packed up his guitar and CDs and left the bar. Enough of that place, he thought. He began walking home towards the Charles River on Mass Ave. He felt good to be out of Billy's even though he knew his temper got the best of him. It's against the rules to lose your cool on stage. He knew it was wrong but still, he had a perverse pleasure from speaking his mind. The compliment from the Liza Minelli looking girl boosted his spirits and made him feel proud. He thought about her as he walked, she was attractive, he desired her and liked her look: big brown dark eyes, white rosy cheeks, and cherry red lips, and not too tall with a full body. Gazing into the stars glowing in the galaxy above, he heard a new song. A song about the girl and the six civil servants, he began to sing to himself.

The Journey of Johnny Vincent

Vampires steal your purpose
I could get it back
Negotiate a deal
Turn fiction into fact
You plant your flowers on Venus
Glued to the TV set
Looking for some kind of meaning
You haven't found it
All the stars shine up above
Two girls in love

Leaving the grief behind him and happy to discover a new song, he forgave himself for losing temper on stage. After a minute of walking he came upon a bar with a luminous blue neon sign that beamed Arrowhead Bar. The bar looked like it belonged in a junkyard. It had one window with a rackety monster air conditioner hanging out of it working at full load buzzing away. The bar was made of clapboard and tin with weeds growing up the sides of it. Thank God those oppressive heat waves of August are gone, Johnny thought.

Chapter 3
Arrowhead Bar

Johnny opened the black steel door that had a faded Boston Red Sox bumper sticker on it. He was immediately greeted by the air conditioned cool air, leaving the warm summer night behind as the heavy door swung shut, loud and hard. Everyone turned to see Johnny enter and quickly went back to drinking. To the right was a horseshoe bar and a big flat-screen TV on the wall. The lights were low and eight to 12 people were elbowed at the bar. It was quiet and calm inside, and the TV gave a campfire glow as the people drank and smoked. A few people talked about the new graphics scrolling across the bottom of the TV with the latest news events. The new graphics were introduced after 9/11. Flat-screen TVs were everywhere now and they were stuck on one channel, the news. It was like no matter what you did, you couldn't escape the news or the war on terror. It was everywhere, whether you're getting a muffler fixed, buying a donut, pumping gas, getting a tooth pulled, waiting for a bus, getting a haircut or a blood test, you're constantly updated on the war on terror, thanks to new graphics and flat-screen TVs. People were hypnotized by the new double mode of news. It was a new way of administering propaganda into society and keeping people afraid. The people at the bar had found their solution to the constant flow of bad news, good old fashion drinking.

The drunk heads at the bar turned and looked at Johnny coming in with his guitar across his back as he shuffled towards them.

"Hey, the entertainment is here," heckled a voice from the bar.

"I ain't no entertainer, that's for sure. I'm a singer-songwriter," Johnny declared while also trying to be friendly.

"Can I get a beer?" Johnny asked and took a seat.

"What are you having?" the bartender quipped.

"Uuh, Rolling Rock, if you got it?"

"Bottle or tap?"

"Bottle, please."

Johnny took a swig of his beer and wished for a cigarette. He fidgeted about as the TV announced a news flash, all conversation stopped and all eyes went on the TV.

A school shooting has happened in Nebraska when one student opened fire on classmates, going on a rampage with an AK-47. 12 people are dead, 10 students and two teachers. The police have the gunman in custody now as we speak.

"Yes, it's a real tragedy that's taken place here at Jones Academy High School in Belmont Nebraska," Commented the reporter. "People are saying the suspect had a history of mental illness but no one expected him to do this."

Everyone moaned and groaned with disgust and disbelief. Instantly they all started weighing in with opinions. One guy, who had a leather jacket and tattoos on his fingers and a shaved head looked at Johnny and said, "What the fuck is this world coming to? I was safer in the joint." Johnny looked at him, knowing the joint was another name for prison and he thought he'd better be careful with this guy.

"Psychos, psychos, and more psychos," added the convict and continued, "probably some nerd kid on medication, playing video games and eating Fruit Loop cereal. Who knows, maybe a teacher was fucking the kid."

"Shut the fuck up," the bartender demanded.

"You never know who the hell you're dealing with, anyone can show up and shoot the place up," the convict mocked.

The bartender looked at Johnny and said, "I hope that's a guitar you got in there."

The convict laughed as he began to tell a story, "There was a kid in Japan who cut his father's head off and then raped his mother. The kid put the head in a bag and brought it to school and bragged about it. I've seen guys in prison as sick as that."

A guy with a beard and glasses joined the discussion, "They call that the Oedipus complex."

"The Oedipus what?" the bartender asked.

The bearded man explained, "The Oedipus complex is when the child wants to fuck the mother and kill the father."

"Get the fuck out of here with that Freud shit!" the convict cringed. "If the teacher or janitor had a weapon, they might've killed the guy before he shot all those kids. Damn shame."

"The second amendment, right to bear arms," replied the bearded man, "they got a do away with that, get the guns off the streets. Who knows, maybe it's a false flag to do just that."

"What the fuck is that?" the bartender barked.

"A covert operation designed to deceive. The deception creates the appearance of a particular party, group, or nation being responsible for some activity, disguising the actual source of the responsibility. It sets the enemy up to be attacked and it makes you look like a victim defending yourself. It's a real coward move, like in Vietnam, the Tonkin

Bay incident. We attacked our battleships and blamed it on the Vietnamese." the bearded man explained.

The bartender looked at him confused and scratched his head.

"Yeah, even 9/11," Johnny said.

"Enough of that bullshit in here. I won't have it," the bartender ordered.

"Yeah, right, none of that conspiracy shit. You get rid of guns, then only criminals will have them, ain't gonna do nothing. They keep coming through the gangs, the Mexicans, the Crips and Bloods, having a gun is as American as apple pie," the convict stated.

"They should send that kid who shot up the school straight to the electric chair and fry his ass," the bartender chided.

Johnny looked a little puzzled, he seemed to be the only person these people wanted to talk to, and he didn't know them, but he was doing his best to show them he was paying attention. Johnny was reminded that throughout his life if he's quiet, he may look smarter than he is. People often gave him the benefit of the doubt. People know only what you want them to know, but they seem to trust and like Johnny. Perhaps this would be a good quality for a priest.

"So what kind of songs do you write?" the bearded man asked Jonny.

"I do all kinds: drinking songs, songs about parties, world wars, plastic hips, loneliness, racism. I write songs about everything," Johnny told him.

"Good answer," the convict said, and continued, "you do any prison songs like 'Folsom Prison Blues'?"

"No, I wouldn't venture to write about something like that not having been in Prison," Johnny explained.

"Johnny Cash was never in prison and he wrote a song about killing a man for fun," the convict said as he swirled his beer in the glass.

"Poetic license," the bearded man added. "Johnny Cash, he had solidarity with the average man."

"Sing us something," the convict demanded, and continued, "write us a song now. Set us up with some shots. Do you want a shot? Come on get to work and write us a song now. Stop fucking around."

"Yeah, go ahead," the bartender piped in as he poured shots for the three of them.

"Here's to the land of the free," the bearded man offered as they all did their shots of whiskey.

"I was just playing at Billy Bob's Bar and they wanted me to sing 'Hotel California'. I couldn't handle it," Johnny confessed.

"You do that here and you got a problem," the convict said. "Come show us what you got. Sing us a Johnny Cash song"

Johnny took out his guitar and tuned it up. He played a few chords and settled on a D chord. Strumming lightly, he began to search for words, "Let's see…"

I severed my father's head
while he was laying in his bed

The men at the bar laughed. Johnny continued

I brought with me to school
Everybody thinks I'm real cool
But I am waiting to wait on the electric chair
I did my mother from behind
Just cause it crossed my mind
Now I am waiting for the electric chair

"That's a weird song but why not, if Johnny Cash shot a man just to watch him die? Then you can sing your killer song too" the convict scoffed, and said, "But I doubt it will be a hit. Do you play on the street in the square? I think I seen you play there"

"Oh yea I do," Johnny admitted.

"Europe is the place to be," the bearded man told Johnny.

"I was in Paris with my wife last year," the bartender recalled, and continued, "they were making good money on the streets, the performers."

"Really?" Johnny asked.

"Sure thing. The Europeans have it in the culture to respect the arts. It's tradition," the bartender stated.

"Maybe I should go there," Johnny wondered.

"Yeah and if you get sick, just go to the hospital and it's free. I thought I was having a heart attack and my wife brought me to the hospital. They did a scan on me and kept me for eight hours. Guess how much it was," quizzed the bartender . Everyone stared blankly at him.

"Nothing, zero. It cost about eight dollars for the paperwork. Here in the States, it would have been about $15,000," the bartender stated.

"I wanna go there," Johnny decided.

The convict pushed Johnny, "Sing us some more songs dude and give us some more shots, set 'em up!"

Johnny happily agreed to play and sang his best drinking song "Poor Poor Me, Pour Me Another Drink". They all liked his song and encouraged him to keep playing. After about an hour of drinking and singing all his hits, Johnny decided to leave to go see his mother for a late night visit. He thanked everyone for the good time, and on his way out, the bartender yelled "Go play in Paris, you'll do good."

Johnny shrugged his shoulders, and said, "Why not."

Chapter 4
Visiting Mother

Johnny walked up the steps leading to his mother's apartment. He knocked on the door and waited on the stoop. She lived on the first floor of a Victorian brick row house in Beacon Hill Boston, a three-room apartment subsidized by the State. Affordable housing was rare in this part of town. Beacon Hill is one of the richest and prettiest neighborhoods of Boston and home to the Gold Dome State House that overlooks the Boston Commons. One of the oldest cities in the country with small cobblestoned streets aligned with gas lanterns. Nice apartments if you can get one, Johnny's mother waited on a list for six years and qualified for it due to back injury disability. He knocked again. "Hey, open up, Mom! It's me, Johnny,"

Looking through the window into the apartment, he could see his mother slumped over asleep in a lazy boy chair. Next to her on a table were boxes of jigsaw puzzles, medications, and a super gulp drink cup from 7-Eleven. On the wall were 60s posters: the Summer Of Love, Easy Rider, The Doors, and Rolling Stones. Johnny could see the TV on and continued to knock. "Come on open up!" he growled. With sleepy eyes and a tired face, his mother opened the door in her nightgown.

"Hello, Johnny, is it you? Come in, oh the air feels so good," she yawned, taking a deep breath.

"Hello mom, how are you?" he asked.

"I'm good," she responded wearily.

Johnny entered the house, his mother stayed at the door. A passing truck took her attention as she surveyed the street.

"What is it?" Johnny asked.

His mother read the sign on the truck. Maggie's Pastries, she thought, what does this name mean?

"What is it?" Johnny asked again.

"Oh nothing," she said and closed the door. "I was just doing a Monet painting puzzle of lily pads and I fell asleep. It's my new puzzle, don't you love it? You know Monet was a gardener."

"It's a great puzzle, mom, really nice. I was passing by and just wanted to say hello."

"Thanks, that's nice of you. Cosmos is missing and Candy went to rehab. I was depressed and my back hurt. I think I might have taken too much medication. I fell asleep watching the news."

"That's good about Candy. It's about time she went back. I hope she gets the help she needs this time," Johnny insisted. "What about baby Priscilla?"

"We have her here until your poor sister gets out of treatment. She's such an adorable baby. She's sleeping right now."

"Isn't this Candy's fourth rehab?"

"Yes, it is, but this one has a 12 step program, and they treat addiction like a disease...because it is a disease, like cancer."

"Like a disease? What are you saying?" Johnny wondered.

His mom continued, "Yes, a disease like cancer or diabetes. Candy can't help it, as soon as she has a drink or a line of crystal, she can't stop. It's not her fault. Back in the 60s, we were having fun taking LSD and smoking grass. We were into peace, love and changing the world. Now it's really ugly, the drugs are very dangerous and everyone has a gun. There have been hundreds of drug overdoses, people are dropping like flies. I'm very happy you don't have this disease, they say it runs in the family." she told him.

Johnny felt the need to share, "I never wanted to use drugs but now and then I would like to. I have my songs and that is more important to me. Candy always wanted to dance and do ballet. She is going to have to find that passion again to beat her addiction, you remember, she was so good at dancing when she was little. She spent so many hours practicing. Yes, she will find that desire again and I will help her. And what about Cosmos?"

"I looked everywhere. He may have gone out the window two days ago," she said as she picked up the A3 paper with a photo of Cosmos on it and handed it to Johnny.

Johnny looked at the photo of a black and white cat sitting in a white wicker chair. The top of the photo read Lost Cat - Please call 617-726-7453.

"I think cats are psychopaths contracted to kill mice. It's like they are a hired gun and will play and torture the poor mouse for fun. Dogs, on the other hand, are pure feelings and emotions, a man's best friend. If a dog kills anything, they put him down," Johnny stated to his mother. He's thought quite hard about his feelings towards cats.

"Not Cosmos, Johnny," she confided. "He has direct contact with the angels, even sees spirits. You know The Egyptians believed cats were magical and brought good luck. After all, they have nine lives and that means rebirth, you know. I need to make more photocopies and hang them up in the neighborhood, but I can't get the printer to work. Maybe you can fix it? You were always good at that."

Johnny entered the salon to try and fix the printer. On the floor were about 20 boxes of puzzles stacked on top of each other. Some of the puzzles had been finished, and glued into frames to look like works of art. On the table was a big black Canon printer next to a half-eaten pizza. He opened the lid to the printer to see if it needed ink. While doing so he heard the front door slam. He looked up to see his detested stepfather Stanley invading the room. Stanley was still wearing a long outdated 80s Members Only jacket that should have been thrown out years ago, and a scaly cap on his bald head. How could my mother be with this guy Johnny thought. He appeared to be a little drunk, as usual, and started in with an aggressive tone of intimidation right away towards Johnny. Stanley always seemed to have gotten up on the wrong side of the bed and was at war with something.

"Hey Johnny, how you doing?" Stanley slurred.

"Pretty good, I guess. Trying to fix the printer. Cosmos is missing, got to print up some missing posters," He told him.

Stanley looked at Johnny trying to make eye contact but Johnny kept focused on the printer hoping he would bug off. The drunk continued "Cosmos hit the road. He's the only one with brains around here. He couldn't take the chaos and split. Oh, and by the way, there's no ink. The last time you were here you printed for hours and used all the paper!"

"No, it wasn't that much, I just printed some of my songs. I had to submit the music for copyright, so I needed to print them," Johnny said, fuming as his teeth started to chatter.

"Printing songs?" Stanley exploded, and continued, "Ha! I told you, you ain't gonna make any money from your music in Boston, it's not the place, you must go to Nashville. I know, I played bass guitar in the band Molly Circus Caravan . I toured with them for 12 gigs, then I met your mother, and fell in love, and we had Candy."

"12 gigs," Johnny retorted with a sarcastic tone, placing the top of the printer back on and sitting down at the table.

"Yeah that's right, 12 gigs and got two co-writes on two songs on their best album "Sun Money". At least it's better than you've ever done." Stanley taunted.

Johnny's teeth continued to chatter, he became afraid.

Stanley continued his bullying. "If it wasn't for Agent Orange fucking up my hand, I would have stayed with them and had a good career as a musician. I should have gone to Canada and avoided the draft, but no, I was a good American and served my country. Now somebody get me a beer."

Johnny's mother looked at the digital clock and informed them it was 11:11. She then shrieked, "We need to do a prayer right now for Candy. The energetic gateway is open to the angels. Please, universe, bring back Cosmos and help Candy, please." Johnny and Stanley sighed. They knew what it meant and were used to her spiritual quirks. Stanley started up again with his opinions,

"Candy has no will power. She's weak. They say it's a disease, what a cop-out. I've never heard of such bullshit in my life." Stanley blurted out.

Johnny became more nervous and angrier. "You know Stanley, what kind of a father are you? Of course, she has problems, anybody who has had to put up with you and your fucking bullshit would be screwed up. You're a fucking jerk!"

"You little shit, I ought to give you one of these!" Stanley said, holding up his right fist. "Don't even tempt me. I swear I'll knock you right across town you little bastard. You've got some nerve. I don't know where you came from, who your daddy was, but I can see he was a no-good loser."

Johnny's mother jumped in, demanding, "Stanley stop it! Please stop it! You are going to wake the baby."

Johnny gave him a mean look but knew he was no physical match and slowly backed down as his teeth continued to chatter. "Fuck you, Stanley!" he shouted and picked up his guitar and stormed out.

Johnny caught the 33 bus home. He sat by an open window and felt the cool evening air passing through the bus. He's always loved the bus. As a child, when he lived in San Francisco, he and his mother would ride the bus to pass time. Not having much money for activities, like an amusement park or movies, they rode the bus for fun, and it was free. Sometimes they could ride all day through San Francisco. They'd look out the window, watching different people get on and off. Johnny enjoyed the comforting sound of the diesel engine, it was almost hypnotic at times.

Johnny first realized he didn't have a father on one of these bus rides. He would see other children with parents, a mommy and daddy, as he understood it. Who were these dads? How did you get one? he'd think. Some days he'd wait by the door for his dad to come home. Johnny thought maybe his dad wasn't around because he wasn't good in school or not tall enough or had the wrong face, head, or body. He couldn't figure out why he didn't have a father. Yet, he kept expecting one to show up, like he'd to come to the house door one day, like Santa Claus. But the father he wanted never came home.

Stanley arrived when Johnny was eight. He couldn't wait to do things that fathers and sons did, like fishing, camping, playing baseball. Instead, Stanley made no effort and sat around drinking beer and giving orders all day. The nights when Stanley got drunk were nights from hell, and they seemed to go on forever. You could hear him fighting with the phone like an animal on the other side of the house. He would flare up about his war experience in Vietnam. Johnny would lie in bed, frozen in fear, hoping he wouldn't come into the room when he was drunk. Some nights, Stanley would make Candy get out of bed and demand she sings songs at three A.M. in the morning. Songs like "When The Lion Sleeps Tonight" or "The Star Spangled Banner". Candy would then go to the school the next day, foggy and in a blur. She couldn't be present at school and looking back Johnny could see she was depressed and non-responsive. Johnny wanted to help his sister but was helpless. He was consumed by trying to pay attention in school and overwhelmed by feelings of failure as his grades suffered. Stanley's drinking bouts and dyslexia got the best of him. Johnny had no choice but to quit and didn't think school was for him anyway.

The bus continued on its route into south Boston. Johnny watched the students and couples bump and sway as the bus drove over the potholes. He thought about the horrible evening he had just had. He knew he would not be able to play at Billy Bob's Bar again, but at the same time, it was a relief to not go back. He also thought about how visiting his mother was a mistake. He often wondered why he even went there. The longest he had gone without speaking to her was six months, and he was proud of it. Maybe it's time to just move on and forget about her, he thought.

Johnny sat watching couples, get on and off the bus, he felt odder and alone as the bus continued. Dating websites were a new thing and he thought it was foolish, but at moments like this he began to think about in a positive way. He wondered "should I get a computer and learn about the information highway and meet a girl that way?" It had been three years since him and Jill Summers broke up and he missed her. He'd slept with different women since then, but nothing had real value in terms of a meaningful relationship. He was good looking enough to get lucky at the nightclubs in Kenmore Square, but he wanted a steady girl. Jill had believed in him, she was fun and loving and very cute, but only to a certain point. They thought they were a good couple, but Johnny wasn't going to give up being a songwriter, and she wanted him to get a regular job. He was able to talk his way into being a manager at a sunglasses store, hoping it would please her, but finally it was too painfully boring and soul-crushing for him. He sincerely did his best to conform but couldn't take it. The regular job experience did inspire him to write one of his best songs "I Know You Did Your Best". All these thoughts swam through his brain, as he sat on the bus, with his teeth-chattering, as they drove through the city.

Once Johnny got home, he went straight upstairs to his room and took out his guitar. No matter how bad things were, he always had his guitar to hold and play. Johnny reflected on his incident with Stanley. If I am to have the burden of knowing such a person, at least may I profit a song from such a horrible encounter, he thought. Johnny then began to sing.

Here he comes
Just crashing through the front door
All the kids run and hide, they've seen it all before
One behind the couch, one underneath the bed
Popa when he's drinking, he's crazy in the head

Johnny found pleasure in this new song and he could tell it would be good, he'd earned it. There was justice for the day if a song has arrived. At least now he could sleep well knowing the horrible evening gave him a song. He lived for the day in the future when his songs would pay his bills. And that would bring all the cash and prizes, a happy relationship, a house, a car and maybe, a son of his own. Johnny knew for certain he would make a good father one day. If there was any value to his existence he knew it was to be guarded in order to share it.

Chapter 5
Coffee with Dotty

On a level from one to 10, on how demanding coffee with Dotty was, Johnny gave it a six. Most of the time, he saw it as an exercise in patience, and enjoyed Dotty's stories about old Boston. Dotty knew all the details of the Boston Strangler, the Coconut Grove fire, where Edgar Allen Poe rented a room, and she told him she'd once met Malcolm X while working downtown at a hotel. Johnny paid Dotty $200 a month for the room and did his best to have a coffee or tea with her each day, as agreed upon. Normally, she had instant coffee ready or a very boring type of generic tea. Dotty was energetic, feisty, and a little gal of 78'. She reminded Johnny of the granny on The Beverly Hillbillies TV show.

Dotty was a true Bostonian and had ancestry as far back as the early settlers from England. She had worked for 30 years as a proofreader for the Boston Herald and had been retired for 15 years. She spent most of her time drinking coffee, speed reading paperback novels, and chain smoking Kent 100 cigarettes. She was always hunkered down at the bottom of the stairs at her makeshift coffee bar or command post as Johnny liked to call it. Before Johnny, there was a Polish carpenter who lived in the house. The carpenter knocked down a wall from Dotty's apartment to make the bar, extending it out into the hallway. It was impossible to leave the building without passing by Dotty. She read murder mysteries, biographies, the classics, and more, but never romance. She had stated on different occasions to Johnny that romance novels were boring, and by writing about love, it killed the romance. Johnny never really understood what that meant, he often thought about it, especially since he had never written a love song.

Dotty was a widow, her husband Frank, had died of a heart attack 10 years ago. Together they had two children and for some unknown reason, the children didn't talk to her anymore. It was rumored Dotty had inherited a large sum of money from her late husband and the kids were always trying to get it. Frank was part of the Gloucester School of Painting, and painted landscapes, portraits, and seascapes. His paintings hung throughout all of the house and you could still smell the oil paint. Dotty kept his studio just the way it was when he worked and nobody was allowed to go in. Johnny sometimes felt his ghost was busy painting in there, he enjoyed looking at the paintings and thought they resembled Winslow Homer but with a touch of Key West. The paintings reminded Johnny of his happiest childhood memories, like taking the train to Revere Beach with his mother. They had only been to the beach around four times and it had morphed into one good beach memory.

"Good morning, Dotty. How are you? Everything ok?" Johnny asked.

"It's ok. I slept all night and just started a new book," She told him, putting on the hot water kettle.

"But you start a new one every day."

"Well, almost every day. When I was younger, I could read a book a day. Now I need about two days."

"What's this new one about?"

Dotty held up the book. "It's about an army brat who grows up to be a serial killer."

"What's an army brat?" He asked.

Dotty slightly surprised that he didn't know calmly explained "An army brat is a child whose parents belonged to the military and the child normally moved around a lot, wherever the parent or parents were stationed."

"Is it a good book?"

"Yes, it's interesting how the child grows up to be a cold-blooded killer."

"I don't know how you can like books like that." He stated.

"The killer mind is something we cannot be afraid to look at. We must deal with it and understand

44

what makes a person so crazy to kill, like the hijackers with box cutters, hijacking planes and crashing them into the World Trade Towers. For example, Osama bin Laden, the terrorist, if he was born in the suburbs of the US, would he be a serial killer? It's interesting to find what causes people to become obsessed and violent."

The water came to a boil and she filled the mugs, stirring in the instant coffee and sliding one across the table for Johnny.

"And you, how was your night? You played, didn't you?"

"It was horrible, not very good," Johnny confessed.

"Why?"

"I played at Billy Bob's Bar. It didn't go well. I just can't do cover songs. The people weren't very respectful either. I tried, but I just can't."

Dotty looked at Johnny, puzzled, "What is a cover song?"

Johnny just as surprised as she just was, about him not knowing what an army brat, explained. "Cover songs are songs that I didn't write. I only want to do my own songs, the ones I wrote."

"That's good. You need to sing your songs, we need original music," Dotty said and lit a cigarette.

"I ended up storming off the stage and made a scene. I can't play there again. I screwed up, kicked the microphone stand over and told the people to go fuck themselves."

"Oh, Johnny, that's not good," Dotty paused. "Did you compromise your integrity?"

"In the end, no, I mean I couldn't take it anymore. I would like to be able to sing cover songs, but I just can't. I wish I could just be simple and easy about it, but I feel divided if I do. I feel broken and unfair, and then feel physically sick."

"We all have our limits Johnny, but you need to work on your temper, maybe."

"But, Dotty, now I feel like a loser. I'm 32 and I have nothing and my music is going nowhere. I can't get on the radio or a decent record deal with a label and now everyone is getting onto the internet where the music's free."

"But, Johnny, you have it. You're an artist."

"You think I'm an artist , for real" He wondered out loud.

"I sure do kid, and I know, I've lived with an artist for 40 years, a real one, a painter." She continued, "Not some silly pop star either, but someone like you, who is dedicated to their craft. You are a poet Johnny and a troubadour."

"What's a troubadour?" He asked.

"They were folk singing poets from France, in the medieval times around the 11th to 13th centuries."

"I've never heard of them."

"You are exactly like them. Like you they spent all the time writing their folks songs of the day, traveling from village to village. They even became knighted and famous."

"What happened to them?"

"I don't know, maybe the Black Plague came and wiped that period out and made the way for the Renaissance, or maybe the church did away with them" She offered.

"I was thinking of going to Paris to play. And now I know I am. Thanks, Dotty. I can't keep playing around here, I must do something. I can't take another winter here, it's too lonely here for me, it's time to carry on. Like this troubadour tradition you are talking about."

"Just keep following your dreams and you will find your way."

"Last night, I met a guy who told me that street performers can get $100 a day playing in the streets of Paris."

"If you need to go, then go! Just go and the universe will follow and provide. All you need to do is have faith." She advised.

Dotty started to sing a French song, "Des yeux qui font baisser les miens, un rire qui se perd sur sa bouche." She reminisced "My husband, Anthony, used to sing this song. It's an Edith Piaf song. It was very popular in the 50s and on the radio all the time. She had such a beautiful voice. She began singing on the streets of Paris as a child."

"Is she still alive?"

"No, she died too," Dotty paused and thought of her husband. "But you know, Edith Piaf did not believe in death. She believed we just went to another dimension and our consciousness went with us and all our ancestors will be there to greet us. It's just part of our journey."

"That's a nice thought" Johnny mused. He didn't know what he believed.

"That's what I always believed too, but sometimes I lose faith and get tired." Dotty stated.

"I can sell my Fender guitar and buy a ticket to Paris. Yes, that's what I can do." Johnny said with enthusiasm.

Dotty shook her head in agreement, lit another cigarette, and said, "Just tell me when you go, and don't worry about the room, it will be here when you get back."

"Thanks, Dotty, I think I won't be leaving for a few days. I must see what money I can get."

Dotty picked up her book, took a drag off her cigarette and placed it in the ashtray and began to read. Their coffee was over for today.

Chapter 6
Selling the Fender guitar

The year was 1979 and Johnny was eight-years-old. The British supergroup Bad Company had a hit song called "Rock And Roll Fantasy". The song played on the radio all the time and was about a boy named Johnny who gets his first guitar and becomes a famous rock and roll star. Johnny naturally thought the song was about him, and for him. When he would hear the song, he felt as though he was levitating with joy, it made him happy beyond belief and he truly believed the singer was singing directly to him. He would play air guitar and sing to the song whenever he heard it.

He begged his mother to get him a guitar. Around this time his mother took him to the Sears Shopping Store to get new school clothes. He saw a guitar in the music section. He fell in love with it right away, a 1971 Harmony acoustic guitar. It was made the same year he was born, and he had to have it. Johnny's mother bought it for him as an early Christmas gift.

A friend of Johnny's mother, who played guitar for Janis Joplin, or so he said, taught Johnny to play the chords. The first chord he learned was E. He learned it while listening to Hank Williams and Johnny Cash songs. Johnny noticed these singers built a lot of their songs around the E chord. These songs were simple and meaningful country songs that Johnny found easy to play only after a month of practice. The E chord resonated like the ohm frequency of Buddhist monks chanting. The vibration carried a peaceful feeling in his heart. He could hold the guitar like a loved one.

Next he learned to play the G chord and some Chuck Berry songs. Berry's songs had a busy energy with a backbeat. Not only that, each song also had a little novel written in them. Then he learned the C chord and Otis Redding songs. Redding's slow soulful ballads gave Johnny an understanding of the heart's groove and how it cried out to be loved. From there on, he got the D chord, which gave him a simple downbeat approach with a broader possibility for a melody. He could play any poem he had written to a D chord.

The A chord presented more possibilities than he knew what to do with, he could write one chord songs all day. Finally, leaving the hardest chords for last, the B and Am chords. Johnny thought these chords invoked a different tone, a darker shade and mood lending toward the sound of danger or tragedy.

He knew dark stories could be expressed with these sounds. He was finding his palette.

Later on Johnny traded in the Harmony guitar and for a Marten Folk guitar. He had saved a little money to buy it along with the value of the trade. Then as time went on, he traded the Marten for the Gibson he has now.

In 1992, Johnny worked as a clerk at Flippies Used Records in Kenmore Square. He loved stalking the shelves, spinning records, and talking about and listening to music with the people who hung out there. The records seemed to go for eternity. How could there have been so many musicians at one time Johnny would think. There were thousands upon thousands of records in Flippies, and Johnny was happy to be a part of it in any way he could. He never felt inadequate or out of place, even when he was silent, being there was good enough. Johnny would have worked there for free.

In 1997, Flippies went out of business because of the free music on the internet and vinyl records were being replaced with CDs. Everyone watched the music industry sink like a rock to the bottom of the sea, and there was nothing anyone could do about it. Johnny thought about how it was already hard to pay your rent as a musician and now it was becoming next to impossible. To add salt to the wound, around the same time, all the clubs and bars became nonsmoking spaces. People also became uptight about the noise from the music venues and social spaces soon began to die. Many of the bars and cafes that were once filled with people high on nicotine and caffeine were now empty, banks or corporate clothing stores. Some unseen force was killing all the fun. Renaissances are great when they begin, even better at the peak, but heart wrenchingly painful on the way out and nobody's not really what's going on, other than "it ain't like it used to be".

Johnny used the money he earned from working at Flippies to buy his first electric guitar, a 1969 black Fender Stratocaster in mint condition. For the last 10 years, no matter where he lived, you could always find the Fender in its original case underneath his bed. The metaphor of a guitar in a case, hiding under the bed was a comforting one. It meant that no bogeyman, no monster or demon, could hide there. That space under his bed was called for by a Strat coming from the stratosphere, or at least Johnny thought.

Johnny bought the Fender from an old blues singer named Eddy Nightfalls. Eddy was playing in a club in Boston around that time, Johnny met up with him later at a party. Eddy needed the money for a plane ticket to get back to Texas to see his kids.

Johnny was happy to buy the guitar from him, especially since it was going to such a good cause. He felt what he was doing for Eddy's kids is what he wished someone had done for him. It was also a good deal at $300. If a father couldn't be present for him as a child , this would be the next best thing, it pleased Johnny tremendously.

The 1969 Fender was an iconic guitar used by all the greats like Buddy Holly, Bob Dylan, Gene Vincent, and Dick Dale. The one Johnny had was in good condition and he figured he could get at least $3,000 for it. Surely enough money to get to Paris. Johnny took the guitar out from under the bed, he always knew he'd sell it someday. He also didn't have an amp and wasn't really into playing electric guitar, writing was his priority, not scales or solos. He was more concerned with melodies, simple rhymes and where his ideas could be easily expressed. This was Johnny's focus, and every good band needed a writer. The only problem was he never fit into any band, but that didn't stop him. He still had hope, it was all he had.

Johnny walked into Rickie's Used Guitar Shop next to the Berklee College of Music. Ricky, the owner, was standing on his boot heels, ready to be of service, while three students talked and tried guitars. Ricky had a lot of guitars. There were about

40 electric guitars on one side of the shop, old Les Pauls, 60s Mustang Fenders, beat up Stratocasters, vintage jazz guitars and 20 feet across on the other side, were about 40 acoustic guitars of all kinds. Ricky had a notorious collection of guitars, was around 68 and resembled Father Time. He was thin and tall with a white beard and silver flowing hair, which he put into a ponytail. Wearing a red velvet jacket, colorful scarves, bandana along with turquoise jewelry, snakeskin boots, a gold tooth, faded tattoos, nicotine stains and long fingernails he used as a guitar pick. He was the guy to go to buy an interesting guitar. He appeared to be very smart, at least you would think so by looking at him. Once you talked to him, you realized he wasn't. He had turned his soul over to guitars. Guitars was his religion, he knew them very well, lived and worked for them all his life. But, like Flippies, the internet was hurting his business and his days were numbered too. All the guitars had a sign on them that read 'Please do not touch. Ask for assistance'.

A student sat on a chair test trying a Gibson SG, playing "Roadhouse Blues" by The Doors. Rick was happy to see Johnny. Johnny visited him regularly and bought his strings and guitar picks from him, about all Johnny could afford.

"What you got?" Ricky asked.

"I'm looking to sell my guitar. An original 1969 Fender Strat." Johnny said proudly.

"Ok, let's see it."

Johnny opened the case and pulled out the Fender and handed it to Ricky. Ricky smiled with delight and began inspecting the guitar very closely. He held the guitar in the air, running his hands down the neck, looking very closely. Drawing deep puffs off his cigarette, which he smoked with an equal amount of interest.

Exhaling a cloud of smoke. "Fake. It's a fake. A good one but it's been messed with." Ricky stated.

"What? Are you serious?" Johnny gasped.

Ricky looked Johnny square in the eye, he hated having to admit it, "Yeah, sorry, but it's a modified fake."

Johnny's jaw dropped. "What the fuck. No, it can't be, please don't say that!"

"Sorry, but this is a Squire guitar that's been made to look like a Fender guitar. See look here." Rick rubbed the Fender mark, pointing to the headstock, and said, "Someone rubbed off the Squire mark." He then held up the guitar to the light and showed Johnny the mark. "Look, you can see the Fender mark, it's a sticker." Johnny's teeth began to chatter, he felt like a fool.

"Yeah, it should be silk screened on there, not a sticker. Also, look at the bridge, the quality is just not the same as a real Fender." Ricky walked over to a wall of guitars and picked a real American Fender to show Johnny the difference. "What you have is a cheaper model, a white Chinese model. And on the saddles, there should be a Fender stamp, but there's not. That's the dead giveaway, and the edges on the frets are too sharp, they should be rounded."

Feelings of failure overwhelmed Johnny. He was speechless. All of sudden memories of not having a father flood back to him. A father would have taught me the difference between a fake Fender and a real one, he thought. Ricky picked up the real American made Fender and showed Johnny the difference between the frets.

"Look," Ricky said rubbing his hands on the frets, "you can feel it, the American made is soft. The fake is hard and rigid."

Johnny rubbed his hand over the frets, he could see the difference. Johnny was now angry and saw Eddy Nightfalls from a different perspective. He wanted revenge.

Ricky offered Johnny $200 for the guitar. Johnny didn't think it would be enough for Paris but he took the money. Ricky gave Johnny the $200 in the $20s, and with a long face, Johnny walked out the door.

How stupid of me to buy the guitar he thought, digging up early childhood memories. Everything was a guessing game with no father to teach him the difference, between a real or fake guitar, a sunfish from a bass fish, a curveball from a knuckleball, a Chevy from a Ford, or even how to change a lightbulb, tie a tie, turn a screwdriver or shave. The list went on and on, and these tasks easily paralyzed Johnny with anxiety. The one good thing Johnny had was moving to Paris and thinking of Eddy Nightfalls made him want to get out of the US even more. In Paris, do fathers know how to be fathers? Johnny wondered.

Chapter 7
Sellout

The next morning, Johnny overslept and joined Dotty for a late coffee. She was sitting at her station, waiting for him. He took a seat, put some sugar in his coffee, and let Dotty start the day with the latest news stories.

"We must keep our eyes open for Al-Qaeda. My guess is there are weapons of mass destruction in Iraq. They could even be right here in this country, hiding out as sleeper cells," Dotty told Johnny.

"What the hell are you talking about?" Johnny asked.

"President Bush Jr. was on TV last night giving a speech and said the terrorist hijackers could attack again. Just like 9/11, you know?" Dotty continued, "we never know when they will attack again. We may have to invade Iraq. The terrorists have no law to their morality and no limit to their violent ambitions. They have weapons of mass destruction and we must stop them before they use them."

"Invade Iraq?"

"Yes, that's right."

"Dotty, please, I just woke up. Let me drink my coffee."

"I think the U.S. will invade very soon."

"We can't invade a country like Iraq, they didn't do anything to us."

"Let me remind you I had a niece who worked at the Trade Center." .

"But Iraq didn't do anything to us, Dotty. Sorry about your niece."

"It's part of the war on terror, that's what Bush said. God told him to attack and invade Iraq, Iraq are sponsors of terrorism and evildoers."

"What?" Johnny objected and couldn't believe what he was hearing. "Dotty, please, what are you saying? evildoers?"

"Yes, the president said this, he calls them evildoers. He appears to see himself as the executor of the divine will," Dotty defended, "he said so on the news."

"He wants to impress his father."

Dotty lit a cigarette, and continued, "That's right, we first invaded Iraq in 1990 with Bush Sr. Bush sent troops into Iraq to get the dictator Saddam Hussein. He didn't succeed in getting him. Now his son is going after him."

"It's all about oil and impressing his father. But, you know, Dotty, I don't care about this war stuff. I had a horrible day yesterday. I went to sell my guitar and it turns out it's a fake! I could only get $200, it was supposed to be over $2,000," Johnny said.

"What?"

"You heard me, it was a fake. All these years I had this guitar under my bed thinking it was an original 1969 Fender."

"Where did you get it?" Offering 100% attention, she could see Johnny needed some love.

"I bought it off an old blues musician who was playing here in Boston. He said he needed money to see his kids. He most likely didn't even have kids!"

"I'm sorry to hear that. You don't deserve that at all, shame on that guy for lying. Karma is not nice. Don't worry I am sure he paid a price for his actions. You are a good boy Johnny and don't you forget it" Dotty said, shaking her head. A moment of silence passed and she remembered the letter she had for him. "Oh by the way, before I forget, you have a letter."

"Where?" He asked excitedly.

"Here you go, and be careful, it could have anthrax in it." Dotty handed Johnny the letter.

"Anthrax?"

"Yes, that's right, you heard me. The terrorists are sending letters with anthrax in them. Don't you watch the news?"

"Ok, I'll take my chances," He opened it and read.

Dear Johnny Vincent,

My name is Baron Von Smith. We met last April at the Sunset cafe in Allston. You were performing there. I signed your mailing list and bought your new CD "Happy Trails". I had a very good time and like your music.

I work for a music agency called Miracle Music LTD. We license music out to commercials and films. A client of ours, Hero Dynamics, would like to use your song "Willy Has A Brand New Hip" for a TV commercial. Hero Dynamics is a prosthetic company. They make artificial body parts. They are willing to pay $1,000 for your song. If this interests you please contact me at my office between 9 A.M. and 5 P.M. at 617-434-5674.

Thank you
BVS

Johnny, surprised, put down the letter on the makeshift coffee bar and looked at Dotty.

"What is it?" asked Dotty.

"Someone wants to use my song 'Willy Has A Brand New Hip' for a TV commercial."

"Who?"

"A prosthetic company. I guess they make fake hips, limbs, and different body parts," Johnny guessed.

"Yes, with the war on terror, there must be a demand for artificial limbs and things. There will be more of a need with the invasion of Iraq. It's good they want your song."

"I'm not selling the song! I'm not a sellout. I don't write TV jingles."

"What? Are you crazy? This is what you've been waiting for! Think of the exposure you will have and the money you can make. I bet they pay a lot."

Johnny started getting angry, "No Dotty, you don't see. This is what has ruined our society. Everyone is selling out. That's how we got this flunky in the White House. His father bought him the job. This is what the world has come to, no more integrity. Everything is up for sale, and no one has any principles."

"If you sell the song, you'll have the money for Paris."

"Hell no! Do you see Leonard Cohen using his music for a toothpaste commercial? Or imagine the song 'Imagine' by John Lennon used for selling soap!"

"Who is Leonard Cohen? I don't know him. He should have sold his music for a commercial. Maybe then I'd know him."

"Leonard Cohen is one of the greatest songwriters of the century. He would never license his music, and I can't either."

"If you say so, Johnny, but you should at least think about it."

"I can't be a sellout like that."

"Ok," Dotty said and moved the conversation back to the war on terror. "They say we need to keep an eye on our neighbors and report any suspicious activity. We are in the orange level for the terror alert. They could attack at any time." Dotty lit a cigarette and offered one to Johnny. Johnny took one and lit it.

"Dotty, I must get out of this country, it's driving me nuts," he told her. They both looked at each other and smiled.

Dotty picked up her new book *The Shining Eye* and began to read. Johnny finished his coffee.

"See you later," he said, getting up from his chair. Part of his rent is paid for the day.

Johnny decided to leave the house and catch the 31 bus to the harbor. Thirty minutes later he was on the Boston waterfront, walking around and enjoying the beautiful sunny day. The harbor was busy with sailboats, yachts, seagulls, good wind, and tourists. On the other side of the harbor, commercial airliners flew in and out of the Logan International

Airport. As a child living in San Francisco, Johnny would lay in the grass all afternoon watching the jumbo jets fly across the blue sky into the clouds. He would fantasize about being a passenger and going to Africa or Australia, like the adventurous places he had seen on the Wild Kingdom TV show. These daydreams could take up an entire afternoon of boredom. He had only been on a jet plane four times in his life. Selling the song just for the sake of going on a plane ride is a good enough reason, Johnny thought. A vacation was something he had never thought of but maybe he needed one.

For now the best he could do for getting away was taking a walk along the waterfront, amongst the high rise luxury hotels, chic restaurants with BMWs and Porsches parked outside. It was like being in another country compared to where he lived just a mile and a half away. He decided then he was going to call Miracle Music and sell his song. Walking past the aquarium, Johnny sat on the bench for another 20 minutes waiting for his bus, anticipating the call he was about to make. On the way back home he sat behind a family of four, a mother and father and a boy and a girl. They were tourists visiting Boston and had just spent the day at the aquarium. Johnny absorbed the love the mother showed her two children. She was like a momma bear with her cubs. She fed and cleaned them, making sure they didn't fall out of their seats as the bus plotted its way back to Southie. The proud father sat in silence and smiled at Johnny, and for a brief moment Johnny felt relieved of any internal strife that was buzzing around him. Maybe one day that will be me, he thought. The man seemed to know what Johnny was feeling and thinking. The look in the man's eye reassured Johnny that one day he would be in his place and have a family of us own. For now it was just a dream.

Johnny arrived home and saw Dotty sitting at the coffee bar. "My mind is made up, I'm selling the song," he announced to her.

"Good news, Johnny! And don't worry, you're not a sellout, you're a survivor," Dotty assured him.

Filled with excitement, Johnny rushed up the stairs to his room and threw all his things on his bed. He picked up the letter and wrote down Baron's number. He then quickly picked up the phone and called. Ring, ring, ring. Ring, ring, ring.

"Hello, you've reached Miracle Music. Please leave a message with your name and number, and we'll get back to you."

"Hello, my name is Johnny Vincent. I'm calling about the song you're interested in. Call me at any time at 878-996-5654. Thank you," Johnny said to the machine.

Johnny hung up and wondered if this was a sign from the universe. Maybe I shouldn't sell the song. Is the voice of my father trying to tell me something? he wondered as his teeth began to chatter. The chatter this time was new. It came in the sequence, "I can, I will, I can, I will, can you hear me?" It was like morse code, coming in as 1-2-1-2-1-2-1-2-3-4. As the code kept on, Johnny started to think of Candy. I may not know my father but I have a sister and a mother, he thought. He decided he needed to see Candy before he left for Paris, and he needed to call his mother.

Johnny waited for the chattering to mellow before calling his mother. When it had slowed down enough, and he was able to speak clearly, he picked up the phone and called her. He needed to find Candy.

"Hello, Mom. It's me, Johnny."

"Hello, Johnny. I'm happy you called. I still haven't found Cosmos. I've put up all the flyers and no one has seen her. Oh and sorry about Stanley,"

"No worries, Mom. That's too bad about Cosmos. I'm sure he'll show up. And Stanley, well, we know he's a royal jackass". Silence. "I want to go see Candy. Where is the rehab she's in?" Asked Johnny.

"She's in Quincy. The place is called Footprints. Take the red line to Quincy Square and it's about a 10 minute walk to 73 Ruby Street, it's next to Starbucks."

"Ok, Mom. I'm going to go first thing tomorrow morning."

"Can you bring her a toothbrush? She called looking for one today but I can't get there. I am watching baby Priscilla."

"Sure, Mom. No problem. Talk to you later."

Johnny hung up the phone and thought more about selling his song. He still wasn't sure. Feeling insecure about his choice, he assured himself that he's done worse things and told himself that no one would ever know. This thought comforted him, and he picked up his guitar and continued to work on his new song "World Gone Bad". His teeth-chatter the tune, playing notes only he could hear.

Chapter 8
Visiting Candy

"Good morning Johnny be careful today, the terrorist alert level is orange. Be on the lookout for any suspicious-looking people," Dotty advised Johnny as he passed her, heading out the door.

"Sorry, I don't have time for a coffee right now. We'll have it later. Have a nice day," he said ignoring the mention of terrorist alerts. He was on his way to see Candy.

To get to the rehab Johnny had to walk 10 minutes from his apartment to Broadway Subway stop. From there he took the Red Line south to Quincy Center. On his way, he stopped at a 24-hour store to get a coffee and some rolling tobacco. After paying for his items , he chatted with the girls who worked there and rolled himself a cigarette for the road. The girls told him the store was held up the previous night, by two very desperate looking armed unmasked white guys. One guy had a pistol and held customers hostage, while the other guy had a knife and took the money from the register. They made off with about $130 and a few cartons of cigarettes. The robbers looked like they were from Charles Town.

With the towny haircuts, jogging suits, and were probably looking for drug money, white as a ghost, sweating and shaking. Charles Town was a section of North Boston with a reputation of bank robbers and thieves.

The robbery brought back a bad memory for Johnny. When he was 23 he had been robbed at knifepoint by a gang of African American teenagers, while busking in the subway. The Red Sox had won an important afternoon game and the fans were in a good mood and gave generously. Johnny had a perfect spot and the fans threw bills and coins into his open guitar case as he played all afternoon. The money, around $300, was out in the open for everyone to see and he was proud of it. The gang stood nearby watching the money pile up in his case. When Johnny went to pack up and leave, they followed him and trapped him in a deserted part of the metro. Two guys stood guard to make sure no one came and one guy put a knife up to Johnny's face while another guy grabbed all the money from him. It was a surreal and traumatic experience that he never quite got over. From that day on, he made sure to never show off the money being made.

Johnny left the 24-hour store and continued on his way. It was a nice morning for a walk and sipped his coffee and enjoyed a freshly rolled cigarette. All the shops on Broadway were opening and the cars were competing for parking spots as everyone scramble to get to work on time. Having made up his mind about going to Paris and selling the song, he walked with a sense of purpose and looked forward to seeing his sister.

Johnny arrived at the Broadway Station and waited on the platform, enjoying the last sips of his coffee. The train arrived, he got on and took a window seat. Picking up speed, he looked out the window at the faded wooden triple-decker houses. The backside of the houses had wooden balcony porches attached to them, with clothes drying on clotheslines. People sitting in tank tops and pajamas having a morning smoke watching the trains go by. Each window had a tragic tale; joy didn't seem to be the feeling evoked. Old workers' flats from years gone by still standing. It was early in the morning, a time Johnny wasn't used to. The morning rush to work was coming into the city, Johnny was going out. He thought about how nice it was to be awake at this time, it made him feel responsible. Maybe I should do this more often, he thought.

The train arrived and Johnny exited the station. The transformation from the city to a small town center was a pleasant one. The square was peaceful and serene and all was quiet. Large clean storefront windows, hand painted signs, and red brick building with neon give it a 1950s feel, like stepping into an Edward Hopper painting. He looked for a pharmacy to buy a toothbrush and a small gift for Candy. Across from the station he could see Danny's Drug Store, and the sign on the door read, "A Neighborhood Legend since 1936".

The bell on the door rang as Johnny entered. These days, independent pharmacies or drug stores were as rare as payphones as most had been bought out by corporations and became a chain. At the counter was a man, and naturally Johnny assumed it was Danny. Johnny quickly found a toothbrush and toothpaste, and then he looked for a gift for Candy. Luck would have it he found an aisle filled with novelty items, books, beach toys, CDs, cassettes, pogo sticks, hula hoops, and dolls. Johnny noticed a little Indian squaw doll with long black hair, a frozen smile, and sparkly brown eyes. She was wearing a dress with beads and had on moccasins. He picked up the doll and gave her a close examination. This was the perfect gift for Candy, he decided. Attached to the doll was a tag that read "Pocahontas Doll Six Dollars". Johnny remembered learning about Pocahontas in school. She was a Native American Indian girl who was kidnapped and held ransom by the Colonist during the hostilities in 1613. During her captivity, she was made to convert to Christianity and baptized under the name Rebecca. After that, she went to England and became a 'civilized savage'. Johnny thought Candy would like the doll and bought it along with the toothbrush.

Footprints was a three-story red brick building built in the 1920s. Daunting and depressing, he thought it looked more like a psychiatric hospital than a rehab. The kind of place you went into and never came out of. Johnny buzzed the door and it opened. Thick wire mesh windows kept happiness out, shatter proof glass, not a common sight he thought. He entered and was greeted by a security officer. The lobby was a mix of white, gray and black concrete and medal. If you fell down here you would get hurt. The floors were waxed and smelled of a disinfectant cleaner of some kind.

"How can I help you?" the security guard asked.

"I'm here to see my sister Candy Vincent," Johnny replied.

"You got ID?"

"Yes, I do," Johnny said and showed him his ID.

"Sign in here and someone will come get you. She's on the third floor," the security guard instructed . "You can take a seat here."

"Thank you," Johnny said and sat down. He didn't wait long before the elevator doors opened and a pudgy man, with curly brown hair, and glasses wearing a Parker vest, jeans, and white sneakers appeared. He was Candy's counselor.

"Hello," he said, "You're here to see Candy?"

"Yes, I am," Johnny said, with a hopeful smile.

The man, quiet and serious, led Johnny into the elevator. Johnny did his best to keep his teeth from chattering or making eye contact. The elevator doors opened onto the floor. Johnny was confronted with a large room of around 100 square feet, with a mishmash of donated tables and chairs, pale green walls with 2 wire mesh windows. Hanging on the walls were hand-painted signs that read 'God does not make junk', 'You are a miracle', 'Just for Today', and 'I can.' The room was active with four or five staff workers, all who had keys hanging around their necks. About 50 people in total were talking and shuffling and milling about. Patients of all ages: young teenagers wearing tee shirts, sweatpants and slippers, hardened addicts from the streets, and a few elderly grandmothers. Candy came walking into the dayroom with a bright bounce in her step. She looked slow, dazed, slightly dizzy, sleepy and medicated. Her face was covered in makeup and it was done badly—too much lipstick and eyeliner. She had on a Prince "Purple Rain" t-shirt with gray sweatpants and green slippers. It looked like her obsession with drugs was transferred to makeup. Candy greeted

Johnny with a big hug and kiss, leaving a smudge of lipstick on his cheek.

"Candy, I'm happy to see you!" he said to her.

"Me too, Johnny, me too. Thank you for coming. I guess Mom told you I was here?" she asked in a slow lethargic tone.

Johnny realized she was on a tranquilizer. "Yes, she did. How are you?" he asked.

"I'm ok. I'm better. The first three days were horrible, but now I like it here. I'm making new friends and have a good therapist and I need to be honest this time," she vowed.

"That's good. I'm proud of you. Here, I brought a little something," He offered.

"You did? That's great. Thank you! What is it?" Johnny handed her the gift bag and her face lit up as she pulled out the doll. She and the doll had found each other. Johnny sighed with relief, the gift was made for her and it pleased him.

"Look at this!" she said, surprised and happy. "It's a Native American girl. I love her, Johnny!" She gave him a big hug.

"Her name is Pocahontas. She can be your guardian angel," He suggested.

"She will be my higher power, they say that I need to find a God to believe in. It will help me stay clean. I was really bad, Johnny. I started doing meth and I couldn't stop. It was horrible. All I cared about was the next fix. I wasn't eating or sleeping. Good thing Mom took Priscilla."

Johnny took a deep breath and looked closely at his sister, concerned and serious. "Yes, for now, she can. But she's been complaining about her back...at least she and Stanley have some money and can help, I hope."

Johnny tried to process the mixed feelings he had about seeing his sister in this condition. Skinny, fragile and pale with a face full of bad makeup.

"How's the food?" he asked.

"It's horrible but at least I'm eating. They have good desserts like brownies and cookies."

"And how about Pete? What's up with him?"

"He's getting help too. He's in another clinic far from here. We have to be separated. When we get together it's not good, Johnny. Not good at all."

"Why all the makeup?"

"I had to. When I looked in the mirror, I saw bugs everywhere on my face. My skin was coming off. I was awake for seven days, I couldn't get any sleep. I was hearing voices and seeing things. I was going crazy, Johnny. Pete and I were living out of his car under a bridge in Roxbury. I am going to go to a halfway house from here. I hope Mom can watch Priscilla, if not, the State will take her in for adoption."

He felt sad seeing Candy in this condition and tried to hold back his tears. "Candy, you need to try to overcome this problem," he pleaded.

"Johnny, I have a disease. Addiction is a disease like any other. What I'm finally learning is the trauma I experienced when we were little is where it begins and—"

Johnny cut her off mid-sentence, "Stanley wasn't good for any of us. It just wasn't good at all. I know he was crazy when he drank."

Candy paused, and then said, "Do you remember his friend Frank? Stanley's friend when we lived in Detroit? He was in the militia group."

"Yes, of course, I remember Frank. He was one of the nicer friends Stan had. Yeah, the militia group...bunch of wild crazies. They weren't hillbillies and not city folk neither. Why Frank?" Johnny looked straight at her, hoping he wasn't about to hear what he knew she was going to tell him.

"He molested me. He did fucking horrible things to me when I was only nine. Can you believe it? That fucking bastard asshole used to come into my bed at night and put his horrible creepy hands all over me when I was sleeping. He told me if I ever said anything, he would kill us all. Johnny, it was horrible," Candy started to break down, tears streamed down her cheeks.

"What? Are you serious?" Johnny exclaimed. He let out a deep breath and stomped his right foot down on the floor. "That no good fucker!" he yelled and took another deep breath and shook his head. "I'm very sorry to hear this Candy." Johnny reached over to her and held her while she cried. Mascara, eyeliner, and blush ran down her face making a painted mess. Johnny was shocked to learn it was Frank. Frank appeared to be one of the nicer friends Stanley had.

"But you know what hurts the most?" Candy asked while crying, "they left the door open at night for him to come in."

Johnny took a deep breath and tried to understand.

Candy continued with her confession, wiping her tears and trembling, "Stan would read me a bedtime story and when he left, he wouldn't close the door." She began to bang on the table crying. "Soon after Frank would come in. It happened a lot that summer we went fishing on the river and hiking. Even mom, she would leave the door open. How could they? How could they leave the door open for him?" Johnny noticed there was a box of tissue on a nearby table. He got up and brought it over to them. Candy pulled herself together and wiped the makeup off her face with a tissue. "Yes, I'm dealing with it in the therapy here. Stanley and mom didn't even do anything to protect me. I think they knew the whole time," she told him. "I don't think mom knew, she would have said something, but Stanley may have known,"

Johnny looked at her and promised, "You are strong, Candy, you can overcome all this. I know you can."

She started to cry again, "I just don't want to lose Priscilla. I'm such a horrible mother. I hate myself, Johnny."

"You're not a horrible mother. Stop thinking that right now. You must pull yourself together and do everything they say here and follow all the rules. It can be worked out and you can get beyond all this. The good thing is you're still alive and Priscilla is with—"

A heavy-set twenty-something in a Stealers football jersey started kicking the coke machine next to them, interrupting their conversation. Johnny and Candy looked at him, and then looked back at each other.

"I've decided to go to Paris and play in the streets, and I may sell a song for a TV commercial," Johnny told Candy as the coke machine and Stealers boy quieted down.

"Wow, that's good news, Johnny," Candy said, wiping the last of her tears away.

"I hope to leave very soon. I will send you a postcard."

"You will do good, I know you will." She offered and looked at the clock on the wall. "I must get going, I have group therapy in 10 minutes."

Johnny handed her $20 and gave her a big hug. She picked up her doll and toothbrush and walked off disappearing into the side door. Johnny looked for the guard and motioned for the elevator.

"Right this way," the guard said and opened the elevator doors. They both stepped inside. Once inside, Johnny burst into tears and held his face in his hands.

"I can't believe it," he said, "she looks really bad. I can't believe it."

"It's all right," the guard assured him, "you can cry. Let it all out. Your sister has a lot of courage. She is strong, she didn't do anything wrong. Addiction is an illness, just like any other. She is brave and you are a good brother. Don't forget that."

The guard handed Johnny a Kleenex and he wiped his tears. The elevator door opened and there before them stood two parents and a sibling on their way to visit someone. Johnny gave a sad smile, they gave a sympathetic smile back. Wiping the tears from his face, Johnny looked at them and without words said, "It's your turn now, good luck, I know how you feel." Johnny walked through the lobby and the security unlocked the front door for him. He left the rehab and was happy to be out on the street and feel the fresh air.

Chapter 9
Making the Deal

After the visit with Candy, Johnny decided to take a walk to a nearby park. He found a bench under a tree and sat to reflect on his visit. He took out his notepad and wrote some ideas for a song. He noted everybody had green slipper shoes and looked malnourished and beat up in one way or another. He started writing a song called "Detox Blues". Sitting and writing, a homeless man approached him and asked for money. Johnny reached into his pocket but didn't have any change to give him. The man scowled and moved on.

Still early in the day, he decided to go home and get his guitar to go busking on Newbury Street in the Back Bay of Boston, a posh area with luxury stores, restaurants and cafes. He felt confident he could make money, and a good way to get his mind off of things.

He arrived at his place and was lucky enough to bypass Dotty and avoid conversation. On the way to his room, he heard the phone ring. He rushed up the stairs, he answered it just in time.

"Hello?" Johnny answered.

"Hello, my name is Baron Von Smith. May I please speak with Johnny Vincent?" Baron said.

"Speaking."

"Hello, Johnny, I guess you read the letter I sent. I also got your message. Thank you for getting back to me. I work for Miracle Music Ltd. I saw you play a few months ago at the Sarra Cafe in Cambridge and bought a few of your CDs, that's how I discovered your music. As it says in the letter, we'd like to use your song. Maybe you remember me?"

"Yes, I do. You were the guy with the Jimmy Buffett t-shirt, right?"

"Yes, exactly. I saw you play with my wife. We love your songs, they're fantastic, really," Baron coughed and cleared his throat. "Well, I have some good news. I have a client who is willing to pay $1,000 to use your song 'Willy Has A Brand New Hip.' They just love it!"

"That's great! Happy to hear."

"Yes, they would like to use it for a TV commercial on a cable network."

"What company is it?"

"They're called Hero Dynamics. They specialize in making prosthetic body parts like hips, arms, legs—you name it, they pretty much do it. They've received government grants and loans from the U.S. military budget. They're getting ready for this thing...the war on terror."

"Wow," Johnny said. Wishing he didn't hear the part about the military grants. "I didn't think of the song this way, but, yes, I guess it makes sense."

"They have the commercial with the music already to go, we took the song off the CD I bought from you, it just needs your approval. It would be on the TV channel right away, in about two nights. I can send you a check."

"Ok. I can deal with that, I need the money," Johnny said and gave Baron his address for the check.

"Very good, they'll be really happy. I'll call you in two days to confirm and send the papers for you to sign. Thanks again Johnny and keep me posted on any concerts you do."

"Ok, I will. Have a nice day. Goodbye," said Johnny. He hung up the phone, still unsure whether it's the right thing to do, but really needs the money if he is to go to Paris. "Why is life like this?" he thought. Having to make a choice like this was not easy. It was already bad enough to be a sellout, but now to be a part of the war on terror? But wasn't everything in the culture centered around profits of the empire. He concluded.

With guitar in hand, Johnny headed to Newbury Street. Once there, he met up with Bud E, an outsider artist from California. Bud was standing next to his canvases with his long blond hair, mustache, and beard, tattoos on his ears and fingers, dressed in sandals, a t-shirt and faded patched jeans. He was chewing gum, smoking buts, snapping his fingers and doing a little dance that seemed to be brewing in him. Bud loved to talk about his paintings and felt they connect with other worlds. With around 25 canvases leaning against a wall and fence and there was extra room for Johnny to play. Johnny songs went well with Buds art brut-like colorful chunky oil paintings. Bud was obsessed with making a masterpiece, painting a woman he'd never seen. He often referred to this woman as 'My Goddess Desire Angel Heart of Pure Love'. Bud's goddess was a cross between Joan Rivers and Mona Lisa, at least that's what she looked like in the paintings. Bud was convinced one day he would meet her. He believed it to be the highest aspiration of nobility that one could live for, the creation of a masterpiece. He even took a total vow of celibacy, a life of sainthood, until he met his goddess.

Johnny began playing as people stopped and looked at Bud's art. Bud sold his paintings for $25, and only needed to sell one painting a day to survive. It was days like this Johnny lived for. If he could do this every day for the rest of his life, his life would be perfect.

Johnny started singing his song "Who Do I Believe", a song about disinformation and propaganda. Out of nowhere, two cops drove up to the corner in an unmarked sedan. The sedan stopped at the curb where Johnny and Bud were. The two cops, rude, rough and undercover, got out of the car and trapped Johnny and Bud.

"You guys got permits?" the short cop wearing a blue cap without any sports insignia demanded.

"No," Bud said, annoyed.

The cops then turned to Johnny.

"Nope," Johnny replied.

"Let's see some ID," the tall skinny cop with a straight nose and blue lips and very pale face demanded.

"I don't have any with me," Johnny confessed.

"Hey, wait a minute. Did I see you at Billy's Bar?" the short cop asked.

"Yes, that's right," Johnny agreed.

"Yeah, you sang some pretty good songs there. I don't know why you got so upset and walked off stage like that," the cop inquired.

"I know, it wasn't cool. I have a hard time doing cover songs," Johnny admitted.

"What's your name?"

"Johnny Vincent."

"Johnny, it sounds like you got some issues. You got a good voice but maybe you need to relax, take it easy. I liked that song you did, 'Just Like Me' or something?"

"No, it was 'I'm Just Like You.'"

"That's right, I remember now, but hey, it ain't gonna hurt you to do a little 'Hotel California' now and then. We all got to pay the rent." He said winking at Johnny.

"How about you?" the short cop asked, looking at Bud, "you got some ID?"

"I left it at home, but don't we have rights? The first amendment protection? It does protect the artist's rights to sell their work, I believe," Bud replied.

"In some situations, yes," the short cop said, and continued, "this is not a designated selling zone and you do not have a permit to sell. I could take all these paintings and confiscate them and arrest you for loitering. Now, do any of you have anything illegal on you?"

"No, nothing," Johnny confessed. "Just a guitar pick and notebook with a pen."

"How about you?" quipped the short cop to Bud.

"No, I got nothing, nothing at all,"

"Let's see, empty your pockets," the cop demanded.

"You need a search warrant," Bud pleaded.

"You want us to arrest you for not having a permit? You're already breaking the law."

Bud emptied his pockets, pulling out his wallet, keys, cigarettes, pipe, and a bag of grass.

"Hold up!" the short cop said, looking at the bag of grass, "what do we have here?"

"A little bit of herb," Bud admitted. "Maybe half an ounce?"

The cop grabbed the bag of weed and gave it a smell, "Looks like you are a dealer."

"A dealer? No way, it's for my personal use!" Bud exclaimed.

"You're under arrest. Put your hands behind your back."

"What are you, crazy? Get your hands off me! I didn't do anything!"

"Don't resist or I will take you down."

"Oh, come on, it's just a little bit of weed, please! I can't go away, please! I have no money for bail and they will keep me! C'mon."

"You should have thought about that before you came and set-up shop in a non-designated zone for artists. You don't want to follow the rules? Now you pay. All these shops here pay taxes and rent and you think you can just jump out on the street and sell your stuff?"

Bud realized he wasn't going to get out of this and complied with the cops. The tall cop began picking up the paintings and loaded them in the trunk of the unmarked sedan. The short cop looked at Johnny,

"You can go. I don't want to see you back here. You got it? Now take care and see you playing at Billy's Bar, not on this street. You guys need proper permits for the designated zones."

"Ok," Johnny said and packed up his CDs and guitar.

The police gathered up around Bud's paintings, put them in the trunk of the car and placed him under arrest. Johnny, depressed and relieved, went home. He felt lucky he didn't get arrested nor get his guitar confiscated.

When Johnny got home he went straight to bed. He managed to avoid Dotty again. For the next three days, he did his best to play on the streets without drawing any attention from the police. He played at Downtown Crossing, Faneuil Hall, and in the North End. He made $160 for his trip. He now had $1,160, enough money to leave.

Johnny started packing up his room and gathering his things for his trip to France. He got his passport ready and started making plans to leave for Paris. He decided to go to the Bank of America to see if he could cash the check without a bank account. With his ID in hand, they give him the money. He then headed to a travel agency to buy a one-way ticket to Paris

The day before Johnny was set to leave, he received a call from Baron at Miracle Music.

"Hello, Johnny. I hope you received the check. I'm calling to mention that we need you to sign the release form we sent. Happy to tell you the commercial will air tonight at eight P.M. on Channel 38. Call when you have a minute. Thank you."

That night Dotty took out her portable TV, the one she brings when she goes camping. Sometimes she brings it out for special occasions, too, like a Red Sox, Celtics, or Bruins game. She set-up the TV and got a bag of Doritos and a six pack of Budweiser Beer. Everything was ready for Johnny to celebrate the TV commercial moment.

Johnny originally wrote the song for an old African American man named Willy. Willy ran a junk shop in Roxbury and needed a walker to walk. He had worn out his hips and couldn't dance anymore. Willy would sit around all day in his junk shop, selling old records, radios, TVs, and stuff. He liked to brag about how good of a dancer he once was back in the 50s right on up to the 80s with disco. He knew them all the dances, or so he said: the boogie-woogie, the swing, the twist, the jive, the jitterbug—you name it, Willy said he knew it. "I'm gonna get me some new hips and hit the town," he vowed. The moment Johnny heard that, the song was written in his head, all he had to do was sit down and enjoy putting it together. Writing a song like that is easier than constructing a bookshelf from a Swedish furniture store. Johnny was so proud of the song that he hired a rockabilly band called The Rollies and recorded it at a professional recording studio.

Dotty and Johnny sat at the make-shift coffee bar watching a rerun of Bonanza impatiently waiting for the TV commercial to come on. Johnny was nervous and hoped no one he knew was watching, especially Willy. There would be a chance Willy would see it because Willy watched a lot of TV at his junk shop. Drinking beer and eating chips, the moment finally came. They watched as the commercial showed a skeleton turning against a blacklight. Johnny was excited to hear his song in the background. The bass and drums kicked in as the guitar riff coincided with the skeleton soaring across the black backdrop. As they continued to watch, the skeleton slowly swirled upward, replicating a DNA hexagon, focusing on the hip of the skeleton.

"Do you experience soreness of the joints? Aching pain? Perhaps you've had a severe injury or arthritis? The demands of life can be rigorous and unfair. Thanks to today's advanced technology, science gives us the ability and chance to have our needs met, even in the most extreme situations. At Hero Dynamics, it's our life's work and mission to meet your needs. Hip replacements, prosthetic limbs, breathing devices, and much more."

Johnny's jaw dropped listening to the narrator talk about Hero Dynamics. As the commercial ended, the skeleton morphed into a tap dancer, tapping off into the galaxy with the stars and lip-synching Johnny's song.

"Pop the champagne! Take a big sip! Willy's got a brand new hip," Johnny voice sang out from the TV. Johnny turned pale. He shook his head and placed his hand to his chest. Is he having a heart attack? Dotty wondered. "Are you ok? Are you ok? Johnny" she could see this was not easy for him.

"No, I am not," Johnny confessed, looking at her. Johnny got up from the bar and ran to the bathroom and vomited beer and Doritos into the toilet. He was disturbed and shocked by the TV commercial. He locked himself in the bathroom and vomited some more. He felt betrayed and sick.

"Hey, you ok?" Dotty asked standing outside the bathroom. Johnny came out with his hair wet and combed. He was white as a ghost.

"You should be proud of yourself," Dotty told him in an effort to cheer him up.

"No, I'm not. It's horrible, just horrible. I can't believe I did that and allowed them to use my song. It's stupid, so stupid. I'm a sellout! I hope no one ever sees it!" Johnny told her.

"Don't worry, no one will!"

"You better not tell anyone. Please don't let anyone know."

Johnny, still feeling sick, headed upstairs to his room to try to forget the TV commercial. Tomorrow was his last day and he had to visit his mother one last time before he left. Johnny finished packing his bag and wished he was sitting in a window seat heading to Paris right now. At least the song paid for the ride in the sky, up in the clouds to get far away.

Johnny laid down on his bed and fell asleep, he was exhausted from the stress of the day. As he began to drift off, he fell into a dream and a silhouette of a man appeared. Johnny didn't know this man and couldn't make out any of his features. The man then faded away, the man was gone. Johnny then fell into a deep square of purple light with a yellow line defining the edges. He couldn't feel any walls around but knew they were there as the square grew bigger and bigger. All of sudden, he heard a voice come from the silhouette, "You are a number, a frequency, a light, a value of information."

"Who are you?" Johnny asked.

"I'm your father, a number, a frequency, a value of light, and do not worry my son, you are not a sellout" a voice with little emotion stated.

Johnny felt his body and mind fill with joy and happiness. "Dad, is it you? I am so happy to see you," Johnny said to the silhouette, as his heart filled with light and love. The silhouette came closer and closer and passed through Johnny, vanishing into thin air. Johnny then saw boxes folding outward and he came to a field with a hillside covered in trees. He was now in the countryside. He didn't recognize the landscape but was overthrown with a feeling of peacefulness and saw his father's back in the distance. Johnny tried to see some of the details, the man appeared to be tall with dark hair, deep dark eyes, and big shoulders. He continued watching the man as he walked into a forest and disappeared. Still sleeping, Johnny was left with a loving feeling that he tried to hold onto as long as he could until he woke up.

The next morning he woke up early with mixed feelings. He was happy about the dream but embarrassed by the TV commercial. The dream was one he would never forget and he knew it was the spirit of his father. He got dressed and went downstairs. Dotty was waiting for him as usual.

"Are you ok?" she inquired, still concerned about last night's reaction.

"Yes, I am. It's ok. I'll be alright. I must go visit my mother today, tell her I'm leaving tomorrow," he explained. He quickly finished his coffee and smiled.

"Be careful on the train. Remember we are at code orange level alert. The terrorists could attack again!" Dotty warned.

Chapter 10
Back to Moms

Johnny arrived at his mother's house and started banging on the door, "Open up! Let me in!" While waiting he stood face to face with an American flag, projecting horizontally out of the porch. The flag brought back memories of first grade and pledging allegiance to it. He was taught to love all it stood for, with its glory, red, white and blue. American exceptionalism ingrained him, it would be hard to shake that off. All the other houses on the street had the same flag sticking out of the same porches, in the same spot. It had been almost a year since the U.S. launched Operation Enduring Freedom. The US and its allies had invaded Afghanistan and began the hunt for the mastermind of the 9/11 terror attacks, Osama bin Laden. Patriotism had never been stronger, American flags were everywhere now. The country had gone flag crazy thought Johnny.

"Hey, come in, Johnny," his mother said, opening the door in her bathrobe, about to sneeze, looking weepy from allergies.

"Hello, Mom."

She closed the door and did a half step circle clockwise, twice, and shuffled into the salon.

"What's that about?" Johnny asked, amused and confused.

"The energy, Johnny, the energy must pass by correctly. It's important to push the negative energy out," she explained.

Johnny could see she was sad, and on rare occasions such as now, he could also see the little girl his mother once was. For a moment without makeup, the mask of weariness and tragedy was lifted. The spirit of her youth and true self shined through the lines and wrinkles of her face. He knew his mother was once a beautiful young woman, with long auburn hair, slender legs, glowing eyes, with a sparkling smile. When she was in her twenties she had a promising career as a model, did runway work and was featured in a calendar for a tool company. She even tried acting and could have been a playboy bunny, so she said. She was in a few films and one of them was with Peter Fonda. She worked as a go-go dancer, and even jumped out of a giant cake. Johnny had seen the photo of her jumping out of a cake when he was 7 and thought it to be the coolest thing ever, but a few years later it only depressed him when he learned it was for a bachelor party. It was hard for Johnny to accept how she'd aged. After the car crash, she was never the same.

A manufacturing defect in the steering wheel was the cause of the accident. The crash left her with a permanent scar on her cheek and a back injury that caused constant pain. After the crash, she was supposed to receive over a million dollars from the insurance company, but she was impatient and opted for a settlement of $80,000. She and Stanley spent all the money in a year. They went to Vegas, bought a jeep, a new dining room set, and threw outrageous parties. Johnny's mother was now overweight, depressed, and worked mostly as a nurse aid, when she could. The days of go-go dancing in L.A. were from another lifetime. Johnny had seen the old photos of her, he knew his mother was a knock-out when she was young. Still Johnny loved his mother deeply.

"Cosmos still hasn't come back," she sniffled to Johnny. "We put flyers everywhere and we have not heard anything. I'm afraid that Cosmos may have fallen into a dry well or attacked by a racoon or something. I don't know what to do. I keep burning candles but nothing yet. Stanley has looked everywhere too." Johnny's mom takes a deep breath. "Are you ready for this?"

"Yeah, what is it, Mom?" He asked.

"Candy left rehab, and she stole Stanley's antique gun collection. Everything is going wrong. I must figure out a way to break this spell."

"What?" Johnny exclaimed, ignoring the conversation about Cosmos and continued.

"Why did she do that? I thought she was doing good. That's horrible! What happened? Did she just walk out?"

"Yes, two nights ago. Pete came to see her and she left with him. We took the baby out to have dinner at the Last Lobster, and when we came back, the house door was open. We could see someone had been here. The only thing missing from the house was Stanley's guns. A musket gun, the pistols...all those stupid guns he had."

Stanley had a mint 1862 Springfield rifle-musket. The model was used extensively by the North during the American Civil War. Even though Stanley was from the South, he often said that the Springfield rifle won the civil war. Candy and Pete also took two snub-nosed pistols and a rare six-inch magnum. The magnum alone was worth $6,000, and with the other guns, the total was valued at $10,000.

"How do you know it was Candy who stole them?" Johnny asked.

"She has a key and we could see it was her because she changed her clothes and left them behind." They both looked at the Purple Rain t-shirt draped on the couch and Johnny shook his head in disbelief.

"Stanley said he could sell them for thousands or that's what the gun show people told him. He's very angry. Let's hope the police find Candy and Pete before he does," his mother added.

"You called the police?"

"Oh yes, we had to for the insurance. The guns are valued at $10,000! "

"That sucks. Candy was doing so good...so good," Johnny said, and paused, unsure what else to say. "Do you have any coffee?"

"Yes, I will go get you one," she said and shuffled into the kitchen.

Johnny looked about the room, shaking his head. He began pacing the salon, upset about Candy. He looked at the candles burning on the table and assumed they were for Cosmos. Annoyed, he walked over and blew them out. These candles should be burning for Candy, not a cat, he thought. Next to the candles was a thousand-piece puzzle of Van Gogh's *Starry Night* in disarray, a Big Gulp soft drink and bottle of Oxycontin. Johnny had heard about Oxycontin on the streets, referred to as 'oxides', a very powerful opiate narcotic given to people in chronic pain. Since 1996, the country has exploded with addictions and overdoses of Oxycontin because the pharmaceutical companies and doctors pushed them on people. Why not help myself, Johnny thought, curious about the high, he opened the bottle and pocketed three. He figured to take them on the plane, to relieve traveling anxiety.

Johnny's mother returned from the kitchen with two coffees, and Johnny, impatient and irritated, jumped right to the point. "Thank you," he said, taking the coffee. "Mom, I came here to tell you I'm going to Paris tomorrow."

"Paris? France? Tomorrow?" she asked, dropping the spoon from her coffee mug.

"Yes, that's right."

She paused and stared into the distance, falling into a mini trance. Something came over her.

"Mom? What is it?" He curiously asked. "What is it?" and continued. "I'm just going to Paris, you know Paris? The Eiffel Tower and all that? I need to see the world and play my songs in new places and get out of this town."

"That's good, Johnny," she sternly stated and confessed. "I think you should go and I think it's time I told you the truth..."

"Truth about what?" He demanded.

All of sudden, a scratching sound came from the door. Both of them looked and wondered where the sound was coming from.

"What is that?" she asked Johnny.

"I don't know. You're the one who has something to say."

"No, the noise..." She stated.

Johnny's mother looked at the unlit candles and they had the feeling of a ghost in the room. The scratching sound continued followed by a meow. Johnny's mother got up and opened the door. It was Cosmos with Stanley only a few feet behind her.

"Cosmos, baby, it's you!" she cheered, reaching down and picking up Cosmos. She hugged and kissed Cosmos with excitement. "Oh, Cosmos, where did you go?"

"I told you, Cosmos couldn't take the chaos around here, she was in an abandoned house up the street," Stanley barked. "I walked by it and saw her in the windowsill, just like she does here, pretty much the same window and same positions." Stanley, proud of himself and looking drunk, stood at the door with his hands on his hips, smiling, giving Johnny a sarcastic look. "You come to use up all the ink in the printer again? Eat all the cookies? Raid the fridge? Steal some guns?"

"Back off, Stan and be quiet, you're going to wake the baby," Johnny's mother ordered.

"The police are looking for Candy. If you see her, tell her the police are gonna get her. It's best if she just turns herself in," Stanley said. His voice started to get louder.

"Hey! Lower your voice, I'm right here," Johnny told him.

"I WILL YELL IF I WANT TO. WHAT ARE YOU GOING TO DO ABOUT?" Stanley badgered, poking Johnny in the chest with his index finger. Johnny glared at him with a menacing look.

"What?" Stanley fumed. "You think you're going to tell me what to do? You better wipe that smirk off your face. You got it you little bastard!" Stanley hit Johnny lightly off the top of his head with an open fist. Johnny backed away, his teeth began to chatter.

"Yeah, that's it, start your stupid teeth-chattering and get the hell out of here! Don't ever think of raising a hand to me. Did you get that? Get the hell out of here!"

Johnny kicked the front door open and walked onto the street, holding back his rage and tears. His mother followed him, holding the baby who was awake and crying, "Wait, wait! Johnny! Come back!"

Chapter 11
Out of Here

Being called a bastard hurt Johnny deeply, like a knife in the heart. The pain was so strong that he considered taking one of the Oxycontin. It would be nice to forget this day, and slip off into a peaceful state of mind, but he feared he'd probably oversleep and miss his flight. He decided he would take one in the morning and save the other two for when he was in Paris. The thought of having a nice buzz while crossing the Atlantic ocean gave him comfort.

Once back at his apartment he jumped straight into bed. He set the alarm clock for seven A.M. and took one good last look around the room. He knew it would most likely be the last night here. It had been a sacred place for him, where he had sought his higher truth and worked on his songs. There were many nights he laid awake staring at the Mexican painting on the wall. Even though the painting was a tragic scenario of a man about to be hung from a tree, the reality of the painting was more interesting than reality itself. This fascinated Johnny. The stark, mysterious and beautiful truth of what art could deliver. He thought the painting was a strong testimony of the perseverance of the human spirit, rising out of pain and poverty, in the same way the blues had. A noose around the condemned man's neck, sitting on a horse, the other end of the rope tied to a tree. Another man was standing next to the horse wearing a poncho and sombrero with a stick in his hand, ready to whip the horse. The mother of the condemned man was kneeling, crying and praying to the Virgin Mary to save her son. The Virgin Mary was sitting up in a cloud looking down on the execution. At the bottom, there was a Spanish prayer. The painting mimicked a religious iconography painting and now belonged to the room, or so Johnny decided. Dotty had promised she'd keep the room for him, but Johnny wasn't sure if he'd be coming back.

Johnny woke to the ringing of the alarm clock after seven hours of rock-solid sleep. It was September 19th, a new day as the sun began to make its presence known. He took a shower and got dressed. For a traveling outfit he decided on his favorite shirt, a retro-mod orange striped t-shirt, old jeans, and loafers with his white tuxedo jacket.

"Good morning, Johnny!" Dotty said, sitting in her usual spot with the TV on and coffee ready. She was excited to see him and felt happy and sad. She loved Johnny like her own child and had enjoyed his nonjudgmental attitude. Finding a replacement for him wouldn't be easy.

"Good morning to you, Dotty. How are you today?"

"I'm good, ready for your trip? Do you have everything? Passport, tickets?"

"Oh yes, I have everything for sure."

"You have francs? They use francs." She asked in her granny like way.

"I will get them when I get there."

Johnny stirred his coffee, took a sip, and was anxious to take the oxy. Making sure the coffee wasn't too hot, he secretly slipped one of the pills into his mouth and washed it down. He felt the pill drop into his belly without a problem. Acting normal, he smiled at Dotty.

"I will be really happy to be in Europe, with the new energy and spirit that awaits for me there," He mumbled with an excited but anxious feeling, unsure of whether he was trying to convince himself or her. He felt nervous like the first day of school and should probably go to the toilet, his body told him. They both looked at the TV in unison and a news alert appeared, breaking the silence.

"Julie Barry here, reporting from the San Francisco commuter train station. The station is temporarily closed down and passengers are stranded due to a powdery substance found on board. A hazmat team and the police are investigating the scene now as a possible terrorist attack."

Johnny and Dotty turned and looked at each other with a confused annoyance and concern, trying to process the news while continuing conversation. Carrying on daily life while the war on terror raged was going to require a certain amount of cognitive dissonance.

"What time is your flight?" she asked, ignoring the TV.

"Three. They said I should be there two hours early because it's an international flight. I have plenty of time, and I enjoy airports,"

The TV continued to show terrorist alerts about anthrax and bombers. They tried to maintain some sort of normalcy while sipping their coffees and waking up. Time was passing quickly and Johnny knew it was time to go.

"Can I use your phone ? I need to call a taxi." He asked.

She slid the phone over to him and he made his call.

"Dotty, I am going to miss you."

"You take care of yourself and send me a postcard of the Eiffel Tower, ok?"

"Sure will," he promised, looking her in the eyes, realizing she had been like a grandmother to him. He leaned over and gave her little fragile body a big hug, "See you when I return. Take care, Dotty, and thank you. You mean a lot to me."

"Good luck!" Dotty wished him as he went out to wait for the taxi.

The taxi pulled up to the house, and with guitar and luggage packed—four pairs of pants, some socks, and a few shirts—he dashed out into the street and into the taxi. "To the airport," He instructed. The driver stepped on the gas and from that moment on, the journey had officially begun. Living in the present is a present, a gift of now, and sometimes it takes a good opiate to magnify it. All fear, anxiety, restlessness and loneliness evaporate into thin air and are replaced with inner comfort and peace. Alive and alert, Johnny opened the window and watched his neighborhood pass by. He told himself he never really felt at home in South Boston. He was not a true 'native Southie' but no one ever made him feel unwelcome, and that was a good enough reason for him to stay. People accepted him as he was and allowed him to be himself. At one time Southie had been a racist part of town and had serious trouble in the 70s do to forced bussing. Johnny knew nothing of that and had met only good people. There was a Dotty on every corner, and the people were open, down to earth, and spoke their minds. He had even sold a CD to Whitey Bulger, the Irish crime boss, while playing in a pub West Broadway. Whitey approached Johnny and said, "Not bad kid, let me get a CD." Whitey then turned to the people at the bar and said, "I expect you all to buy his CD." Johnny sold 30 CDs that night, if he had known who Bulger was at the time, he would have given the CD to him for free.

Johnny began reminiscing about the moments he had in Boston. He enjoyed many summer nights at Castle Island eating ice cream cones and lobster rolls, but there was always a longing to be closer to the people. He thought back to the times at the video store when he would see families choosing films and wished he could join them or have Sunday dinner at their house. It never happened. There was a barrier he could not break, but who knows, maybe everyone else was looking for the same thing? Human connection had always eluded him. He also knew in his heart he would leave Boston one day. He didn't know when or how or why but he knew the day would come, and here it was. He looked at the streets as they passed, and knew he may never see these streets again, and that was ok with him, time to say goodbye to Boston.

Johnny started to feel the oxy, his blood pressure dropped and the taxi sped up. The suspension and shock absorbers in the car must have been brand new because the taxi felt like a waterbed on wheels. The warm sensation of the painkiller started to take full effect, a glowing feeling of calm and peace filled Johnny's body. The taxi swiftly sailed up L street bouncing over the potholes amid construction to the Callahan Tunnel going under the Boston Harbor and out to Logan Airport. Johnny gazed out the window passing by the sight of the Boston Tea party, sailing ships, 17th-century brick buildings, the same buildings that once housed the ideas of the American Revolution of 1776, now all overshadowed by skyscrapers in the financial center.

"Hey, Mon, how are you?" the taxi driver, a Rastafarian man with dreadlocks and a heavy Jamaican accent, belted out.

"Good!" Johnny yelled out, and asked, "You like music?"

"Sure do," the driver said, smiling at Johnny in the rearview mirror, turning up the radio.
Bob Marley and the Wailers song "Trenchtown Rock" came blasting out of the speakers. Johnny and the driver looked at each other in the rearview mirror and gave approving smiles. The taxi arrived at Terminal C for international departures. Johnny paid the Rastafarian, and tipped him five-dollars, and went straight to check-in for his flight. He glided along with his legs numb. Found a stroller for his suitcase and guitar and rolled on like a roman in a

chariot going to the colosseum. The buzz was working and it was fun to be at the airport.

"Hello, sir. Welcome to Delta. Passport and ticket," the gate agent asked.

"Here you go," The passport led the way as his hand numb from the opiate followed.

"Very well. Do you have any carry-on luggage?" she asked, smiling at Johnny.

"No, just my guitar."

"I'm afraid you must check your guitar into cargo hold."

"What? I can't, it's my guitar." He objected with a sad frown, imagining the guitar alone in the freezing belly of the plane.

"I'm sorry, Sir, but there is a code orange terrorist alert and you must check it in. We can put a fragile sticker on it." She offered as her words sounded very far and insulated from his ears.

"Ok. What can I do? I have no choice?" Nothing is a problem when high on an opiate, everything is met with ease and grace. If only he could feel like this all the time , he thought.

As the words came out of Johnny's mouth, he could see them in the air, but was genuinely worried about his guitar. He looked around for something to make the guitar stand out,and there on the counter was a white marker. "Hold on," he said to the agent.

"May I use your marker to write my name and address on it, in case it gets lost?" Thinking of the guitar as if it were a child needing a name tag.

"Sure, go right ahead," she told him.

Johnny took the marker, wrote his coordinates, and 'FRAGILE' in big letters. What can I add to it? he wondered. He wanted everyone who saw his guitar to treat it like the Holy Grail. "Oh I know" he thought , excited by his bright idea smiling like a little kid. In white marker he wrote 'GOD IS FRAGILE' on both sides of the case. How he came up with that, he didn't know. Why not? If God can be dead, like some German philosopher said, he can also be fragile, he thought. He figured this was sure to work. In his mind he saw the safe journey of the guitar, being gently handled every step of the way.

At Homeland Security, the guard directed the passengers to one of the five X-ray machines. Johnny remembered when going through security used to be a simple process of strolling past a metal detector, but now with the war on terror, it was time-consuming: shoes, belts, all contents in your pockets, all electronic devices, and carry-on bags must go on the conveyor belt to be X-rayed. Johnny threw all his things into a tray, hoping security wouldn't make him empty his pockets and find the Oxycontin. The guard signaled Johnny to walk through the metal detector. He made it by without any problem, turned and smiled. He had happily strolled through security to get to the departure gate. There was a long line of morning travelers with babies in strollers, kids with stuffed animals, businessmen with state of the art luggage, French tourists, and the odd soldier. Johnny, observed the crowd, noticed everyone looking nervously at the Muslim couple in the line.

He had two hours before his flight and the time went by quickly. He sat and nodded out and came too, to watch the news. The big TVs were everywhere and always within listening distance or sight. The reporters were incessant with the war rhetoric, terrorist alerts, describing weapon systems, latest jet fighters, types of bombs, how fast tanks can go, where the battleships are stationed, and of course, where Osama bin Laden may be hiding. A few months of this and a soccer Mom would be able to talk shop, with a hardened battlefield general. As the reporter continued with the call for war, Johnny heard the gate attendant announce boarding.

He got in line and waited for first class to board, then he followed suit with economy. The line passed quickly and Johnny walked down the hallway jet bridge, feeling like he was in a Stanley Kubrick film. The pain killer was in full effect. Legs numb, the smell of jet diesel and the sound of the engines idling created a Zen like sensation. Finally, on the aircraft, he found his window seat, buckled up and waited for take-off. The seat next to him was empty, he hoped and prayed a very pretty girl of his dreams would have it. No such luck however, the seat belonged to the Muslim man he saw waiting in line. The guy everyone was afraid of because; brown skin, moustache and beard, with deep dark demonic eyes, and a wife wearing a scarf meant; suicide bomber and hijackers with box cutters.

Johnny looked around to see everyone staring at the couple. The man sat down next to Johnny and buckled up. Johnny decided to be friendly and wanted to find out right away if this guy was a terrorist or not. Johnny would know instantly and struck up a conversation. After 10 minutes of friendly conversation he learned; His name was Abdul and was originally from Syria, living in Cambridge, was professor at MIT University, and was on his way to Paris, to give a talk about environmental issues and climate crises. Johnny felt ashamed for thinking such thoughts but also felt he interrogated the man for his fellow passengers. The trauma of 9/11 was still fresh and the media wasn't helping none.

Within a few minutes, the engines were roaring and the jumbo jet was speeding down the runway. The plane lifted, steadily climbing to 30,000 feet. Outside the window, Johnny watched the city get further and further away.

He had the view over Castle Island and all of the south shore. He spotted the gas tanks that had the rainbow swish painted on it, next to the Dorchester Yacht Club, and the Southeast Expressway with its usual bumper-to-bumper traffic. The plane followed the coastline over Buzzards Bay of Cape Cod, and then went over Nantucket Shoals, flying over George's Bank fishing ground. Johnny looked down at the fishing boats, tankers, and cruise ships that became specks in the Atlantic ocean. The East Coast of New England was now visible . He couldn't help thinking about the Native Americans who used to live there: The Wampanoag, Nipmuc, Shinnecock, and Penobscot who had lived there for 10,000 years before the Europeans arrived.

Johnny's ears popped and his teeth started to chatter. He could feel himself falling into a haze of deep thought which was amplified by the Oxycontin. The inner voice in his head spoke up clearly, and directly with an announcement "The corporations are taking over the country. The poor and marginalized are targeted for private prisons or a hospital they can't afford. If you can't find a place in the matrix, one will be found for you. You are no longer a citizen but only a consumer. People are being fed diets that keep them in permanent malnutrition. There's no profit to be made from the dead so they keep people ill and barely alive and paying". Tucked away in his window seat alongside Abdul, Johnny drifted off into a deep nod.

"Thank you for flying Delta and my name Captain Nelson and I am your pilot. If there is anything we can do to make your flight more enjoyable please let one of our attendants know," the captain announced on the loudspeaker. Johnny woke and saw the seatbelt sign was off. He unbuckled himself, put the seat back, and stretched his feet out. Enjoying the cool air blowing into his face from the tiny plane air conditioner, he thought back to when he was a child laying in the grass dreaming of being on a plane. He wondered if there was a child down there doing the same thing. If this was all he got from selling the song, it was good enough. A ride in the clouds, high on a narcotic and meeting a man named Abdul, was better than hanging around Boston.

Chapter 12
The Eagle has Landed

Five hours later, the plane circled Paris waiting for its turn to land at the Charles Du Gaulle airport. Johnny's ears began to pop as the altitude of the plane dropped. Looking out the window in the countryside, Johnny started thinking of WWII and the Americans who liberated the city from the Nazis. He naturally imagined tanks rolling in, B52 bombers, lost parachuters meeting the resistance and bridges being blown up. Johnny had seen too many movies and Stanly never stopped talking about the great war as he called it. It was six A.M. in France and the sun was rising on a new day. More French was being spoken and Johnny only knew the basics: Bonjour, ca va? Comment ça va? Comment tu t'appelles? Enchanté! Puis-je vous offrir un verre? As the plane landed safely and approached its gate, the captain welcomed the passengers to Paris. The seatbelt light turned off and everyone began scrambling for the door. Johnny got up, stretched his legs and head, feeling groggy and no longer high, wished Abdul and his wife a good stay in Paris. Time to see the city, he exited the plane and headed for customs.

"Purpose of your stay, Sir?" the customs agent asked Johnny. Johnny thought for a moment, unprepared for the question, wanting to brush his teeth and wash his face. He still wasn't fully awake. "Sir, the purpose of your stay?" the customs agent asked again.

"I don't know," Johnny answered. "What do you mean 'purpose'?"

"Are you here on business, visiting family, vacation...?"

"I haven't thought about...well I guess it would be business cause I want to write some better songs," Johnny told the agent.

The agent gave Johnny a very serious look, stamped his passport and returned it to him.

"Welcome to France," he said with a smile.

Johnny passed through customs and into the airport. Roaming around, he started looking for a money exchange booth to change his $1,300 American dollars. His eyes scanned the airport until he found one, and then he went and exchanged his money. At the exchange, the agent gave back 7,000 francs for his $1,300. Johnny looked at the francs and noticed they had an artist on them, Paul Cezanne the impressionist painter. Will the U.S. put Jimi Hendrix on a hundred dollar bill one day? He wondered.

After a bit of confusion, trying to read the signs in French, he found the exit and a taxi. The driver spoke broken English to Johnny and was friendly enough to make him feel comfortable, he also felt fuzzy, tired and hung over from the oxy.

"May I smoke?" Johnny asked the driver.

"Sure, no problem," the driver told Johnny. Johnny's mood changed quickly, and he was glad to be on the road again. "Where exactly do you want to go?"

"Take me to the center of the city. I'm a musician and want to play in the streets."

"I take you to Saint-Michel, Latin Quarter. I take you there." Said the driver in broken English.

Johnny sat in the back of the speedy Peugeot, looking out the window at the sky, it was overcast and the sun was hard to find in the milky hazy grey sky. The buildings looked colorless, lonely, and old. Standing guard on the horizon was about a dozen white tower buildings around forty stories high—a depressing sight. This could easily be Detroit, New York City or Chicago where poverty is pushed out. In Paris, they called it 'Les banlieue', which means 'to banish.'

The taxi entered Paris and the sights became more desirable, livable and noble. The cab arrived and dropped Johnny off at the Saint-Michel fountain in the sixth arrondissement of Paris. Johnny got out of the cab and to his astonishment and relief, the area was beautiful. He looked at the fountain and saw a huge statue of the heroic Saint-Michel with a sword in one hand, leading God's army against Satan's evil forces. A biblical superhero of its day. The statue sat at the top of the fountain overflowing with water into a large pool. Built after the Second French Empire in1860, it still looked brand new with dragons and eagles hanging onto it. With Saint-Michel using his mighty sword to slash away the snakes and demons crawling at his feet. Johnny took in all vibrancy of the square. This was not a place for anyone with an attention disorder, it was hard to focus with all the chaos: little speedy cars, electric buses, obnoxious motorcyclists, fragile bicycle riders, day-glow rollerbladers, classic 1950s style dog walkers, moms and dads, free gangs of kids, pickpocket gypsies, beggars dropping to their knees, an Athenian looking pigeon feeder. Johnny had never seen so many people on cell phones either; back in the States, only the trendy people had cell phones.

Johnny put his suitcase down, pulled out his guitar and started singing his song "The Devil Didn't Scare You None" in front of the fountain. He wrote this song a few years back, it was about how most men would rather face death and destruction than summon the courage or emotional fortitude to face love; they'd rather kill than love. Johnny thought this was the perfect song for Saint-Michel as Saint-

Michel was not a coward and the song was about cowards.

The larger than life presence of the fountain gave off the feeling of an ocean with the fresh air and pigeons. As Johnny sang, Europeans, Parisians, and tourists all gathered around to listen to him. He laid out his guitar case and people were tossing coins in as they passed. Johnny had been playing at the fountain for around 20 minutes when he spotted one of the most beautiful women he'd ever seen. He then looked around and noticed all the women in Paris were romantic, dreamy, and cinematic, not trashy and pornographic like the girls he saw back home. With all the newness and beauty of the old world around him, Johnny felt more alive than ever. He trembled with excitement as he thought about how he was playing in the land of his ancestors. He felt a connection to what little roots he did have or thought he had, even if imaginary. He never knew his grandparents but had heard they were Irish and Swedish. As he played in the early morning sunlight he couldn't get over how simple it was to be standing there and playing, as if the subway from Boston had a stop called Paris. In little than eight hours he was far removed from what he knew. Sometimes life is just that easy.

Johnny played for another two hours and made 500 francs. This is by far the best I've ever done, I should have come to Paris sooner, he thought. Overjoyed by how the first day went, he packed up his guitar and went looking for a hotel to catch some sleep. His eyes were getting droopy and the jet lag was catching up but the excitement of being there was hard to contain.

Johnny roamed the narrow streets of Saint-Germain and was amazed at how the liveliness of the city grew more and more, as he dodged cars, buses, and people. The eye was confronted with so much at once in Paris it was hard to have a focus point: shops, cafes, restaurants, hundreds of people moving through the city. Observing the new world around him and following his intuition, he arrived at Rue Gît-le-Cœur. Johnny noticed how simple the street was with only a few shops and a quiet eight-story hotel with 46 rooms, The Royal Flush, it was close to everything too. This is the perfect hotel, he thought.

Johnny walked into the hotel and saw a man at the front desk. The lobby was quiet and looked comfortable with a gold and red colored canopy and matching wallpaper with rope designs on it. A big coffee table with leather chairs, a Persian rug, a bookshelf, and black and white photos on the walls . The man at the front desk looked to be of Indian descent with black hair and deep dark eyes and a medium build. He was probably around 45 and was dressed in a blue suit with a black tie. He moved incredibly slow, like slow motion in a video. Johnny had never seen a man move so slow.

"Bonjour Monsieur," said the desk clerk very slowly and softly.

"Hello," said Johnny, slowing himself down.
The desk agent instantly realized Johnny was American and began speaking English with an Indian accent. "Hello, how may I help you?" the desk agent asked.

"I'm looking for a room," Johnny told the desk agent as he looked closely at his eyes at what looked to be eyeliner.

"We have single or double rooms available. How many nights are you staying?"

"Oh, I only need a single room and for at least three days."

"Very good. It's 400 francs a night. I will need your ID."
Johnny paid the desk agent and handed him his ID.

"Here you go," said the desk agent in slow motion handing Johnny the keys to a room, "you have room 16 on the third floor to the left. The lift is broken at the moment so you will have to take the stairs." He smiled graciously at Johnny.

Johnny took the key, his suitcase and guitar and peacefully made his way up the stairs to his room. The front desk man's calm and grace gave Johnny the feeling of serenity. He must meditate or be enlightened, Johnny thought. As he made his way up to his room, he noticed the hotel was narrow just like the Paris streets. He liked the close feeling of the city, he felt less alone even if he didn't know anyone or speak French. It was comforting and to feel the human connection and touch everywhere, centuries upon centuries of it.

Johnny found his room, unlocked the door and entered. The room was small with a window overlooking the street and a little shower with a toilet. The double bed looked inviting, wide, heavy and comfortable. The ceiling had large beams running across it and had been painted black. The walls were wall papered in a flowery light blue green, it made Johnny feel calm and relaxed. Dropping his suitcase and placing his guitar to the side, Johnny laid on the soft bed and fell fast asleep, allowing himself to give in to his exhaustion without restraint. Within minutes he was fast asleep with the lights still on.

Chapter 13
Making New Friends

Ten hours later, Johnny woke to the sound of a police siren. He wasn't familiar with the sound but he recognized it from the movies. He remembered it from the 70s American film *The French Connection*. The sound wasn't as sharp and punctuating as an American police siren. The French siren was long and drawn out with a lower pitch near the end. He looked out the window and saw two blue economy police cars speeding up the narrow street. The people crowded onto the sidewalk to let them pass.

A fresh new day awaited him outside, blue sky, vivid and alive with color, the people and buildings appeared saturated. Amazing what a good sleep can do. Shifting his eyes up from the street, Johnny saw a beautiful mature woman across from his window putting on her bra. The woman could easily satisfy any young man's fantasy for a mature woman. She looked a bit like Sophia Loren. Johnny and the woman made eye contact and she smiled at him. He did his best not to stare, was taken by this desirable coincidence and quickly turned his business back to minding his own. He decided to take a shower and the image of the woman was still with him. He thought about masturbating, but vowed " none of that, I need a real lover, not an imaginary one".

Once out of the shower, and dried off, he put on a black t-shirt, jeans, loafers, and his favorite white tuxedo jacket. He now needed a coffee. He combed his hair and wished he had some gel, then went down to the lobby to get breakfast. On his way down the stairs, he heard a deep loud voice speaking in English. He listened closely, trying to make out what was being said. As he listened, he recognized the voice but didn't know where from. The voice continued.

"The best fucking president in the United States we ever had was shot by a crazy actor, John Wilkes Booth, and he was the son of an actor as well," the voice said.

The voice was describing the assassination of Abraham Lincoln, the 16th American president. Johnny reached the bottom of the stairs, he saw the man talking to a middle-aged German couple who were also guests at the hotel.

Johnny was sure he knew the man but couldn't place where from. He was tall with a full head of gray hair, strong features and looked to be of Italian descent. Johnny decided to join the morning group of three for breakfast. He instantly liked the man and admired his presence. He listened closely to him making eye contact. Johnny poured a coffee, took a croissant, and sat down in an armchair next to the fireplace. The man continued to talk while resting one hand on his wooden cane, the head of the cane had an eagle carved on it. Enjoying the audience of the two German travelers and now Johnny, he continued.

"So wouldn't you know, the best president the United States ever had was killed by an actor and the worst president we ever had was an actor. My father wanted me to be a doctor but my mother wanted me to do theatre. I was happy to do theatre," the man told them.

Johnny smiled as it came to him: the man was Nick Costello, the American TV actor who starred in a show in the 80s called *Angel Hour*. He played Detective Ray and had the ability to communicate with angels to solve cases. Johnny loved the show and watched it every day after school. He would come home to an empty house, turn on the TV, and watch *Angel Hour* while eating peanut butter cookies and drinking Pepsi. Johnny even bought a detective coat similar to Nick's, a short tan colored trench coat with side pockets and a belt. Nick's role as the detective was one of the few male role models Johnny admired and when faced with tough situations he couldn't deal with, he would ask himself, What would Nick do?

"Good morning young man," Nick said to Johnny. Johnny, somewhat excited, wasted no time connecting with Nick.

"Good morning. My name is Johnny Vincent and I used to watch your show, *Angel Hour*. I loved that show. I would watch it every day after school, and I watched all the reruns. You were the best. What was that phrase you used to say?" Johnny asked.

"Open your eyes and ears, solve the case in the days, not years," Nick said with a smile.

The German couple who had been talking with Nick decided to leave, they excused themselves, wished everyone a nice day. Johnny, feeling slightly nervous about meeting someone famous, especially Nick, jumped right in, "My favorite episode was the one where the angels contacted you through a parrot. There was an innocent man on death row wrongly accused of murder. The parrot was able to speak the name of the real murderer but the real murderer was dead and buried. And with the help of the parrot, you were able to find the grave, dig it up for a DNA sample, and free the innocent man."

Nick, amused and happy to receive Johnny as a fan, said, "Yes, that was one of our best shows for sure, *Case 119 The Trail of Bobby Baxter*. I remember it very well. My co-star, Barbara Brooks, and I ended up getting married and then divorced some years later...but that's another story." Nick thanked Johnny and felt very flattered. "What brings you to Paris Johnny?"

"I had to get out of the States, I just can't take it after 9/11 and the war on terror stuff and all the police and drugs. I flew in from Boston last night and came here to Paris to write my songs and sing them, like a troubadour. And you?" Johnny asked .

"Very good. You are an artist too," Nick said smiling. "I'm starring in a film about Gregory Corso. We are supposed to start shooting next week. We're still waiting for the camera operator."

"Who is Gregory Corso?"
Nick lit a cigarette and started to tell Johnny, "Gregory Corso was the youngest of the beat poets. You don't know him?"

"No I can't say I do but I heard about Jack Kerouac, Allen Ginsberg..." Johnny confessed.

"That's all right, Johnny, Gregory is lesser-known but in some ways more the poet and real deal, in my opinion. This is the hotel they all stayed in the late 50s.
Look, their photos are on the wall." Johnny, surprised to be in a hotel where the Beat Poets stayed, got up and examined the photos. On the wall hung 10 black and white labeled photos of Kerouac, Ginsberg, Gysin, Burroughs, Orlovsky, and Corso.

The photos showed them clowning around in the streets of Paris.

Johnny stopped at Gregory Corso and asked, "You do look like him and why do you say he is the more interesting?"

"Well, pour us another coffee and I'll tell you about him since I am him," Nick said laughing with a mad look in his eye. "Gregory was born in 1930 in Greenwich Village in New York City at St. Vincent's Hospital, the same hospital Dylan Thomas died in. They call it the poet's hospital."

"Hey, that's my last name, too," Johnny exclaimed.

"Maybe you are related…" Nick offered before continuing, "so, Corso's parents were Italian teenage immigrants and his mother moved back to Italy when he was a little child. Corso was then put in an orphanage. When he was young, at the orphanage, he had to transport a toaster across town but on his way he decided to sell it to get money to go to the movies. He was caught and sentenced to three years in an adult prison. Imagine that? They put the kid in a hardcore prison. While Corso was in prison, he created a crazy story about taking over New York City with a gang he controlled. He told the other inmates that his members had walkie talkies and were situated throughout the city and would act when he told them to. He was afraid of being raped and concocted the story to impress the other inmates. There was a New York Italian mafia crime boss who was also in the prison and heard the story and thought it was quite imaginative. The mafia boss found Corso entertaining and since he was so young, the boss decided to make him a mascot, for him and his crew. On top of that it just so happened that Lucky Luciano, also an Italian American crime boss, had recently donated a library to the prison, after he had recently been imprisoned there. Corso learned about poetry from that library and discovered his favorite poet, Percy Bysshe Shelley and that's how he began writing poetry."

"Wow! That's fascinating, and you're making a movie about him here?" Johnny asked.

"Yes, that's right, this was the place where the beatniks came to stay, right here in this hotel. It's changed but like you they were fed up with the States and had to get out to create. So you are in the right place," Nick assured him.

Johnny and Nick looked around the stylish lobby with its cozy warm settings. The colorful wallpaper with red and gold design, oriental rugs, three leather fauteuil chairs, a modest size red couch, a wooden writing desk, coffee table with art books on it, and of course the black and white photographs of the beat poets, a fireplace, and a bookshelf which led to a three-step walk up into a dining room that could seat twelve people.

"I had no idea about the history of the Hotel. I just followed my intuition to get here" Johnny admitted to Nick.

"Paris is the place, Johnny. Every important artist of the last 500 years has spent time here. In Paris, 'Poverty is a Luxury', to quote poet Jean Cocteau. Ideas and creativity have flourished here in the city of lights for centuries. You're in the right place."

"Thanks, Nick. Say, do you think it would be ok if I watched you on the set of this film you're in?"

"It might be kind of boring, but if you want to, sure. I think it would be ok."

"Yes, I would like that a lot, seriously."

"Ok then, I will know more later but in the meantime, nice to meet you, Johnny."

"Nice to meet you too, Nick."

"Please excuse me, I must go up to my room and study the script for the film. Let's get together and talk some more while you are here. I'm around for a few weeks anyhow."

"For sure! I'd like that!"

"Great," Nick said, getting up off the sofa to go upstairs. "Good luck and bon inspiration."

Johnny finished his coffee, felt excited and privileged to meet a movie star. He couldn't believe it and was proud of himself for not getting too nervous. Johnny then went to get his guitar, to find the place he played yesterday.

Chapter 14
Down by the Riverside

Was it left or right? Johnny asked himself trying to remember how to get back to the Saint-Michel fountain. With each hour the air became fresher, the skies bluer, the sun brighter, and the day hotter. The Parisians had slowly started to integrate back into their normal routine from their month-long vacation in August. They still retained their tans and positive mindsets, which would slowly fade until their next holiday break. Johnny eagerly followed his intuition, turning right and walking onward dodging swarms of people, cars, and buses. He knew he had to pay attention and stay on the narrow sidewalk or he could get easily clipped.

"Extra! Extra! Read all about it! The United States declares World War III. George Bush Jr. starts World War III! The war has begun! Read all about it!" a voice yelled out from down the street. Johnny was soon face-to-face with a middle-aged man of Pakistani descent who was declaring the bad news. He was waving the newspaper in the air and shouting headlines with vitality and optimism, reminiscent of how papers were sold during the Great Depression.

The Journey of Johnny Vincent

The newspaper seller was selling the French newspaper *Le Monde* creating a wake of confusion as he moved through the street. Johnny stood there with a group of tourists ready to buy the paper, only to discover they'd been duped by the sensational fake headlines. The seller was known to all the locals and had an effective and charming way of selling the paper, all the while making people feel welcomed and pranked. Straight away the American tourists were set up and felt ashamed of their countries foreign policy and embarrassed by their own naivety.

Johnny continued wandering, looking for the fountain, mesmerized by the grandiose architecture and symbolism that found its way into every facet of Paris. The city was overflowing with ornamentation, symbols, statues, and monuments. There was a gargoyle behind every nook and cranny. The proximity of the Parisian architecture allowed him to observe everything intimately. Passing by open windows, Johnny saw a woman fixing her makeup, children learning piano, the elderly in moments of lost gaze, couples fighting, and the everyday drama of living. Johnny then came across a small park that looked to be around 200 square meters with an iron-wrought fence around it. The iron bars on the fence were sharpened at the top in a spear-like fashion, making it dangerous to climb. Johnny once heard a story of a man who was struck by lightning in a park in Paris. The man died because he was too close to the fence, no doubt it was this kind of fence. Danny thought to himself. Half the park was grass and the other was clay gravel, the clay gravel left dust on your shoes that could stay for days. A few cherry blossom trees, a statue of a ballerina girl, a trash can, four dark green painted steel chairs, and three granite slab benches all surrounded the statue of the ballerina girl.

Johnny opened the heavy door, it squeaked as it opened, it could use some oil he thought as he entered. He walked over to one of the granite benches and sat down. He stared at the statue of the ballerina. She resembled Candy—thin and lanky—and looked to be around 13 with one arm stretched out and the other on her hip. Johnny was amazed at the likeness and sat in silence staring at her. The serendipity of the moment felt unforgettable, and for a minute, the park felt like utopia. Johnny began to think about Candy and her suffering. He felt horrible that he trusted Dave and he couldn't protect his sister. He wished there was something he could have done but there was nothing he could do now. It was out of his hands and her and Pete were another run. " C'est la vie" Johnny mumbled to himself.

Across from Johnny, outside the park, stood a wall or the side of a building, he really couldn't tell which. It was an enormous structure left standing that didn't appear to belong to any of the buildings around it. It was about 10 feet in height, gray, green, ochre color, and had centuries worth of lines, cracks, pockmarks, and gouges. It could have been standing there since when the Romans ruled. Staring at it he found forms, and images, hands, faces, landscapes, and clouds that seemed to come to life. It was a mystery what lay on the other side. Small sparrows flew around a huge cherry blossom tree, like big flies looking to attack and kill anything smaller than them. Thank god they're tiny, he thought.

Johnny heard the gate to the park squeak, a young man with curly black hair around Johnny's age came strangling in with a bottle of wine. The young man was dressed in a blue velvet smoking jacket, bell-bottom jeans, shiny black hipster boots, and a dark red scarf. He looked at Johnny and asked for a cigarette in French. Johnny didn't understand and the young man quickly realized Johnny was American.

"A cigarette? Have you a cigarette? Please," the young man asked in broken English.

"Sure," said Johnny and pulled out his pouch of tobacco and rolling papers.

"My name is Alex."

"I'm Johnny," he replied and put a pinch of tobacco into a paper for the slightly drunk stranger. Alex rolled the cigarette and looked at Johnny for a light. Neither of them had a lighter. Alex continued to speak, holding the unlit cigarette and slurring his words, "Your country made Michael Jackson. He is the greatest musician ever. "Billie Jean Is Not My Lover" is the best song ever written." Johnny wondered how everyone knew he was American. The young Parisian man continued, "Poor Michael. He just wanted to make music for us and he had this groupie woman who claimed that Michael had a child with her. Michael didn't deserve this." Alex's eyes started to water as he sang the song. "Michael had to deal with this stuff all the time. In the song it says for 40 days and 40 nights the law was on her side. Can you imagine what Michael went through for 40 days and nights? Michael can fill soccer stadiums around the world everywhere! Tens of thousands of people! Just think about that!"

"You're right, he is the greatest," Johnny told Alex, pretending to be a fan.

"I saw Michael on his last tour, it was the most amazing thing I've ever seen."

Johnny didn't know what to say and suspected Alex had forgotten his medication. He was slightly drunk but seemed sharp and lucid. Johnny had never met anyone as passionate about Michael Jackson, he never really cared about Michael but listening to the young Parisian man, he concluded he was probably right. How could you argue against that? Michael was a genius and the world's most famous Pop Star, The King Of Pop.

"It was nice to meet you, Alex. See you around," Johnny said looking to get out of the conversation and leave the guy to his own Michael Jackson fantasy.

"Ok, you be cool, Johnny. I'm always here in this park if you want to talk."

Johnny picked up his guitar, exited the park to see the wall, he was looking at before he was interrupted. He got closer, investigating the cracks and studying the tiny details of its weathered history. The left side of the wall had a plaque with the names of four Frenchman who were lined up against it on August 17, 1944 and executed by the Nazis. It was easy to imagine the firing squad. Perhaps a high ranking SS agent and six soldiers, the poor ragged, hungry frightened condemned locals who were caught, who were maybe caught hiding Jews. Just like in the movies but here was the place, the exact spot, their names on the plaque, on the street they were probably born on. On the other side of the wall, a few yards away, Johnny could see down to the banks of River Seine.

To the right of the bank sat the enormous Musee Du Louvre. Johnny had no idea what he was looking at. The Quai De Conti had a steady flow of traffic that kept him separated from the river. Parallel to the river, along both sides, were vendors selling posters, rare books, and old French novelty items. Johnny waited for the traffic and walked down to the river onto the Pont des Art Bridge. The sunlight and scenery of the setting were familiar to him but only as a memory of a dream. He could see and feel what must have been the inspiration for the impressionist painters. On the wooden bridge were artists and their easels, an accordion player, small groups having little picnics, lovers gazing into each other's eyes and little dogs running around unattended. This place is perfect for busking, Johnny thought as he watched barges and tourist boats flow with the river passing under the bridge.

Johnny found a free spot on the bridge that had enough room for him to perform. He began singing and playing with his guitar case open. People passed by and smiled, occasionally throwing a franc into the case, requesting Elvis songs, Johnny reluctantly played "You Ain't Nothing But A Hound Dog" for them.

After about 30 minutes of playing, Johnny bent down to get a cigarette and a roller skater dressed in very baggy orange pants, a sweatshirt with dreadlocks came crashing into him. The roller skater pretended it was an accident. Johnny fell on his guitar and cracked the back of it.

He got up, pissed off and yelled, "WHAT'S WRONG WITH YOU?"
The roller skater responded in an angry tone in French. "Fais attention, stupid idiot!" Johnny could tell it was something of the effect that the crash was an accident.

The man spoke a little English, "Stupid American. Go back to your country!" he shouted. A young woman around 25 with jet black hair, a black leather jacket, jeans, and white Doc Marten shoes, saw what was happening. She wasted no time to help Johnny. The young woman started yelling in French at the aggressive roller skater and they started to argue. The roller skater had other friends, who arrived and set-up cones for their roller skating dances and tricks. They were street performers and wanted Johnny's spot.

"THAT FUCKER CRACKED MY GUITAR" Johnny shouted.

"Don't mind those assholes, they're fucked up and just want the spot," the young woman told Johnny. "Let me see your guitar." She then turned to the skaters and yelled at them. "Connard! Tu as cassé se guitare !"

"I'm so sorry, it was an accident. He should look where he is playing, I was just going by and he moved in front of me," Lied the roller skater.

"They make me so angry! They do this to my friends all the time. They want to have the spot and are just stupid roller skaters, not musicians," she told Johnny.

"Who is he?" Johnny asked.

"That's Jacques. He lives at the squat and is not cool at all," she told him. "I know someone who can fix your guitar if you like."

"Yes, that'd be very nice of you."

The girl smiled at Johnny, "I like your songs, I was just listening to you. My name is Carol. Welcome to Paris. Would you like to go for a drink?"

"I would love to. My name is Johnny."

The roller skaters, trying to draw a crowd, set up their cones and started blasting a boombox. They were doing jumps and dances. Johnny and Carol packed their things and left, crossing the otherside of the river.

Chapter 15
Getting to know Carol

The one o'clock sun shone brightly onto the enormous courtyard to the Louvre, leaving no shadow, as Johnny and Carol made their way across it. Johnny stood in awe of being at one of the world's greatest museums. He felt the magic of its wizardry, greatness and sensibility of something sacred. He had the impression it was connected to another dimension and certainly another time, that was obvious. A steel and glass pyramid had been planted in the courtyard, as if it was dropped from the sky, clashing with the 15th century. How bizarre he thought.

He knew he'd never forget this moment, standing at the doorstep of this fortress, a palace that held some of the most famous art treasures in the world. The past French Empire had pillaged the world and now had all its treasures here. New York City had the Empire State Building but Europe had renaissance style buildings that seemed to span for miles. Nature had produced beautiful mountains, canyons, valleys, and rivers, and Paris was man's attempt at an equivalent. Johnny was not used to such monumental beauty and style.

As they walked, a young African man approached them, selling Eiffel Tower key chains and postcards. Carol tried to push the street vendor away but Johnny stopped her and bought a little Eiffel Tower from him for 20 francs. He was delighted to have his first souvenir and carefully put it in his pocket believing it would bring good luck. He was happy to discover that the word souvenir was the same in French as in English. In French it meant a good memory but to the Americans it was associated with cheap marketable trinkets of tourism.

Carol took Johnny to O Bla De Bla Da Café, a café near the Louvre, on Rue De Nevers. The café was clean, hip and pleasant with 60s décor. Orange booths with a red and white tile floor, a jukebox and pinball machine; it had managed to retain its originality and didn't undergo any stupid renovations in an attempt to look contemporary. The people were happy, talkative, drinking coffee, beer, wine and smoking like mad. Along the mirrored wall there were six booths, they sat in one of them and ordered omelets and coffee.

Johnny found Carol to be beautiful and sweet. He was mystified in ways he couldn't understand. The mystery of love had him fucked up in thought. Her eyes, nose, ears and mouth and hair—he fell in love right then and there, under the UFO-shaped orange hanging lamp . Johnny wasn't sure of her ethnicity. He wondered if she was Spanish or maybe Polynesian or maybe part Japanese. It was hard to place her roots. He looked closely at her, he noticed her fingernails had nicotine stains on them and were dirty and needed to be cut. For an instance he saw her from her perspective and felt close to her, just looking at her warmed his heart. He even understood her smell, taking it in ,without looking too obvious. She smelled like a mix of coconut and flowers.

Johnny tried to explain to Carol why he was in Paris. He was conscious of his words and story, while doing his best to impress her. He had thought hard about leaving Boston long before he left. He wasn't sure what the truth was. There were different layers to the question and it wasn't as simple as 'I'm on vacation.'

"Are you from here?" He asked .

"Not originally. I was born in Vietnam and came here in 1975 with my mother when I was just a baby," she confided. He smiled and looked into her eyes with sincerity and compassion, trying to hide his mixed feelings about the Vietnam War. He was anti-war, but he felt guilty for just being American, by association. He felt the need to say something, not condoning was approval of it.

"Horrible what my country did to such a beautiful place. I'm totally against the war machine for profit, it's part of why I left America. I won't pay any taxes to a place that destroys weaker countries for profit," he confessed, knowing it was a bit of an empty declaration, he had never paid taxes because he never made enough money to do so.

"Hey, it's ok, not your fault. All these governments are the same everywhere. We are just people, but it was hard for my grandparents and uncles, they all died." Johnny was speechless. He had never heard those words come from another person in his entire life. He looked into her deep dark peaceful eyes and felt more about the Vietnam war in those seconds, than he had ever felt from a film or documentary.

Carol ordered a carafe d'eau, a small free pitcher of water, a little secret the Parisians do to save money, so they don't buy overpriced drinks. The omelets and fries arrived, he asked for ketchup and they quietly began eating. They smiled and chewed politely, while looking at each other innocently. The jukebox played "Bonnie and Clyde" by Serge Gainsbourg. The sound evoked an ambience of a foreign land, cool and hip where danger could happen. The song was based on a poem by Clyde Parker, he wrote it weeks before they were gunned down by the FBI. The music seemed to take over the café, filling the room with emotion; it owned the café.

Carol started singing along, "*Alors voilà Clyde un petit amie, elle est belle et son prénom ce Bonnie,*" she stopped and started to tell Johnny about the singer, "It's Serge Gainsbourg singing, he's like our Mick Jagger."

"I like it, it's very cool. I want to hear more," He said.

"Stick around and you will for sure, but you're going to have to learn some French."

"Oh, I will, I will."

"Johnny is such an American name, oh boy. But you don't seem like a typical American but I see you like ketchup, like all Americans do."

"Thank you. My mother named me that, she said it was after her great-grandfather who was a gold miner in California. He played guitar and piano and wrote songs. He never found gold but he met a lot of people playing music, so my mother named me after him."

"And your father?" A solemn mood swept over Johnny, and she saw the change in his demeanor. "I've never known my father. I don't know who he is," Johnny confessed. Johnny's face became blank

146

and he shook his head as he took a deep breath and exhaled slowly. He didn't intend on becoming too emotional, open, and honest so quickly, but something about her made him feel like he could lower his guard. It was beyond his control. He looked up at her with a blank expression. She put her hand on his, he wanted to cry but made sure he didn't.

"Oh geez, I am getting too emotional, sorry about that," he apologized.

"It's ok , you have the right," She assured him.

Johnny continued, "Never knowing who, what, and why is what drives me crazy, it's just not fair. There's always something that feels like it's missing," he told her, his teeth started to chatter nervously and quickly.

"Are you cold?" she asked.

"No, when I get nervous my teeth chatter." He continued, "I think not knowing who my father is or was...it feels like you're reaching for something and it's never there but you keep reaching and it's always empty. It makes me nervous and my teeth chatter."

"I know how you feel," she said. Her words echoed and resonated the truth. He looked at her with a smile to understand more.

"My father was an American soldier in the Vietnam war and I never met him either. His name was Carl and he is from Texas. When the Vietcong took over Saigon he had to leave immediately. The

Vietcong destroyed all the birth records and would kill anyone associated with the enemy. My mother and I hid in the jungle. We made a hut of mud and sticks and had nothing to eat. My mother kept me, she could have left me in the orphanage but she didn't. She was able to get us out and escaped to France and then to Paris. I'm lucky to be here," Carol shared.

"Wow, that's an incredible story. And your mother, does she live with you now?"

"No, I have my place and she lives with a French man named Jean Yves here in Paris. They have a photography studio together. I work with them too. It's a nice job I am able to have my time off."

They finished eating their omelets, then ordered cheesecake and coffee for desert.

"This is turning out to be a fun day. I didn't expect to meet you," she said with a warm smile and twinkle in her eye.

" Same for me, thank you for coming to my rescue, it was worth getting a crack in my guitar."

"My friend can fix it. She's a really good luthier, repairs and makes guitars. I can meet you tomorrow and we can take it to her. I can't do it today, I have to work at the studio in an hour, so I must go soon."

"That's very nice of you. Yes, please, let's meet tomorrow and see your friend. I have lots of time and no place to be. " The cheesecake arrived and they took their time eating, looking into each other's eyes and smiling. Johnny's heart felt alive and he did his best to maintain the excitement of being with her. It had been a long time since he'd felt emotions for a woman. Carol was beautiful and his interest in her overrode the lustful feelings he felt for her. He felt emotionally, spiritually and physically connected all at once. This was rare and Johnny knew that when you connected on those three levels, it was mirrored and would grow. He knew in order for love to last it had to grow. He was excited and getting way ahead of himself. In his mind he saw a match made in heaven.

"So you're a photographer?" he asked, coming back down to earth.

"Yes, but I mostly do commercial work. I work for my mother doing passport and school photos. Sometimes I work at the Moulin Rouge taking photos of the guests who want to be photographed with the dancers. But my real work is taking photos of street scenes and people. Recently, I've been doing behind-the-scenes photo shoots with the dancers at Moulin Rouge and transvestites at drag bars," she told him.

"That's great. I would love to see them."

"You will, I'm sure."

They finished their cheesecake and agreed to meet the next day at 1;00 P.M.

"Let me buy your lunch since you saved me. I'm really happy to meet you," He said to her.

"Likewise," she said. They then got up from the booth and made their way to the street.

"Do you know the place Odien?" she asked him.

"No, but I can find it."

"Ok, let's meet there. See you at one tomorrow," Carol confirmed and leaned in and to kiss the sides of both of his cheeks. "We kiss in France, but just on the cheeks." She looked at him seriously, "Kissing on the lips is for your lover."

"Ok, see you tomorrow," He said, smiling and trying to act cool and calm.

He watched her walk away towards the metro and disappear into the underground. Johnny could have jumped for joy, skipping and running down the street. He felt like he could touch the clouds and cry. As he walked away from the café, he started to sing a little ditty to himself. With guitar in hand, he decided to go back to the hotel and find Nick and relax. Everything was alive with color, sensation, and sound; it all vibrated with the frequency of love. All around him the people were in harmony and in sync with another. People smiling, laughing, and making sense. He couldn't get Carol out of his mind, her beauty permeated his being. Like he had on a new pair of glasses, everything in perspective.

Chapter 16
There are no Shortcuts

"If the doors of perception were cleansed everything to man would appear to man as is, infinite..." Expressed Nick, reciting a William Blake poem from memory to Phillip, a young French jazz musician of 25 with curly black hair. Nick continued, "For man has closed himself up, he sees things through chinks of his cavern," Nick paused. "Just think about that my friend. That's a poem by William Blake and Aldous Huxley wrote the book *Doors of Perception*, based on it.

"What are chinks?" asked Phillip in a heavy French accent.

"They are cracks and narrow openings," Nick explained.

"And the cavern is his head?"

"Yes, cavern from the word cave, a large enclosed dark space."

"Maybe it is for our good that we cannot see the infinite reality. We might go mad."

"You have a point Phillip, and let's not forget Aldous Huxley wrote the *Doors of Perception* on LSD."

"I don't want to take LSD to be able to see. I have music, poetry, theatre, art...they all cleanse the perception of reality. Knowledge gives power and your heart gives it wisdom,"

"You're right, Phillip! There are no shortcuts to the infinite but dropping some LSD can help you cut through all the disinformation and propaganda, and from there you have an imprint of expanded consciousness that you can recall. The challenge is to make sure you can return," Nick replied.
Phillip laughed and lit a cigarette, "You mean the door might be closed?"

"But of course. It would be you who needs the key to get back, and if you do make it back through the door...well, you've got it."

"It?" asked Phillip, "what is 'it'?"

"'It', you know 'IT'. I can't explain it. You know it when you see 'IT'."

"Ok, yes, I see. Not sure how to answer."

"We know 'IT' when we see it." Nick paused for a moment to think how to best describe this so-called 'it'. "The pathos of wisdom and the direction of father intellect. I don't know, let me say this. The journey is paramount to the traveler. All that is required of the journey is that 'truth' is the ultimate goal, not the destination. Like a dance, there is no specific place for the dance to begin or end. 'IT' cannot be contained in words. You either have 'IT' or you don't. But like Jack Kerouac said..." Nick then pointed to the photo of Jack Kerouac on the wall, and continued, "The only people for me are the mad ones. The mad to live, mad to talk, you know mad with desire and passion. So the key here is to survive your madness and to translate that which is beyond words," Nick finished. He wasn't even quite sure if he understood what he was saying.

Johnny lost outside and in love, wandered in amazement, blindly trying to find the hotel. The narrow streets, twisting and turning, always leading to the boulevard. Using the River Seine, the Louvre and Notre Dame as points of reference, he tried to guess his way. Confused and frustrated, Johnny stopped to ask for directions. "Excuse me, can you tell me where nine rue Git Le Coeur is?" He asked strangers . No one stopped, they all ignored him as if he were a beggar. After a few failed attempts, he lost confidence and became insecure. He tried again but with a little French accent, pretending he spoke French. He spotted a young professional man with horned rim glasses, a tweed coat, and a small dog and thought "maybe this guy could help me". The young man welcomed Johnny's asking for help, it must have been the way he threw his hand out and shrugged his left shoulder and rolled an R. The man took the opportunity to practice his English. He pointed Johnny in the right direction and gave him a Paris map book, and quickly explained how to use it. Johnny happily thanked the young man and felt embarrassed to find out he was closer to the hotel than he thought.

Nick saw Johnny entering the hotel lobby and welcomed him. "Hello Johnny, how are you today?" Hearing his name called by the voice of the actor he loved to watch as a child was a sobering sound, he almost turned around to see if he was talking to someone else.

"Hey Nick, I'm really good, I'm happy to be back at the hotel and you?"

"I'm ok," responded Nick and introduced Phillip.

"Hello, nice to meet you," Phillip said to Johnny in a heavy French accent. "Welcome to Paris," extending his hand.

"Thanks," Johnny replied.

"What brings you to Paris?" Phillip asked.

"I was bored with the U.S. and it was getting too fucked over there: school shootings, private prison for-profit, bad food and so much worse. I couldn't take it."

Nick interjected and spoke for Johnny. "He outgrew the culture. It happens, especially for creative types. Johnny's a singer-songwriter too." Johnny beamed with happiness to learn that one could outgrow culture. He had never even used the word 'culture' before. And was honored to have Nick sticking up for him.

He looked at Phillip and agreed with Nick, "Yeah, that's right."

"I see," said Phillip with a smile, he continued, "I play guitar too." He looked at the guitar case in the corner, got up, opened it and pulled out a beautiful mahogany coffee-colored 1957 Gibson ES 125 and handed it to Johnny. Johnny took the guitar, surprised at having such a beautiful guitar in such good condition before him, "Wow, perfect condition. Where did you get it?"

"I bought it from an old-time jazz player here, Little Jimmy from New Orleans. He came here during the war as a soldier and helped liberate Paris from the Nazis and never returned. A real good guy, he played with all the greats: Coltrane, Ella Fitzgerald, Miles Davis...you name it. He taught me everything I know about jazz. He died last year and I bought it from him before he passed," Phillip explained with a mood of sorrow.

"Sorry to hear that," Johnny said while doing the scales on the guitar.

"Yeah, he was something else. He lived a good life, he was 84 when he died."

Johnny felt the presence of Little Jimmy in the hollow body guitar. He had never met him but imagined a small smiling African-American with a mustache and beard. You can feel the blood and sweat that had seeped into the maple wood of the guitar. You could also feel the jam sessions, concerts, and after-hour parties. The worn-out frets and low action on the neck made the guitar a pleasure to play; it was made in a factory in Kalamazoo, Michigan, and had aged like fine wine. Guitars like this have a lot of confessions layered in them. Johnny thought of his own Gibson and how it was damaged and scarred.

"I have a Gibson too but it's cracked on the back of the body," Johnny told Phillip while closely inspecting Little Jimmy's guitar. Johnny looked up at both Nick and Phillip, and started to tell them what happened, "I was playing on the wooden bridge and after about 20 minutes, I bent down to get a cigarette and a fucking big goofy guy on rollerblades came crashing into me. He pretended it was an accident and I fell on my guitar and cracked the back."

"What?" Nick exclaimed, "are you serious?"

"Yes, I am."

Phillip chimed in, "That fucking asshole, it was Jack. I know these people. They are always pushing people around, real jerks. I play at the bridge too and they are always fighting for the spot. We musicians, find good spots and create the energy, and the street performers and beggars come and try to take them."

Nick in a fatherly way looked at Johnny and cleared his throat. " I suggest you take your time on this and figure out the lay of the land. You can't let him push you around. If you're gonna stay here, you're going to need to defend your ground, but take your time."

Johnny, hanging onto every word, understood what Nick meant. Johnny had never been one to fight, he had been bullied throughout his childhood, and at home by Stanley. One day, when he was walking home from school, he saw about five or six kids from the neighborhood playing jump rope and kicking a ball. Johnny being around ten, stopped to see what was going on and the kids invited him to join. The kids asked Johnny many questions. They began running around him like a pack of hummingbirds asking who he was, where he lived, why he lived there, who his father was, and more. It was an interrogation, that turned into an initiation with mild torture. The kids circling him like that, and all the questions were too much for Johnny. When they saw how afraid and sad he was, one of the kids put the jump rope around him and they tied him to a tree. They then all ran away and left him all alone tied to the tree. Johnny's mother found him an hour later as the sun was setting. It was a traumatic experience for him and he still had nightmares about it. Johnny never took that route home from school again and avoided many places after, taking the long way home or looking for shortcuts. As a result of that experience, he was never able to defend himself or raise a hand to someone, it was next to impossible for him.

Johnny handed the guitar back to Phillip.

"Remember the greatest victories require no battle," Nick advised Johnny. Nick excused himself to go upstairs to rehearse his lines for the Corso film. Phillip and Johnny continued to talk, hitting it off very well. Phillip invited him to a party.

Chapter 17
The Squat Party

"The very concentration of vision and intensity of purpose which is the characteristic of the artistic temperament is in itself a mode limitation. To those who are preoccupied with the beauty of form nothing else seems of much importance." — Oscar Wilde

Johnny and Phillip left the hotel to go to the party. Johnny realized that while he and Phillip had come from different backgrounds, there was a mutual understanding between them; they viewed each other as the same. Phillip came from a 'Famille bourgeoisie de Paris' and received what was called 'a bonne education'. He had read all the classic literature and considered himself an artist. He rejected and rebelled against the social conformity of being a French bourgeoisie and instead chose the lifestyle of an artist living in a chamber du bain as a poor musician. He was a very good guitarist, inspired by Django Reinhardt and played gypsy jazz.

Walking to the Odeon Metro, Johnny and Phillip eagerly exchanged ideas and opinions on music. Phillip led the way and explained to Johnny how the Paris metro system worked and showed him how to buy tickets in the machine. Johnny didn't understand but he went along with it. They took line two to the Pigalle Metro in Montmartre, the 18th arrondissement, where the party was. On the train there was a proud defiant homeless man, who made Johnny think of Napoleon. He was very short, walking through the train car, asking for money, explaining his misfortune with the charisma of a theater actor. He was struck by the caliber of the begging that took place in Paris; it was a legit fixture, an authentic archetype, as old as the city itself. Phillip explained to Johnny that the man was out of work and now asked for handouts. They arrived at the Pigalle Metro and were greeted by a fountain sitting at the bottom of a hill in Montmartre. The neighborhood had a grittier feel than the hotel's as it was filled with sex shops, clubs, and cafes with lots of movement from tourists and locals. Phillip told Johnny to watch his wallet as there were many pickpockets.

The party was hosted in an old bank that was turned into a squat. There were about a 100 people living in the five-story building, and had been taken over by artists, refugees, and homeless people. They had changed the locks on the doors and claimed the building. The laws in France favored tenants over landowners, and it would take a court order to make them leave, and that could take years. In the meantime, the groups were living as a cooperative community, organizing different events, and working and living there. Johnny had never heard of such a thing and the word 'squat' itself did not sound very inviting to him.

The party was packed with about 300 people, young Parisians, Ibiza hippie types, world travelers, and many dropouts of society who just couldn't stop partnering. Johnny and Phillip moved through the crowd to the bar and bought some beers. Outside the building, in the back, there was a courtyard and you could smell chicken grilling on a fire in a barrel. On the red brick wall beside the courtyard was a huge mural of a nude woman. On the other walls, there were murals of different types of landscape art, brut art, pop art, and graffiti. Smoke from hashish and cigarettes floated above the crowd in the open space, creating a blue hue of light that came down from the top of the building. Rap music was blasting from large speakers and people were milling around with plastic cups of beer and wine, smoking, drinking and laughing. Downstairs, in the cave, a rock band with guitar and drums were playing. Johnny had never seen so many pretty girls in one place. The courtyard had an open-air feel and was filled with a huge cloud of tobacco and marijuana smoke rising to the evening sky. If Johnny knew Paris was going to be like this, he would have come a long time ago.

Johnny left Phillip and decided to explore the party on his own and made his way upstairs. Upstairs he found single rooms that had been turned into ateliers for painters and sculptors. All the doors were open and there were micro-parties in each atelier. It was amusing to think these rooms were once bank offices and now they were used to make art. Johnny walked into the atelier of a French Algerian artist named BizziBoy, a graffiti artist from the banlieue of Paris. BizziBoy's paintings of tigers, snakes, and African women were hung everywhere and all had his signature tag. BizziBoy was dressed in a red Adidas tracksuit and was full of energy explaining his style in French slang. Johnny had no idea what everyone was talking about but felt close to them; it felt like home. The atelier had around 20 people in it, all from different parts of the world. There was a tin tub of beers on ice and joints being passed around freely. Another young African man, Balu from Togo, was freestyle rapping to a rhythm track. Balu had a microphone in his hand and was dressed like a typical L.A. rapper with baggy pants, an oversized Lakers jersey and a backward L.A. cap. Balu spotted Johnny at the door and motioned for him to come in. He continued to rap but Johnny didn't understand what he was saying, it was part English and part French.

Say no to all you haters
Feed you to the alligators
Then I can hear you cry
Here I am, a young lion
Fire and burn justified
Can't keep me down
Even if you tried
Fire and burn justified
Justified boom boom!
Can't keep me down if you tried

Johnny was amused by Balu. After Balu finished his song, he put the microphone down and came over to introduce himself to Johnny.

"Salut, ça va? Bienvenue," Balu said to Johnny, placing his on his heart and giving a handshake known as 'pulling one'. Balu instantly realized Johnny was from the U.S. and switched to English, "Welcome, my name is Balu."

"Merci," Johnny said using the little French he knew.

"Don't worry, I speak English."

"Are you from L.A.?"

"No, I'm from Togo, Africa, and I live here in Paris but one day I'm going to live in L.A. and rap like Tupac!" Balu professed then asked, "Where in the U.S. did you come from?"

"I'm from Boston,"

"Boston! Said Balu and went on "Celtics, Larry Bird, Magic Johnson...the best basketball ever," Balu looked to Johnny for his approval.

"No doubt," Johnny agreed, bluffing that he knew about basketball, but more impressed by Balu's knowledge of his home team The Celtics. Balu continued excited to meet an American.

"I love America. Tupac, Biggie Smalls, Snoop Dog, Eminem..."

"You like Muddy waters?" Asked Johnny.

"I don't know him."

"You mean you don't know the blues? Robert Johnson, Howlin' Wolf?"

"No, I don't know them, Howlin' who?" Balu revealed.

"Howlin' Wolf. How about Chuck Berry?" Quizzed Johnny.

"No, I don't know him either."

"Oh my God. They're the greatest Americans ever. They created the blues and the blues had a baby and it was called rock 'n' roll. If it wasn't for African Americans, who came to the U.S. as slaves, we would have the most boring culture ever imaginable."

"You think so?" Balu asked.

"Yes, and there's James Brown, the Godfather of Soul, Little Richie, Fats Domino, John Coltrane, Miles Davis...there are hundreds of other great artists, all African American. How can you be African and not know these people?" Johnny preached.

Balu beamed with pride to be African. He had never heard a white person talk like that. He was impressed by Johnny.

Balu shifted in posture and cleared his throat and began to speak seriously, "I can see you have a good soul. You are a good man. I like you, you are my friend."

"Thank you. I'm honored, that means a lot to me." Johnny stated.

When Johnny was around seven, his first friend ever was an African American boy named Teddy. They were best friends and had matching shirts at one time: purple velour t-shirts with zippers instead of buttons. The matching shirts made Johnny and Teddy feel like twins and they knew they were kindred spirits. Johnny and Teddy had met at school and lived on the same street and played at each other's houses. One day, Johnny's stepfather Stanley, called little Teddy a nigger boy and it all changed. Johnny would return from visiting Teddy's house and Stanley would say Johnny stank from the visit. Teddy's parents found out what was happening and Johnny and Teddy never saw each other again. The last Johnny heard, Teddy was in a gang and had been shot dead in a shootout. Johnny always thought of Teddy as a twin but never saw him again. Johnny was happy to have this moment with Balu. He was never able to reconcile the hurt of losing his friendship with Teddy, all from the racism projected onto him by Stanley. The trip to Paris was starting to make more sense than he imagined.

Johnny saw Teddy in Balu. "Good to meet you Balu, let me get you a beer," He offered full-heartedly. Phillip came into the room and was happy to see everyone. Johnny introduced Balu to Phillip. Balu continued to perform some more rap songs from his new album *Justified*. The three of them drank beer all night, trading stories, and Johnny happily preached to Balu about the American Blues. They partied all night, becoming the best of friends.

Chapter 18
Happy Hangover

Johnny opened his eyes and had no idea where he was. Panic set in. Within an instant, the reality hit him; "I am in a hotel room in Paris". What the fuck he gasped and let out a deep breath as if coming up for air from under water. Head pounding with a massive headache, his mouth parched and dry like the desert. He looked at the clock on the nightstand, checking the time, relieved to see it was only 11:30 A.M. He still had time before meeting Carol.

He fumbled out of bed and made it to the sink, turned on the tap, splashed his face with the coldest water he could force from the faucet, turning it as far as it could go. It felt good, fresh and alive. Drinking as much as possible in between splashes. Shaking off the hangover, he remembered meeting Balu with Phillip at the squat. The fun moments of the night came tumbling back to him through the haze of his pounding head. He checked his pants pockets looking for their phone numbers, hoping he remembered to take them, and he did. He was pleased to have Balu's number and to still have a good amount of francs as well.

The hangover was a small price to pay for such a great evening, he figured. He went back to bed and took his time waking up, trying to piece together the previous night's events. As far as he could remember, it was all right, good and innocent, nothing to be ashamed of, even if some of the events were foggy. Even with a hangover, it was better than how he felt in Boston. There wasn't much back home for him, just after two days it was more than obvious he had made the right choice by leaving.

After taking a cold shower and putting on the same clothes from the day before, he went downstairs to see what was going on. He found Nick in Gregory Corso character rehearsing. Dressed in a flannel shirt, work pants, looking like a hobo studying his lines for the film. Pacing around the lobby by himself, with his script in one hand, and a cigarette in the other. Nick perked up seeing Johnny, and turned on his craft, reciting his lines with a New York accent, "This is America where it's all fun and games. In California, I sang my song into the ears of a dying Mexican. He died with a smile on his lips. That bastard had two gold teeth, an ounce of hash, a button of peyote and a 14-year-old wife. This is America! It was all fun and games!" Nick turned to Johnny and smiled with a fresh set of new teeth.

"That was good!" Johnny said, clapping lightly pouring himself a cup of coffee, still a little shaky from the night on the town. "Is that for the film?"

"Yes, it is. I'm getting there," Nick admitted, stopping and sitting down. He looked at Johnny squarely and began to unload his thoughts, "Let me tell you something: if you wanna be a poet, you're gonna have a heavy cross to bear and you're not going to have much money. It's a heavy price to pay to reach the divine, and it gets lonely." Nick confessed while smiling at Johnny with sincere compassion.

Johnny felt compelled to share his thoughts, which was easy, still being slightly drunk from the night. "I need music to write, some kind of melody and rhythm. I don't know if I would call it poetry…"

"I think so. You are condensing and compressing language to convey ideas and emotions to bring about a higher sense of being, shining a light on what makes us human. To me, that's poetry." Offered Nick.

"I never felt smart enough to do real poetry like Wordsworth or Winslow Homer," Johnny admitted. He then paused; it was the first time he'd heard himself say those words out loud.

Nick laughed and said, "Winslow Homer is a painter."

"Oh, I meant the guy who wrote *Blades of Grass*."

"Walt Whitman and its *Leaves of Grass*. Whitman, Shelley, Keats, Blake...they're all romantic poets," Nick said. "They can be very healing."

"Healing?" Johnny asked.

"Yes, life was very hard in 1850, people died of disease, famine, starvation, wars, and so on, and they shared perspectives of the supernatural and natural. I suggest you read some while you are here. Like I said, very healing."

Johnny had been waiting a long time to hear those words of wisdom. He felt speechless, feeling every word Nick said. Johnny had lost hope of meeting someone who could offer such advice, and now here he was in Paris, talking with a man dressed like a mechanic or a janitor; Nick looked like an ordinary suburban American dad working in the yard. Nick had been in many films but never had a Star Wars blockbuster. He painted, wrote poetry, did theatre, truly lived the life of an artist, and didn't get the acclaim he deserved. Hollywood had given him all the wrong friends, wives, addictions, and thieving agents. You would have thought it left him bitter and broke, but he was still faithful to his heart, holding a steady course and remaining true to his creative self. After all, here he was doing a low-budget film of a poet. A poet no one knew, at the Beat Hotel, long and forgotten after the fact but ready to receive Johnny. Nick was at his post ready to receive, holding down the fort.

"Now, if you're a writer, you can keep the day job, but if you're a poet, there's no place for anything else but your poetry. By poetry, I mean painting, sculpting, acting, or music. People are going to judge you, not an easy ride, but that's the price to reach the divine," Nick said. "It's the journey, Johnny, it's all about the journey. Keep your mind open and follow your heart. Keep writing your songs, don't give up, you'll be fine. I know it, after all, here we are in the beat hotel. The universe is looking after us Johnny."

Johnny didn't know what to say and was astonished by Nick's advice. Where does he get these ideas from? He wondered. "Thank you Nick, that means a lot to me seriously. I have never had such good advice," He said, excusing himself to get his guitar to meet Carol.

Nick stayed at the hotel and continued studying his lines. Johnny walked away, trying to remember what Nick said, hoping he didn't seem rude by leaving so quickly.

He had left his notepad up in the room and felt he needed to write it all down. He was just going to have to remember it.

Chapter 19
Fixing the Guitar

Johnny sat at the base of the giant Danton statue along with 20 other people. Space in Paris was limited and people had no problem brushing elbows with one another. Mostly students from the Sorbonne University, mixed with tourists and locals waiting for a rendezvous. The square was busy with buses, motorcycles, bicycles and cars. The statue was in front of a movie theatre with many restaurants and the entrance to the Odeon metro. For a city center, this little space had the right amount of trees flush with green leaves, creating just the right amount of light and shade.

Johnny wondered who Danton was. Judging from the statue, he must have been a heroic figure. Danton stood gallantly, pointing the way to victory with an arm stretched out. At his feet, a falling soldier and a man holding a flower . Johnny turned to the girl on his left and asked, "Excuse me, could you tell me who Danton was?" The young girl looked almost insulted and gave Johnny a 'Bonjour'. He quickly realized he had disrespected the social code of the Parisian greeting.

"Bonjour, bonjour," he said nervously.

172

The young girl smiled and responded, "Parle française?"

"Ah, no...sorry, parle English?"

The young girl sighed and smiled. She dropped her French, and like a shapeshifter, started speaking perfect English with no accent, "You want to know who Danton was?"

"Yes, please," He asked.

"Danton fought for the liberty of the people. His famous quote is 'Either I do away with the guillotine, or it does away with me'."

"Ok..." Johnny said with a lump in his throat.

"They chopped off his head, but he was essential in the revolution and inspired the poor to rise," she explained to him and asked. "Are you here on vacation?"

"Yes, but I think I'm going to stay," he admitted, realizing that's what he wanted to do.

"If you choose to live here, you must learn French. You do not want to be living in Paris for 20 years and not speak French. There are lots of Americans here who don't learn the language," She told him, turning to see her boyfriend who had just arrived. She wished Johnny well and went off with her date, a handsome well-groomed lean guy of about 30.

Carol arrived a few minutes later. She was on a beautifully restored classic shiny red Vespa with white-walled tires. She pulled up to the curb and shut off the engine. Straddling the bike, she waved her hand and yelled out to Johnny, "Hey! Over here!" He turned to see her. She looked sexy dressed in a black leather jacket and boots and a white helmet. Johnny picked up his guitar and went over. She kissed him on the cheek, still wearing her helmet. Johnny was impressed by the innocent presence of her face coming from the white helmet; it showed only her face without the distraction of her hair. He noticed how clean and clear her skin was, how full and red her lips were and how dark and mysterious eyes were. A slight separation in her nostrils gave her the appearance of being in deep thought. Johnny found all this extremely fascinating. Carol wore no makeup and the memory he had of her didn't compare to how beautiful she looked today. She must have more of her father's genes than her mother's he assumed. He was very happy to see her and could spend the rest of the day just looking at her.

"Wow!" he said, "that's a beautiful scooter."

"Thank you, I finally got it. I'd been waiting two years to get the money for it."

"Very nice," he complimented.

"Come on, get on the back." She handed him a black helmet and helped him put it on.

"I've never been on one of these," he confessed.

"Don't worry," she assured him. Johnny got on, and she started the motor and continued with instructions. "Just be like a sack of potatoes," she instructed, grabbing his right hand and placing it around her belly. "You'll be fine. Hold onto me, and don't drop your guitar. I'll take you on the scenic route." She kicked the Vespa into gear and released the clutch, driving out into the busy, chaotic street. She swerved in-and-out of traffic alongside buses and angry, aggressive Parisians pushing and honking their way through traffic. Johnny held his guitar case in his hand as it acted as a shield on his left side. The case still read 'GOD IS FRAGILE'.

She sped onto Boulevard Saint-Michael heading north, passing the fountain where Johnny first played. Staying on the same road, he noticed the name of the road changed twice. She then turned onto Boulevard de Sebastopol. Johnny was excited to be this close to her with his legs around her outer thighs. He had her safe in his embrace with his right hand firmly around her waist. She led the way with her long soft black hair in his face; her softness and smell intoxicated him. It was the same scent from lunch, like roses and the ocean. She made another turn, this time right onto Rue Faubourg Montmartre. As they turned they came across a garbage truck making its rounds. The men were dressed in green as they quickly went up the street tossing green plastic trash bins in the back of the truck. Their route was holding up traffic. Carol swiftly maneuvered the scooter up onto the sidewalk and weaved in-and-out of pedestrians before driving back onto the street. She knew the city well. Johnny, quite surprised by the sudden jump onto the sidewalk, did his best to deal with the scowls and insults the people made as the Vespa passed them. This would never happen in the U.S., he thought. Before he knew it, they were at the bottom of Rue des Martyrs, outside Christelle Luthier's guitar shop.

Johnny and Carol went into the shop. Christelle was hard at work, calm and concentrated, working very quietly, fixing a wooden guitar that was in a vice. There were guitars and tools all over the table and on the walls. Two beautiful Gypsy jazz guitars sat in the shop window for sale.

Christelle and Carol had been friends for many years. Christelle came from a long tradition of luthiers, and she was known all around the world for making high-quality classical guitars. Many such artisans lived in Paris and had been working for centuries on wooden instruments. Carol also took photos of the guitars Christelle made. Christelle looked up from her workbench with a smile, happy to see Carol and Johnny. Carol introduced Johnny to

Christelle, and they got along instantly. Christelle complimented Johnny on his white tuxedo jacket, which made him feel right at home. Christelle offered Johnny a cigarette and coffee. He readily accepted, still feeling a bit hungover from the night before. Handing Johnny the coffee and smoke, Christelle looked at Johnny's guitar case and smiled, reading GOD IS FRAGILE on the side.

"God is making a comeback?" she asked.

"No, why?" Johnny responded.

"Nietzsche said he was dead, and you say he is fragile. It makes me think he's coming back to life but in a fragile condition," she said with a smile.

"Oh, I just wrote that cause it came to mind. I was hoping that when the baggage handlers at the airport saw it, they would treat it as the Holy Grail, assuming they were God-fearing people."

"Smart thinking."

Christelle opened Johnny's guitar case and pulled out his Gibson, admiring its beauty. She then turned it over and saw the crack. "Ok, here we are," she said, examining the six-inch split.

"Yes, I can fix this with some glue. No problem, but it'll have a scar."

Carol then let out a gasp of frustration, thinking of how the crack happened. "The stupid, dangerous roller skater named Jack did this!"

"What?" asked Christelle, confused, and amused by the roller skater being the culprit.

Still in disbelief of what had happened, Johnny explained the incident to Christelle. She listened carefully to Johnny, relaying all the details of what happened. Christelle shook her head, confused by the act of aggression.

"I'll have it ready for you in about a day or two," She offered. "Wow that's great!" Johnny said, thanking her. Christelle offered to fix the guitar for free, giving him a proper welcome to Paris, making up for the bad incident he had with Jack. She handed him her number and got back to work. Carol and Johnny thanked her again and left the shop.

Johnny and Carol got on the back of the scooter. He felt compensated for the violent act that had happened. It was kind of Christelle to fix his guitar for free. He held onto Carol as they sped away up Rue des Martyrs.

Chapter 20
The Top of the Mountain

Johnny was impressed with Carol's driving skills as they sped up Rue des Martyrs. He kept thinking about the street name, wondered where it came from. He knew what a martyr was but how could they name a street after one? And it was plural, he imagined hundreds of martyrs shuffling up the street with heads drooped, frowning, hooded and cloaked. Paris offered much for the imagination in this way, of its medieval and gothic period. Taking in the sights from the Vespa, Johnny recognized where they were. He was pretty sure, it was where the squat party was but couldn't be certain.

Continuing down the street, they stopped at a traffic light, pulling up alongside a butcher truck who was unloading four quarters of beef. At eye level, Johnny was two feet away from a cow carcass dangling from a hook. The carcass was freshly cut and raw, showing its blood, meat, and bone. He counted the ribs, not accustomed to such a sight. Carol, seeing the carcass, turned her head towards Johnny and said, "I'm a vegetarian." She then revved up the Vespa, and they went flying through intersection, passing guitar shops, cafés, wine bistros, and cheese shops. They continued up a big hill, finally making their way to the steps of the Sacré-Cœur church at the very top of Montmartre, the highest point in Paris. Carol parked the Vespa under a tree by the side of the church, and she and Johnny got off, placing their helmets with it.

The Sacré-Cœur church was enormous. Originally it was built as an appeasement for the people of France after the French government executed 25,000 people during the Paris Commune of 1870. The government built the church shortly after, completing it in 1923. Hundreds of people were gathered outside the church's entrance enjoying the panoramic view of Paris. Johnny took in the overwhelming view of the city, noting the millions of little gray, tan, and brown cement and stone buildings; they seemed to be all thrown together. Two thousand years of fighting for an extra foot of space, from this point of view, Johnny could see that Paris was one of the most populated cities in Europe. The view from the church was beautiful and spanned for miles and miles. Johnny thought it resembled an ant farm. A few gold domes shone through amongst the homogeneous view: the Arch De Triumph, the Eiffel Tower, and the Montparnasse one skyscraper, were the only recognizable sights.

They decided to go inside the church. Carol led the way as Johnny read a sign on the entrance wall 'A sanctuary of Eucharistic worship divine mercy'. He wasn't sure what it meant exactly, but he liked the idea of divine mercy; it sounded like a good song title. Johnny had always believed in God but never went to church or practiced any religion. He did feel there was a force greater than himself at work, and he thought it was based on love or giving and receiving. He figured this force was similar to how the sun and rain provided life to the trees and how the trees provided oxygen through photosynthesis. He assumed everything in nature operated on the principle of function and need. The challenge was to find your own function in this process, but once you did you would be ok. He arrived at the fundamental question of "what does it mean to be human?" He considered the question and felt being human was about following your heart and expressing your talent. He could not come up with more.

Carol continued to lead the way, telling Johnny how she came to the church when she felt overwhelmed and confused by life. Together they stood at the top of the aisle, which had a red carpet leading up to the altar. On the altar, there were beautiful fresh flowers, gold statues, ribbons, and wreaths with light radiating from the large stained glass opening in the dome overhead. Painted on the dome in cobalt blue and gold was a huge Jesus Christ. The big Jesus was floating above them with arms stretched out to greet all who entered the church. Stained glass windows with biblical scenes lined the side walls letting in the diffused natural light throughout the day, creating a contrast of light from above and darkness at the ground level. A steady line of people entering followed each other, making the customary sign of the cross with holy water at the font. Neither Carol nor Johnny knew the custom but continued anyway with curiosity. The inside of the church was spacious and dark, and it was filled with hundreds of people slumbering through in a zombie-like fashion. The mood was somber, quiet, and peaceful. There were paintings and religious statues with ornamentation everywhere. The suffering of all the world seemed to pass through here and had been transcended. Carol took Johnny's hand, and they wandered deeper into the church passing, lit candles and people praying. The crowd seemed to flow like a lazy river ride at the waterpark Waterworld, entering left and going clockwise around the altar and exiting out the opposite side of the entrance. Johnny decided to duck into a smaller altar to have a moment alone. Carol continued with the flow of the tourists. Johnny lit a candle and said a prayer for Candy and hoped she was doing alright. In the small altar, Johnny admired a painting of the Virgin Mary and baby Jesus. He wondered about Priscilla and Candy. He gave his best at a sincere and concentrated prayer and hoped they would be taken care of and have a good life. Satisfied with the intent of the prayer, Johnny turned and rejoined the flow and looked for Carol. Unable to find her through the shades and shadows of people, Johnny decided to exit the church. As he came back onto the steps in the sunlight, he saw Carol waiting for him with a smile.

"I have never seen such a beautiful church. Where I'm from, we have nothing that big and old," He confessed to Carol.

"Come this way," She motioned. She wanted to take Johnny to visit Place du Tertre, situated alongside the church. Walking through the crowded little cobblestone streets of Place du Tertre, they passed shops, cafés, painters with easels, and artists offering portraits for 30 francs. The square was full of life and tourists from all over the world.

After passing through the street of Place du Tertre, they decided to go to a restaurant advertising itself as a traditional guinguette, Café Des Artistes Cabaret. The café was full of about 50 people singing and drinking the local guinguette wine. There was a man wearing a beret playing the accordion and another man with a straw hat at the piano. "What is a guinguette?" Johnny asked.

"It's a..." Carol searched for the right words, "a nostalgic happening, a very traditional party from the suburbs, but since the 80s, there's been a revival of the festive party. Guinguettes were popular in the 1920s, but television took its place. I love it here! Come on!" Carol always had a fun and heartfelt time whenever she went, the festive guinguette parties always made her feel at home.

Johnny and Carol took a seat at a table and joined the party. Everyone was welcomed at the guinguette, and someone poured Johnny and Carol a glass of wine as Carol sang along with the songs. The guinguette reminded Johnny of one of his mother's French Impressionism puzzles. He smiled as he enjoyed his glass of wine agreeing with everyone. Not knowing what they were saying, watching them sing and talk in French with laughter and enthusiasm. Johnny felt lost in translation but was blissfully content. Carol ordered them a plate of ham bone and potatoes. Johnny was very hungry and devoured the plate, hoping not to insult Carol, remembering she was a vegetarian. Carol ate the plate of vegetables the server offered her. The ham Johnny ate was thick with a pineapple glaze sauce and oil, and the wine was dense and hearty. After three glasses, he and Carol were on the dance floor, doing their best to dance with the others; the dance was somewhere between a waltz and a tango. They held onto one another spinning around, pretending they knew what they were doing. They looked deeply into each other's eyes, dancing as people clapped, trying to keep up with the fast tempo of the accordion and piano music.

After 20 minutes they were exhausted. They sat down and ordered dessert, a profiterole topped with ice cream, and two cafés. Johnny was beside himself with joy, and so was Carol. Huddled alongside one another, they shared the dessert and cafés. In between bites of vanilla ice cream, Johnny gave Carol a sweet innocent kiss that was light and meaningful; it felt magical. A woman with a big blue dress and long blond hair got up and started singing "Ca S'est Passé Un Dimanche" by Maurice Chevalier. Johnny had no idea what the song was about but felt all the sparks of the moment. Who needs words when such feelings are so powerful and filled with sincerity and color, he thought. Everyone sang along with the woman, and Johnny and Carol continued to kiss.

Hand in hand, Johnny and Carol paid for their dinners and said goodbye to the new 'friends for life' they had made. Johnny knew he'd never forget this beautiful and magical moment for the rest of his life. Stepping out onto the small cobblestone street not far from where Picasso and Braque invented cubism, Johnny heard a man singing and playing guitar. Carol and Johnny went to find where the singing was coming from.

"Can I play here too?" He asked.

"Of course you can. As soon as your guitar's ready, we can come here," She informed him.

Hand in hand they wandered down the street. Following the singing and came across a young man playing French folk songs. The singer was happy to see them. Johnny and Carol stopped and listened to him. The man finished his song and asked Johnny where he was from.

"Boston," Johnny said out loud. The singer offered to sing Johnny a song he wrote in English, about a girl he loved who wouldn't see him anymore. He began singing and playing. At the third verse after the harmonica solo, Jack the roller skater and his friends appeared on the corner. "There's that asshole who broke my guitar," Johnny exclaimed. Carol looked, the singer kept singing. Jack skated towards them and began circling Johnny, Carol and the singer, while his friends looked on. The singer started to get nervous but continued. He finished the song, and Jack yelled out at them French to leave. Johnny was angry with Jack's interruption. He and Carol loved the song; the singer, who had just given his all in a fragile performance of a beautiful innocent song, was disrespected. Johnny thought the singer had sang with courage in a language not his own and had exposed himself in such a vulnerable manner out on the street. The least Jack could do was show respect.

"It was great, just beautiful, keep singing," Johnny told the singer and gave him ten francs, encouraging him to ignore Jack. " Keep singing" Advised Johnny. Jack yelled out one more time while his friends set up cones on the street. "To hell with you!" Johnny shouted back at him. Jack recognized Johnny and remembered the incident from a few days ago.

"Oh, it's the little American in his wedding jacket," Jack shouted at Johnny.

"Keep playing," Johnny told the singer. "And it's about time for you to go!" he shouted at Jack.

"Ha! What are you going to do about it?" Jacked laughed.

"What am I going to do? I'll tell you," Johnny said as he walked towards Jack, who was a foot taller with his rollerblades and appeared to be in good physical shape. Johnny looked him straight in the eye and said, "Your nothing, now it's time for you to get lost." Jack skated up to Johnny and turned around, doing a kick on the come back to intimidate Johnny. It didn't work. Jack then took it a step further and faked a kick and punched Johnny in his right eye, knocking him down and giving him a classic shiner. Johnny fired back up and punched Jack in the chest, knocking the wind out of him. Jack bent over and as his head went down, Johnny uppercut his face with his fist, breaking Jack's jaw. He screamed in pain and fell to the ground.

"Ma mâchoire!" Jack said, speaking from the side of his mouth while holding his face and rolling on the ground. "Ma mâchoire! Tu es un connard, je t'aurai. Merde!" Jack's friends rushed to help him up. Carol came running over to Johnny.

"My hero," Carol shouted. She was proud of Johnny. Carol looked at his black eye and cleaned it with a napkin. He had a big shiner and was surprised at his swift punch that landed perfectly on Jack. The singer thanked them both. They hung around for a few more minutes to make sure Johnny was alright. They walked back to the Vespa taking their time enjoying the night. After the walk they went to Carol's apartment to clean Johnny's eye.

Chapter 21
Carol's Flat

A luminous haze of purple light was setting on Paris and the streetlights were about to be turned on. This is what gave Paris "the city of lights name", it being one of the first cities in the world to have streetlights. The Parisians were being freed from work, making their way to either an apéro at a local café or home. They showed no mercy in this pursuit and could become brutal, cutting each other off and honking their horns furiously. The traffic was tight, and Johnny held onto Carol as she confidently drove the Vespa to her flat in the sixth arrondissement, Saint-Germain-des-Prés. Johnny could feel her muscles twitch as she turned left and then right, charging forward. Carol shifted gears quickly and the motion gently pushed Johnny forward. He felt comfortable nestled on the back of the Vespa, resting his head on her, feeling more and more of her life force as she heroically led the way. This feeling caused Johnny to be lost in the moment as the motor created a hypnotic vibration matching Carol's life force. As they swerved through the traffic and side streets, the Paris skyline peeked through and Johnny caught glimpses of the Eiffel Tower all lit up and sparkling like a sparkler on top of a birthday cake.

Crossing the Seine river, Carol and Johnny were bestowed with an astonishing full view of the orange, purple, and blue sky, and the Eiffel Tower. "So this is what all the fuss is about," Johnny exclaimed. Feeling happy to see the beautiful view. "Extraordinary," he yelled out loud to Carol. He had heard Parisians use this word 'extraordinary' a lot. He was fascinated by how something just ordinary could become 'extra'—extraordinary.

"Oui, j'adore," She agreed as they went up Rue De Seine, getting closer to her place.

They arrived at her flat on Rue Mazarine. She was lucky to find a chamber de bain on the top floor of an eight-story building, especially one she could afford. They parked the Vespa and went into the building, taking a small lift that brought them directly to her apartment. Her flat was located directly under the roof, and the ceiling was angled, cutting through a 20 square meter room with old oak beams supporting the ceiling. On the low end of the room, there was a queen size mattress on the floor with dark blue sheets and a rose-patterned quilt with two yellow pillows. On the high end of the room, where you could fully stand up, there was a window with a small circular table for two decorated with a red checkered tablecloth. The view from the window overlooked the courtyard of another building, to the east you could see the Montparnasse skyscraper and Eiffel Tower. Johnny was amazed at how peaceful and quiet her place was, all was still and seemed to have been that way for centuries. Looking out the window he was fascinated by how far removed he was from the chaos of the city, and how behind every door waited another world. There was a small kitchenette in the flat, and a decent size bath and toilet—a rarity in a Parisian flat like this one. The room was painted pale yellow and pink. On the walls hung the backstage photos Carol took of Moulin Rouge dancers getting ready for their shows. In the corner, there was another window with a medium ficus tree in a hand-painted clay pot. On the wall beside the mirror was a shelf, and on the shelf was a toy G.I. Joe soldier in army fatigues. The toy soldier sat there with his arms raised and a permanent smile. Next to him was a small Buddha and incense burner. There were also five little drawings of a man's face pinned to the wall behind the incense burner. Johnny noticed all the items together made a shrine-like presentation. "What is this?" Johnny asked.

"That's my father," Carol responded confidently.

"Ha!" Johnny said with a surprised smile, "I thought you didn't know him."

"Not well, no. I don't know him personally, but this is what I've created for me to believe. I believe in this image I have created with what information I have, and it helps me. Having an image saves me from not knowing. His name was Carl and that's why my mother named me Carol," She confessed and picked up the toy G.I. Joe and kissed him. "Dad, meet Johnny."

Johnny responded quickly playing along. "Hello Sir, a pleasure to meet you. My name is Johnny Vincent and I was born in San Francisco before moving to Detroit and then settling in Boston."

Carol started speaking the role of her father, talking from the side of her mouth in a low tone. "Now Johnny, you seem like a fine man. What is it you want with my daughter?" She smiled and made eye contact with Johnny, waiting for his answer. Johnny confidently reached for her hand, and pulled her close. They were now face to face. Carol smiled with a warm glow feeling flustered.

"I want to get to know her better. She is the most beautiful woman I've ever seen," Johnny admitted, pulling her closer and giving her a passionate kiss. She kissed him back and the two of them fell into a long and deep kiss. She then pulled back and kissed his black eye and went to get a towel from the bathroom to clean it.

"I think I have some ice you could put on it," She offered opening the small freezer in the fridge, taking out a bag of frozen peas. He placed the peas on his eye. They then laid down on her bed. Johnny put his right arm around her and his left arm held the bag of peas. She felt safe between Johnny and the wall. He drifted to sleep as the bag of peas fell to his side. She got up, put the peas back in the freezer and turned on a Billie Holiday album. She delighted in him falling fast asleep, admiring his boy-like qualities that appeared in the moment. She took off his shoes and socks to make him more comfortable. She then took off her pants and shirt, leaving just her red panties on, the same color as her Vespa. She laid down close to him and crawled under the sheets. They both fell into a deep quiet, and much needed sleep. Holding each other close and tight.

During the night, Johnny woke up to take a pee. In the washroom, he found a small turtle on the floor. Confused, he wondered how a turtle could be here. He gently picked up the turtle and placed him in the soap dish by the sink. While Johnny peed, the turtle sat in the soap dish, moving slightly, ignoring the soap. Johnny finished and washed his hands. He then examined the turtle carefully, thinking about the turtle he had when he was a kid. He hadn't seen one since then. How could there be a turtle in here, he wondered. He looked in the mirror and inspected his swollen, bloodshot black eye. It was black and blue and swollen so much so that it almost shut his entire eye. It's beautiful, a perfect shiner, he thought. It was the first time his outside appearance matched how he felt on the inside. A badge of courage had been earned. Will the turtle bite me? He wondered as he picked up him.

"Carol, wake up," he said quietly, tapping her on the shoulder, "look what I found." He held the turtle in front of her face. Her left eye slowly opened up as she squinted in the darkness of the night, trying to see what he was showing her.

"Zeus. You found Zeus! I've been looking for him since yesterday. He escaped from the pot," She exclaimed. She then jumped out of bed, taking Zeus from Johnny's hands and kissed Zeus.

"Zeus, my baby, where did you go? I was looking for you everywhere!" She said, speaking like a baby. She gently placed him back in the flowerpot by the window. Johnny noticed there was just enough space for the turtle; the pot was 14 inches and had a small bowl of water. She continued talking to Zeus, "You went on a journey, didn't you? Maybe I should get you a bigger pot or maybe a girlfriend." She smiled at Johnny and put her arms around him. They fell into each other and onto the bed. Carol began unbuttoning Johnny's pants, slowly taking them off. Impressed by her directness, he took off his shirt and shorts and laid completely naked with Carol. He began to feel excited and it showed. They started kissing even more deeply and passionately, becoming aroused with each other's touch and caress. He had not been this close to a woman in a long time. She moved her hand down to feel him. She then smiled at him while gently touching him. "We need to wait," she whispered into his ear as she felt his hand slide up her thighs and into her. She began to moan. He was thrilled to discover she was just as excited as him. "Wait, I need to get a condom." She got up off the bed and looked through her dresser drawer. "Merde, je n'en ai pas, je pensais l'avoir fait."

"What?" He asked.

"I thought I had some. I don't. Oh well," She said, sighing and getting back into bed.

They continued to kiss and caress each other. He kissed her ear and neck. They both became overwhelmed by desire and passion. They started making love—a purely natural act of a sexual union motivated by genuine love. How can it be wrong when it's so pure? he thought. With instinct and intuition, she held him close as they continued to make love. Johnny held himself back from orgasming and knew he'd ejaculate soon if he didn't move. "On top," he whispered to her. She happily maneuvered herself , feeling him deeper inside her, as she slowly moved from front to back in a riding style. He was afraid he'd soon orgasm and began thinking about the turtle eating the soap. The distraction worked. The soap would taste horrible if you were a turtle, he thought. This thought stopped the surge of his climax. From his perspective he saw her form and soft breasts; they were perfect for his hands. Her hips and thighs were tight, her skin soft and smooth. He was stunned with amazement at the ecstasy of the passion of her. He watched her silhouette against the darkness of the night, enjoying her moans of joy and pleasure.

"Oh, mon Dieu!" She yelled out. He began pulling himself away from the thoughts of the turtle eating the soap. She was orgasming, and he was now ready to join her. He let go of any inhibition and pushed the turtle thoughts out of his mind. Exhaling and breathing deep, he counted. ONE, TWO, THREE! Both let out sounds of excited relief and pleasure. She screamed and collapsed on him. It was an amazing moment in his life, he managed to satisfy her and himself and orgasm together at the same time. This had never happened for him and it was the first time. Normally he needed at least three times together before it all fell into place. He did his best not to fall off the bed because he felt incredibly sensitive. They both started laughing and she laid on him, putting her head on his chest. They drifted into a deep, deep sleep.

They slept for seven hours, waking to the chirping of a little bird perched on the open windowsill. He was lost in her black hair as he opened his eyes and peered through the thick strands. The room looked like another place in the natural light with the warm pastel colors. She turned towards him and he gave her a soft morning kiss and caress. She began to wake up, smiling as her eyes opened slowly. She looked at his eye, "It looks better," she said and leaned over and kissed it. She smiled at him again, looking into his eyes, "Café?" she asked.

"That would be great," he replied.

She got up and walked to the kitchenette and put on a small Italian coffee pot, and then went into the bathroom. Johnny looked around the room in amazement, being in her flat with her felt surreal. I need to call Candy or Mom to tell someone what's happening and how good things are. Everything had happened so fast and he still hadn't had much time to reflect on all the events that had transpired. He didn't even know where he was. He thought about the view from Sacré-Cœur, and now here he was in one of the tiny gray-brown boxes crammed into the city. Carol came back from the bathroom and brought the coffees to the bed.

"Would you like a tartine?" she asked.

"What's that?" He asked with a smile.

"Toasted bread with butter and strawberry jam."

"Sure would!"

Johnny got up and put on his boxers. She sat at the table and he joined her. The two of them sat together, eating their tartines and drinking their coffees, smiling and talking with each other as the sound of the birds flying around the courtyard filled the background.

"I've never had a tartine," He told her as he caressed her foot with his.

"Today is a beautiful day," She added.

They both smiled at each other.

"I have to go to work. If you want, I can give you a ride back to your hotel," Johnny agreed and put down his tartine and coffee. They kissed and felt tempted to go back to bed. They finished their coffees, and she drove him back to his hotel.

Chapter 22
Promenade

Carol and Johnny pulled up to the hotel on the Vespa. The street was quiet, and it was another beautiful sunny day in Paris, just like the previous one. Pigeons and little sparrows intermingled in flight on the shaded street. Johnny got off the Vespa, unstrapped the helmet and gave it to Carol, she fastened it to the sidebar on the seat, and gave Johnny a deep kiss on the lips. He felt cool and proud to be seen with her.

"That is a kiss, just for you. Would you like me to come see you tonight around nine?" She asked.

"Yes, that would be really nice," He replied, excited to see her again.

"Ok, see you later. Have a good day," she said and drove off.

Johnny walked towards the hotel and saw Nick leaving. Nick was wearing a white cotton suit with sneakers and was on his way to the film set. Johnny was thrilled to see him.

"What happened to you?" Nick asked, looking at Johnny's eye.

"What do you mean?" Johnny replied. He'd forgotten about his black eye.

"Your eye, what happened?"

"Oh, that," Johnny smiled, "the roller skater, the guy Phillip was talking about who broke my guitar."

"Yeah?" Nick asked.

"Well, I think I broke his jaw. He sucker-punched me, but I got him two times, and the second punch did him in. One punch to the gut and the next to his jaw while he was on the way down. Bam!" As he reenacted the punch.

"I'm happy it worked out for you, Johnny! Wow! I must be honest, I didn't think you had it in you. Let me see that eye," Nick walked closer to Johnny and inspected his eye. "Make sure you keep it clean," He said with a smile. "Say, I'm going to Place de l'Opéra to shoot a scene for the movie if you wanna join me, you can. I'm walking there now."

"Yes, that's great! I would enjoy that."

"Here, I have the address," Nick pulled a piece of paper from his pocket, "22 Rue Vice."

"Let me see," Johnny said and pulled out the little map book the stranger gave him a few days ago. Johnny looked up the address, and they began their walk to Place de l'Opéra. "Let's see, we go straight to the river and make a left, then take a right on Rue Dauphine. Then go over the bridge and then towards the left, kinda," Johnny said as he checked the route on the little map.

Nick gave Johnny an approving smile. "So tell me, what have you discovered since you've arrived?" Nick asked.

"Where do I start?" Johnny said rhetorically.

"First thing that comes to mind,"

"Well…" Johnny took a deep breath and thought about Carol, "I'm in love."

"Already? You just got here."

"Yes, she just dropped me off on her Vespa," Johnny took another deep breath and beamed with joy. "Yes, I met her two days ago at the bridge. Her name is Carol. She helped me after my guitar was damaged by the fight with that jerk roller skater. Then we went up to the Sacré-Cœur church. After that, we went to what they call a guinguette restaurant. At the restaurant there was beautiful French music with an accordion and a piano player, cheap wine, and ham and potatoes—a real traditional French time like in a Renoir painting. Then I got in the fight, and I won! That bully came around intimidating a street singer for the spot. I called him out on it."

"That's great, Johnny, you are living life, your life, following your truth."

"Oh, it doesn't stop there!"

"Go ahead, tell me more," Nick encouraged him as they walked toward the Seine River.

"From there, I went back home with Carol, and we spent the night together. Sleeping with her was beautiful." They stopped to let the cars go and looked both ways, crossing over to Rue Dauphine. "It's been a while since I was with a woman, and it went really well. I'm surprised we hit it off. She's super cool and wonderful."

"Who is she?"

"Her name is Carol, and she was born in Vietnam. She and her mother came to Paris as refugees in the early seventies. She has never met her father. He was an American soldier stationed there and had to leave very quickly once the Viet Cong took over the country."

"Ok, I remember that period. I was doing theatre in Vancouver at the time. I went there, so I didn't get drafted, but many of my friends went and didn't come back. No good fucking war. They died for nothing! I am sorry Johnny. I lose my cool when I think about it. Please tell me more about your new girlfriend. It sounds like Carol has an interesting story."

"It's ok Nick, I understand." Johnny got back to his story, "And you know what else?"

"No, what? Tell me."

Johnny took a deep breath and Nick could see his emotions rising to the surface.

"Like me, she doesn't know who her father is," Nick stopped walking and looked at Johnny very seriously and asked, "you don't know who your father is?"

"No, I don't, and it pisses me off. I don't! It's not fair!" Johnny's mood changed.

"How come you don't know?" demanded Nick.

"They never told me. I asked when I was younger, and my mother told me he worked on a pipeline and left when I was little. For many years, I pretended it didn't bother me, but then I didn't know, but now I want to know. I wouldn't know him if he walked by us right now." Both their eyes scanned the people walking by them and returned to the topic.

"You have a right to know Johnny, ask and it shall be received. It's the cosmic law of the universe." Explained Nick.

"What? Say that again. It's what law?"

"Yes, it's the law of creation to ask, and you shall receive. Ask out loud to the universe source of creation, and you will receive an answer. You may not like the answer, but you'll get one."

"Wow, I like that." Expressed Johnny with a hopeful smile. They continued walking.

They came to the Seine River bridge and stopped in the middle to take in the sights of the old world city. It was here you could see where the old world met the new world. The scenery of the Eiffel Tower to the right and the Notre-Dame cathedral on the other side. The power of the flowing river underneath the bridge brought the new and old world together. Nick stopped and earnestly looked at Johnny and spoke, "If you are serious, look out over the river and ask, use the power of the word. Ask out loud. Go ahead, Johnny. You can do it. It's ok."Johnny stared out at the river's horizon as a barge of coal passed underneath the bridge, followed by a tourist boat filled with sightseers.

"Who is my father? Who? I want to know. Please, universe, tell me. Who is my father! I want to know!" Johnny's tone turned angry. Nick stood beside him, stern and supportive. Johnny turned to Nick.

"Ask is all you need to do," Nick assured him.

They both looked out onto the river.

"WHO IS MY FATHER!" Johnny yelled. "WHO!"

"That's good, Johnny. You don't have to yell, but if you're angry, you can tell me."

"Yes, I am! It's not fair I didn't have a father," Johnny said as he broke down into tears.

Nick placed his arm around him. "It's ok son, you can cry. It's ok, let it all out. Nothing to be ashamed of," Nick reassured him. Johnny cried and wiped his tears away with his sleeve, feeling his swollen black eye. "No need to be carrying that sadness and anger anymore. You are a good person, Johnny. You could have easily gone the wrong way, but you held steady to who you are. You're going to be ok. Don't worry, and trust life."

Johnny felt good about his call to the universe. They smiled at each other and continued to walk towards the opera. They enjoyed the stillness of the peaceful silence shared in the moment, understanding there was no need to talk; they're bond was created. Johnny felt a new peace of mind, something he wasn't used to but welcomed with joy. Life was beginning to make sense and have meaning. He'd waited a long time for these small signs.

They walked onto Rue de Rivoli and turned up onto Avenue de l'Opéra. After around ten minutes of walking, Nick broke their pleasant silence. "I have a son. I haven't spoken to him in fifteen years," he confessed. Johnny gave him a surprised look. "He lives in Hollywood with his mother, my first wife. I just wasn't a good father or family man at the time. I started getting good roles in films and then the TV show. I was making lots of money and got caught up in the fast lane with the parties, drinking, gambling, and flying around the world. It was a crazy life, and I couldn't see it at the time, and by the time I could, it was too late. His name is Carlton and he would be around 28. And from what I know, he's a genius kid. He lives in Seattle working at some type of internet business." Johnny turned to Nick, squinting with the sun in his eyes. Johnny found it hard to believe that his son wouldn't forgive him. How could he live like that, it's pretty cold, he thought.

"I'm sure he will forgive you someday soon," Johnny offered to Nick, trying to give support, especially after how he just helped him.

"I hope so, Johnny. I sure do," Nick replied.

They continued to talk in silence, soon finding themselves at the opera. Johnny caught a glimpse of his reflection in a store window. At first, he didn't believe it was him; he was impressed with the person he saw. That's me? That person is beautiful, he wondered. He wasn't used to having a positive inner dialogue. The voice he heard didn't feel forced; it came with ease. He felt a new sense of self. He looked closer at the reflection and examined the black eye. It was still a dark blue and purple color, but the redness inside his eye had gone away. I love my black eye look, it gives me character, he thought with admiration.

"Is everything ok?" Nick asked.

"Yes, like they say, It's all good wouldn't change a thing, even if I could," Johnny boasted and pulled out the map book to look up the street again.

They finally arrived at the Opera. Johnny was blown away by its beauty. "Incredible," He shouted as he marveled in awe at the majestic Opera building, with massive pillars and statues of angels and naked dancers. Sitting on top of each side of the Opera house were two large angels with two smaller ones at the bottom. People rested on the entrance steps huddled in groups and some even had tour guides who were busy giving mini history lessons. Johnny remembered what Dotty had told him about the troubadours; he felt the presence of that period, alive and well at the opera. He imagined the troubadours playing here and felt the spirit of the angels in the statues. When did people stop believing in angels? "These angel statues have enormous wings" Johnny exclaimed.

A thin man dressed in denim with a ponytail started to play guitar singing "Yellow Submarine" by the Beatles. He was facing the steps where around 30 or 40 people were sitting and watching him. Without a guitar amp or microphone, the singer entertained the free audience. Johnny looked on with envy. The singer carried the melody with ease and delight as he sang. The singer had perfected his song and knew it inside-out, his guitar strumming was minimal and muted as his voice carried to the crowd; he could feed himself for the day with this one song. Johnny wished he could perform like the street singer. He had never been an entertainer but did consider himself an original songwriter. He didn't want to admit it, but he wasn't sure of his skills as a guitar player and singer. He felt he had missed out on the music scene during Boston and Seattle's grunge period. Missing these important musical moments made Johnny doubt himself.

Johnny and Nick stood among the children running around with the balloons. Together they looked up at a statue of a naked man with curly hair, waving a tambourine in the air like he was dancing.

"Who's that?" Johnny asked.

"That my friend is Bachus,"

"Bachus like Bach Beethoven?"

"No, like Bachus, the God of wine, dancing and poetry."

"I've never heard of him." Johnny admitted.

"Bachus is part of Greek mythology, also known as Dionysus God of wine, theatre and fertility."

"You mean the God of parties?"

"Yes, intoxication."

"I'm happy to meet you, Bachus," Johnny said to the statue.

Johnny and Nick turned to one another, smiled and walked on.

Chapter 23
Action

Johnny and Nick arrived at the studio loft on time. The camera operator, makeup artist, sound technician, and young assistant were all waiting and ready to work. The director Marco was not there yet. The assistant, a young girl, was overdressed for the shoot. She looked like she belonged in a nightclub wearing a low cut white flowery blouse, with a black leather mini skirt and high heels. Everyone looked boring and dull alongside her, in their parker vests with sneakers and jeans; they wore the kind of outfits you'd buy at a camping store. The young girl smiled and enjoyed the attention she received from the two young 20-something guys, while the makeup artist, a gay African American man who looked like Little Richie set up his cosmetics on a small table. Nick introduced Johnny to everyone, and they were all happy to meet him.

The makeup artist began to work on Nick's face applying some blush with light cotton.

"Not too much," Nick insisted. "Remember Greggory Corso was from the streets"

"We just need to enhance the positive attributes you already have and hide those little flaws with just a little foundation," lisped the makeup artist.

The space was ample and about a 100 square meters with high ceilings and three large windows overlooking a perfect courtyard that resembled a Zen garden. A fashion designer previously used the studio, and they had left their armless mannequins, empty clothing racks, and strips of colored tissue on the floor. On the walls hung a series of several large colorful abstract figurative paintings with text written on them. In the corner of the room, there was a wooden table with four old school wooden chairs. The table hosted coffee, bottled water, and pastries in a basket. Johnny eyed up the pie with delight and did his best not to appear too eager to eat one.

Johnny took a seat at the table and poured himself a coffee and took a croissant and watched everyone on the film set. Around fives minute into their arrival, the makeup artist made Nick look ten years younger. Nick started pacing up and down the room in front of the paintings, repeating a mantra. A few minutes into Nick's mantra, the director arrived. He was an Italian American man from New York City who looked to be around 45-years-old. He was of medium build, dressed in black with glasses. Holding a clipboard and a light meter, he glanced at Nick, happy to see him. The director's name was

Marco. Marco had made several independent films and was pleased to have Nick acting in his latest one.

"Hello, everyone, sorry I'm late. I was stuck on the metro, I still haven't figured it out," Marco confessed, while chewing his gum. Nick introduced Johnny to Marco.

"Nice Shiner! Maybe we could use you for a fight scene," Marco joked.

"Fight scene?" Johnny replied puzzled.

"You know Gregory was a tough guy, a fighter,"

"Sure why not," Johnny shrugged.

Marco turned to the set team and began to explain what they needed to do. "Today we are just going to be doing close ups on Nick reciting poetry. We will use the images later to fade in and out with the beach scenes that we are still yet to do. Hopefully we will do the beach scenes next week." The camera operator put the camera on the tripod, and the sound guy got his boom ready. The assistant smiled. Everyone seemed excited to be on set and ready to start filming.

"Ok, you ready, Nick? Let's take it from where we were yesterday: scene 25," Marco told him.

"Ready when you are," Nick replied.

"Ok, quiet everyone," Marco said. "Action!" Nick casually walked with a bit of a sway from the corner of the room to the center and turned and looked into the camera. Taking a deep breath and began a poetry monologue.

The Journey of Johnny Vincent

I am the American man,
the dreamer, the giver, the seer,
the statue of liberty with a handful of rain.
I'm the lightning, the thunder,
a dead coffee stain.
I'm the money in your mix, the graffiti on your
soul, the monkey on your lips, the fire in the hole.

Johnny looked at the director, who appeared content
with Nick's acting; it was a good start. Johnny
enjoyed getting this glimpse into the reality of Nick's
world. Nick continued, rolling his head with a grin
and trying to crack his neck.

I'm crazy about Zelda
in my angel boots
with broken brains and zoot suits.
I'm searching for my taste
With your burned out eyes
She's laying me to waste
With all them other guys
Oh see sister velvet
Won't you hold my hand
With a rose and stiletto
Do it if you can
She picked my pocket
Slow dancing with a beer

Can't find Zelda anywhere

Johnny sipped his coffee and watched intently, excited to see his favorite actor in action. He was trying to understand the rattling of the poetry. It was clear to Johnny that these beat poets didn't sell out. They lived for the moment and stood with the naked truth and had access to their subconscious. Johnny thought about the TV commercial and his song "Willy Has A Brand New Hip". He pushed the thoughts away; now was not the time to dwell. Johnny continued to focus on Nick.

Let's play hoops with Balzac
and go one for one at his gravesite.
We can spit out gum chewing geniuses
and blow bubbles filled with love
that kill your brightest gadgets
laced with cancer cells.
Throw darts at Wall Street trades
leaping off the Empire State
into the blackness of the pavement.
Look at me, Mom,
I'm coming home
into the afterlife in a limousine.

Johnny wasn't used to this kind of poetry, it seemed crazy and sloppy like reckless talk. The words were held together with such colorful imagery and rhythm, and at the same time, the poem had a personal tone. The words spilled out into the room and swam around in a steady stream of consciousness. Looking at the paintings on the walls, Johnny saw they respected no academic rules of perspective and compositions. They had little faces, symbols, and doodles that juxtaposed against the wild sporadic forms and gestures; the paintings showed aggressive brushstrokes that looked to be painted with anger. Soft and frail, the lines in the paintings traveled through the composition. The bright and bold colors contrasted with the high intensified complimentary colors. Is this what the mind looks like? Johnny wondered.

Johnny's attention went back to observing Nick was doing his best to be this poet Gregory Corso. It was hard to see the actor that Johnny knew from the TV show *Angel Hour*. The straight-laced clean-cut detective who had slow, deliberate moves, with deep thought out sentences, was now talking from his hip, sharp and fasted with wild gestures.

Frightened to death to death of death
of the nuclear inhalation
getting scolded from
preachers and teachers.
We're at it again

Chrysler and Christ
We're at it again and again.
We're at it again we're at it again
again and again and again.

Nick broke out in laughter, Marco yelled cut. Nick gave Marco a friendly glance, suggesting a break. Nick then swaggered to the table and pulled out a chair to join Johnny. "These Beat poets planted the seeds for 60s music: the Beatles, Bob Dylan, The Doors, and all that stuff. A mix of the blues, jazz, and James Dean, and we have rock n' roll." Nick shared with Johnny, who nodded his head in agreement, delighted to have Nick tell him about the Beats. Nick got up and returned to work. After another ten minutes Johnny became restless and felt it was time to leave and go back to the hotel. He needed to change his clothes. He'd been wearing the same ones for a few days now and probably stunk. Johnny waited for the next break and then said goodbye to everyone.

Walking back to the hotel, Johnny stopped at the opera to see if the street singer was still there. The man stood in the same spot still singing more well-known songs to happy tourists. A person could survive on these streets as an artist, Johnny thought, remembering what the guy from the bar in Boston said. For a 100 francs, a person could rent a hotel or rooming house room without an ID or credit card. Rooming houses or cheap hotels were disappearing in the States—how could an artist community exist with no affordable housing? Johnny always dreamt of a time when a city, like NYC in the 80s or Paris in the 30s, would have had a real art scene. There wasn't really one in Boston anymore. The Seattle scene with its grunge was good, but it was too far away, and over now. Johnny wished he had been part of the Greenwich Village scene in the 80s. In his mind, that was the last significant moment where all the arts collided: painting, theatre, music, and others. He knew Boston had a decent vibe during the 90s with the Cambridge and Berkley school of music students, but it had faded out.

Standing in front of the Le Dance statue, Johnny listened and watched the singer. He had the audience in the palm of his hand. Johnny wished he could command an audience that way, but he couldn't play other people's songs well. He also didn't feel confident about his voice or guitar playing. He knew he could write a good song, and even when he tried to quit writing songs, they would still come to him. That was the way it was: his best songs always came to him when he wasn't trying. It was as if a spirit was talking to him. Who was the spirit? Johnny wondered. It was at this moment

Johnny realized he was a creator with a gift for songwriting. He didn't need to be an entertainer—he was a creator.

Johnny continued to stare at the La Dance statue, while this beautiful new revelation swept over his mind. He looked to Bacchus for an answer about the mysterious spirit. Johnny felt it was a curse at times to feel like such a clumsy musician. The thought of this bothered him, but he knew in his heart, the only time he really felt free and alive was when he was writing and singing his songs. He took one last look around Place de l'Opéra and walked back to the hotel with these thoughts running through his head. He stopped at a small gift shop and bought postcards to send to Dotty, his mother and Candy.

Johnny arrived at the hotel 30 minutes later. A new person was working the front desk. It was a young girl from Lithuania. Her name was Vita. She was a 23-years-old and a strong looking girl with short brown hair, brown eyes, and a big smile. She wasn't very tall and reminded Johnny of a Russian gymnast he'd seen on TV during the Olympics in the early 80s. The new girl Vita told Johnny that an African man named Balu had been looking for him. Johnny was happy to meet Vita, and to hear Balu had come by to see him. "I will be in my room if he returns," Johnny told Vita.

"Ok, I will ring you if he comes back," she replied.

Johnny thanked her and went upstairs to change and have a rest.

Once back to the room, he changed his clothes and went through the little belongings he had in his pockets and found the two oxy pills. Should I take one or both? It would be nice to soak in a hot bath and feel the sedation and euphoria from the oxy, he told himself. He looked at the pills in his hand and looked at his reflection in the mirror but thought about the toxic side effects. A deep voice from the bottom of his being shouted, "NO!" This is strange, he thought, I've never heard this voice before. The voice felt strong and wise. It was different from his own, almost separate. Johnny knew this was a turning point; he couldn't repeat the mistakes of his family. He felt he must walk away and choose an honest life and feel his feelings and not want to escape them. He moved away from the mirror and went to the toilet and flushed the two pills. That's the way it goes, he thought to himself, listening to the toilet digest the narcotic. I am on a new road, and a new destiny awaits me. He then went and laid down on the bed to take a nap.

Chapter 24
Memories of Detroit

Johnny laid on the bed listening to the sounds of the building. He could hear the man in the room above peeing. He wished the sound was muffled or elsewhere, but in the silence of the hotel, he could hear everything. The walls were thin, and if you were still and silent, you heard all the movements of the people in the adjoining rooms. Right after the man finished peeing, his female partner came into the bathroom and yelled at him in French. She then slammed the toilet seat down. Johnny liked this feeling of being close to people. It didn't matter if he spoke the language or not. It seemed that he was always only a few feet from someone. Above or below, alongside or behind a wall, there was always someone nearby doing something. The Parisians didn't have a problem with personal space. Americans however, need at least six feet of social distance, a wide berth for a Cadalac, and are trigger happy about it. Johnny felt good to be in a soft nonaggressive culture and not know every nuance of the language. Just listening to the tone of the French language was a relief.

The Journey of Johnny Vincent

He hadn't had much time to reflect on what Candy had told him. His mind drifted to that period of their childhoods. He had no idea she was sexually abused, it was a complete shock. How could this guy Dave pretend to be a friend and come and go like that? More importantly, did Stanley know what was going on?

It was when they lived in a three-bedroom wooden house in a suburb of Detroit, alongside the Detroit River. They had just moved there from San Francisco, and Stanley took a job at a car factory. Johnny's mother worked as a secretary at an insurance office. On the weekends they would have cookouts, softball games, and go fishing on the lake. Stanley belonged to a militia group called The Torch and Dave was his best friend.

The Torch was a paramilitary organization formed in the 80s. The group was created in response to the perceived encroachments by the federal government on citizens' rights. The group also had roots in racism. The Torch sponsored the weekend outings, camping trips, and softball games. They believed in no federal taxes, anti-immigration, and held Libertarian and constitutional ideas about governance. They said things like "the government was going to put them in concentration camps" and "there was a new world order conspiracy to destroy all sovereign nations to create a one-world

220

government". The Torch spent their weekends preparing for the day the government was going to come and take their guns. They felt that day was getting closer and closer, "a well-armed militia is the best defense against an excessive government," they would say.

In the beginning Johnny and Candy had fun. It was nice to get out of the city and be in the forest. Soon Johnny began to dislike The Torch and noticed Candy was their favorite. She received a lot of attention, and Stanley and Dave thought it was cute to see a little girl handle a firearm so well. Johnny would go camping with Stanley and the group. The camping weekends turned into military-like training exercises with live drills, hiking excursions and lots of beer drinking by the campfires. Stanley hoped to build some sort of camaraderie with Johnny and the Torch members. Stanley had said on several occasions that he needed to make a man of Johnny.

The Torch was a group of around 60 men, all out of shape and overweight, but energetic and alert. They needed to prove to themselves, to be ready for battle and dressed in camouflage military fatigues. Johnny wanted no part of this training; setting up booby traps and playing war games didn't interest him. He refused to join in the military exercises. Stanley called him a pussy and baby, who was going to get his ass kicked by people and life. Johnny couldn't see any sense in what The Torch was doing, plus they frightened him. They were crazy, violent, and paranoid with a perverted sense of humor. Being near them made him feel uneasy.

Johnny often brought his radio on the camping trips so he could tune them out as much as possible. The radio meant everything to him. No matter where he was, it brought music from all over the world straight to him. The transistor frequency in mono sound was comforting and familiar. Made for one ear ; it knew what you needed at the right time. Johnny thought the radio seemed connected to another world that was helping this world. He figured if there were such a thing as angels, they were working in music.

What was so surprising and hard to grasp was, Dave was the kindest of Stanley's friends from The Torch. It baffled Johnny that Dave would hurt Candy. On one of the weekends Johnny had refused to participate in the field drills, it was Dave who stood up for him, telling Stanley to back off. Dave was around 45, big and chubby, always with a smile on his face. He never had kids of his own, and for that reason, Johnny thought that's why he liked him and Candy so much. Dave always had a solution and a calming demeanor, especially when explaining things. He drove a family station wagon with seats that lowered in the back making room for the camping gear and more kids. He was always ready to help. He took Johnny and Candy fishing to the good parts of the river. He cared about the environment and agriculture; he checked all the boxes for a 'good guy'. How could it be Dave? Only an evil person would tell her that he'd kill her and the family, if she told anyone. It must have been horrifying and frightening for Candy. How many other kids had Dave sexually abused? Johnny asked himself.

Candy was always going to the shooting range with Stanley and Dave. They often gave her a ride home after her dance recitals. Looking back, it was apparent to see when her behavior changed. At 12 years of age she was arrested for shoplifting, in trouble at school and with the police. She then started taking drugs and eventually dropped ballet. Poor Candy thought Johnny. Life had not been easy for her and that stupid fuck of a father couldn't protect her. Johnny could see how her life began a downward spiral around the same time Dave must have assaulted her.

Johnny laid on the bed resting his head on the pillow. The couple above continued with their argument. Outside the window, he could hear cars, buses, and motorcycles in the distance; they all sounded like a waterfall to him. Johnny fell into a deep sleep and was woken by the phone ringing a few hours later.

Chapter 25
Hanging with Balu

The phone kept ringing while Johnny slept. He could hear the sound but couldn't move. It took more than a few rings to wake him from his siesta coma. He fumbled for the phone, picked it up, and put the receiver to his ear.

"Hello Mr. Vincent, it's me Vita, from the front desk. Your friend Balu is here to see you,"

"Ok, I'll be right there. Thank you," Yawned Johnny and hung up the phone. He looked out the window, guessing it was about six in the evening. It felt nice to be woken up with a friend waiting for you. He washed his face with cold water, put on a clean pair of pants, red flannel cotton shirt and shoes, and went downstairs to see his new friend.

Johnny had learned a few things about Balu from the squat party; he came from Togo, his father was a politician with five wives, he had 25 brothers, 15 sisters, and was in Paris because it was safer than Togo right now. The Elections were taking place in Togo and Balu's father was an important official, things could be violent during this period. Balu preferred Paris and it was safer. Johnny found Balu waiting in the lobby. He was sitting on the couch dressed in a L.A. shirt and baggy jeans with Nike Air Jordan's and a Boston Celtics hat on his head.

"Hey Balu, how's it going?"

"Hello, my brother. I'm good, and you. What's this?" he asked, looking at his black eye. By now Johnny was getting better at telling the story. Balu laughed "You are a young lion," He said.

"No, I was lucky," They both laughed and Johnny changed the subject.

"How is it you have a Boston Celtics hat on?"

"Yes, to show you my solidarity as a fan of your hometown team." He replied with a big smile.

"That's great. Thank you!" Johnny gave Balu a hug, not sure what 'solidarity' meant, but he figured it was something positive. He had never heard that word before. "I like that word, 'solidarity.' In the U.S., we don't use that word."

"It's an important word," Balu explained, "Together we stand, divided we fall. We're all in this together." Johnny agreed and wondered why the word 'solidarity' wasn't more common in the U.S. "I was in the quartier and wanted to stop by and say hello," Balu said. "Would you like to go for a drink or a walk or something?"

"Sure, that sounds good. I have to be back around nine tonight."

"Cool! We can go to the Bar Du Marche on Rue de Buci. I want to tell you my latest rhymes on the way, and you can correct my English."

"Sounds good, let's go!"

They left the hotel and within minutes they were on Rue Saint-André-des-Arts heading towards Rue de Buci. Balu started right away with his new raps, turning into a human beatbox. As they walked down the street, he snapped his fingers, keeping time and replicating the sound of a drum and bass, rapping about Africa.

My mother, Africa
the spirit of the sun
she breathes
land of the ancestor
hand in hand
one love for the sun
my mother, Africa
you are the only one
land of living sun
mother to everyone

Balu looked up at the buildings and the blue sky, spying the clouds in the late afternoon sun. He smiled and continued.

The Journey of Johnny Vincent

Happy days in the sun
follow freedom for
we the fortunate one
oh, Africa, Africa
Boom boom boom

"This is the new rap I'm working on, it has a way to go," He explained .

"It's good, I like it," Johnny replied, impressed by his enthusiasm and passion for life. Johnny liked Balus' charismatic and inspiring energy. He had something money couldn't buy, he was high on life, and his enthusiasm was contagious.

"Tell me something," Balu asked .

"What?"

"In the U.S., do all the rappers use this word 'nigger'? Do I have to use it?"

Johnny, quite surprised by the question, thought for a few minutes. He wanted to think about how to properly address such a serious question. "No, you don't have to use it. If you want to, you can, but one thing is, I cannot use that word. That's for sure," Johnny said and explained more about the word, "some people think if the word is used enough, it won't be hurtful anymore and lose its negative power. Other people like Martin Luther King believed we shouldn't use it all."

"Who is Martin Luther King?"

"You don't know who he is?"

"No, is he a boxer?"

"You're thinking of Muhammad Ali."

"Yes, the Muhammad Ali and George Foreman fight was epic! My father took me to see the match in Zaire, they called it 'Rumble in the jungle' and Ali won. It was a great time," Balu recounted and asked, "so who is Martin Luther King?"

Johnny was surprised he didn't know who Martin Luther King was, but then remembered Balu didn't know much about African American culture. "Martin Luther King was a civil rights activist. He led one of the most important civil rights movements in the States to help end segregation. He gave a famous speech 'I Have a Dream'." Johnny paused and tried to remember some of the speech, "I have a dream that one day we will all be created equal and not be judged for the color of our skin"

"Where is Martin Luther King now?" Balu asked.

"They shot him dead," .

Balu shook his head in despair and continued speaking, "I am from Africa, so I don't know much about America. Thank you for telling me. God made us all equal, we are all brothers and sisters."

"Yes, we are."

Johnny and Balu continued walking down the street towards the bar. Johnny raved on about

American jazz musicians who shaped American culture like John Coltrane, Miles Davis, and Ray Charles.

"My music is not about gangs, sex, drugs, street life, and prison. I will not use this word 'nigger', I don't like it. My music is about beauty, love, women, equality, and nature. I think I want to be more like Bob Marley than Tupac," Balu admitted.

The café was full of fashionable people, tourists, and locals having an early evening apéro. Johnny and Balu found a little table on the terrace and ordered some beers. A handsome slim-fit waiter spun around with a tray of beers, dressed in jean overalls and a marine shirt. He flipped two coasters down the on table, like an acrobat, then quickly and delicately placed each full beer on them, and offered them a small bowl of salty popcorn.

"Cheers," offered Balu. They toasted their mugs tipping them and took a big sip of cold beer. Johnny took a moment and decided to share a personal story. "My very first best friend in life was an African American boy named Teddy Shears. We were both around six and seven at the time. We met at school, and we were the same in every way: same height, weight, body type, and similar personalities. Our only difference was skin color. Our inner selves were truly mirrored, and you could see this in our smiles and body language. We even had the same shirts and called ourselves twins. We used to have sleepovers on the weekends and spent many hours playing with trucks at the playground and creating imaginary adventures in the yard. It was all good until one day, my stepfather got drunk and started making racist comments about our friendship, using that word you mentioned before."

"What?" Balu said and shook his head with disbelief. "That is horrible, that is just fucking horrible, man. I'm sorry you had a father like that!"

"Stepfather," Johnny said. He wanted to make sure Balu knew it wasn't his real dad.

"Yes, it is. I never understood why we stopped hanging out, and then it all came back to me. I was too young to recognize it at the time, but thinking back, I see it now, and meeting you has brought back the ugly truth of how racist my stepfather is. I'm very pleased to meet you Balu."

"Thank you, my brother. You are good people. I'll take you to meet my family one day," Balu said as he put his arm around Johnny and smiled. They both drank their beers and reflected on what Johnny shared about Teddy and his experience with racism. Johnny and Balu watched the people, cars, and bikes pass the terrasse, enjoying the moment of silence. While sitting there, Phillip passed by and saw Johnny and Balu, he came over to their table happy to see them.

"Hello!" Phillip said. "So good to see you guys. I'm on my way to Saint-Sulpice to hear the organ music, do you two want to join me?" Johnny and Balu were surprised by the idea of going to hear church music.

"Organ music?" Johnny asked.

"Yes, I know it sounds a bit weird, but trust me, it's good. The organ at Saint-Sulpice is one of the biggest in the world, and the church was made for its acoustics," Phillip explained and continued, "they're playing Beethoven Moonlight Sonata 27. Come and check it out! You guys will like it."

"Why not!" They agreed. They finished their almost-empty beers and paid, and the three left for the Saint-Sulpice Church. The two happily followed Phillip as he explained his theory about the organ; Phillip believed the organ could heal the body.

"I think sound vibrations can heal the body," Phillip told them.

"How so?" Balu asked.

"What is the body?" Phillip asked rhetorically and continued, "a body is made up of organs, organs like the instrument. It's the same word."

"Yes," Agreed Johnny and Balu. They both listened, curious to know more about what Philip meant. It made sense to them both.

"Well, it's the same word. Isn't that a coincidence? And the skin of the body, it's an organ as well. The sound frequency can kill any virus, and the right sounds can raise our DNA level and increase the immune system," Phillip told them and continued. "If an opera singer can break glass, it's obvious that sound has real power to change material physically."

"That's the power of the blues," Johnny added. Balu looked at Johnny, expecting him to start preaching about American music again.

The three of them arrived at Place Saint-Sulpice. A beautiful square in the 6th arrondissement of Paris. A few hundred feet in diameter with a massive fountain in the middle. The fountain had a shrine dedicated to Sulpitius the Pius, at the top of it. About 50 feet high with water flowing out and around him. With four statues of a lion, at each corner of the fountain, guarding the saint. And unforgettable an impression. Johnny stood amazed by its power and detail.

On the way into the church, they passed an old woman, begging on her knees. She was dressed in rags, dirty and frail. Her face expressed despair and tragedy, as though from another century. Once inside the church, Johnny felt like he had been swallowed and was in the stomach of a giant whale.

The ceiling of the church had large stone columns that arched into ribs to support the enormous painted ceiling. There were beautiful hallucinogenic stained glass windows with worlds in them: suns, moons, planets, birds, demons, angels, and creatures of all kinds from land to sea to air, and of course, baby Jesus was everywhere. This was the second time Johnny had been in a church this week, and these two visits were more than he'd had in the last ten years. Johnny preferred the Saint-Sulpice church to Sacré-Cœur; Saint-Sulpice was bigger with fewer tourists and smelled like softwood, like a forest, clean and rich. Johnny assumed there was incense burning.

They continued to wander around the church, and the organ concert began. Johnny looked up to see the vast pipes and took a seat in the wooden pew. A bass frequency filled up every inch of the church, breathing long notes in and out. The higher tones on the keyboard set a range of notes that were lighter and playful. There was no escaping the waves of sound. The emotion of the Sonata was warm, tender, and extremely intimate. A strong slow vibration of sound vibrated through the church. Johnny sensed his emotions rising and became teary-eyed. He felt the hairs on the back of his neck stand up. Johnny imagined somewhere in the church a person was playing the gigantic organ. It reminded him of the

Red Sox baseball games, he never knew where the organ player was hiding, but he or she was out there.

Phillip looked at Balu and Johnny, "Well, pretty impressive?" They both nodded in agreement.

Johnny invited Balu and Phillip to hang out and meet Carol. The three left the church for the hotel. Johnny was sure he was a better person after this experience, he didn't know how or why, but figured it had to be that way. What was all of this for? The church, the statues, the organ; Wasn't it to make us better somehow? For the first time in his life he considered the good that maybe a church could do. He wasn't exactly sure, or able to pinpoint how he was better, but just figured it had to be better. It just had to be.

Chapter 26
Hotel Party

Johnny, Balu, and Phillip arrived at the hotel in good spirits. They were greeted by Vita and Nick, who were discussing the war on terror. They were sharing a bottle of Bordeaux and a charcuterie plate. It was Friday and everyone was in a good mood. Johnny introduced everyone, and Vita kindly offered a glass of wine, which they happily accepted.

Nick raised his glass and proposed a toast, "To good friends and world peace!"

"Too good friends and world peace," they all repeated, smiling and making eye contact as they raised their glasses to cheer each other. Everyone took a mouthful of the soft tasting wine.

"C'est du bon vin" Phillip said, licking his lip and continued, "world peace, is such a thing possible?" His tone turned from joyous to hopeless.

Nick fired back quickly, "Of course there is! The battle is within us, and the outside world is a projection of our collective consciousness."

"We have a long way to go before that changes. War is a part of our nature," Vita said.

"We must never lose hope. We must always strive for peace, love, and justice," Balu added.

"Rich people start a war, and the poor people die in them," Phillip chimed .

They looked at Johnny for his opinion. He took a sip of wine and thought about a response.

"There will always be conflicts, but how to resolve them will coincide with our communication skills and emotional maturity, But, I like what Phillip said."

The five of them continued to discuss the latest news about the U.S. and its war on terror. The newspapers and TV were dominated by the US and its build up to war. The world was debating on whether to intervene in Iraq or not. George Bush Jr. had been promoting Operation Iraqi Freedom in the news. The U.S. government was claiming they needed to restore democracy in Iraq and save the world from Sadam Hussein, and Iraq's weapons of mass destruction. France was opposed to the intervention, and their opposition was poorly received by the US and its allies. Politicians in the U.S. media were encouraging Americans to boycott products with the name "French" in them. French fries became "freedom fries" and French kiss a "free kiss".

"TO FREEDOM FRIES!" shouted Phillip, raising his glass. Everyone laughed, astonished by the pathetic absurdity of such a smear campaign and the bullying by a nation.

Carol arrived at the hotel, interrupting the conversation. She had Johnny's guitar. Johnny saw her coming in and smiled, putting down his glass of wine and greeting her with a kiss on the lips. Johnny introduced Carol to the group and poured her a glass of wine. They were all happy to meet her.

"So good to see you, and you have my guitar already," Johnny said with a smile.

"Yes, I do. I stopped by her place after work, and it was ready. She said it was an easy fix," Carol said, taking the guitar out of its case and handing it to Johnny.

"Thank you!" He inspected his guitar, feeling the place where the crack was on the back. It was now nice and smooth but had a slight bump. Christelle had smoothed out the crack with some wood glue and filler. Unlike Johnny's black eye, the crack would never fade, and the memory of his fight with Jack would live with him and his guitar forever. It would remind him of the day he stood up to the roller skater and won. A minor dragon had been defeated but a victory just the same—he had won.

"It's great! Tell Christelle I say, 'thank you very much'," Johnny said happily reunited with his Gibson.

"Play us a song, my brother," Balu asked. Everyone welcomed the idea and cheered Johnny on. Johnny thought for a minute about what to play. It felt good to be holding his guitar again; it was a secure and familiar feeling. Johnny strummed his fingers on the strings, and to his amazement, Christelle had also changed the strings. This small act of kindness meant a lot to Johnny, and the sound was sharp, bright, and crisp. "She changed the strings," Johnny told everyone with a big smile on his face. It seemed like weeks since he had last played, but it had only been five days. "Ok," Johnny said, looking at his guitar case and the 'God Is Fragile' message he wrote on it at the airport. A song had been brewing within him on the idea about being fragile and what it meant. It had been festering in the mud of his subconscious and it was time to dig it up.

"Ok, I have been thinking about a new song based on what I wrote on my guitar case," he told them. They all looked at his case and smiled with interest. Johnny started strumming in a Dixieland type tempo.

"Come on, sing it out, Johnny!" Carol encouraged him.

"Show us what you got!" Vita added.

I have been reborn used and abused
Kicked around like an old pair of shoes

The Journey of Johnny Vincent

I'm fragile

Johnny sang softly, playing his guitar.

"Hey, that's good," Nick said. Johnny continued.

Vision gets blurred, might need surgery
What's that I heard, you laughing at me?
I'm fragile

The group cheered Johnny on, enjoying his spontaneous melody and catchy phrases. They were happy to hear him sing and play. "Someone get a pen," Johnny asked. Carol reached into her purse and pulled out a sharpie marker, and Vita got a piece of paper from the printer. Carol started to write the lyrics down as Johnny continued to sing and play.

Where's the umbrella cause it's gonna rain
I need an aspirin cause I'm in pain
I'm fragile

Balu joined. "Hold on, let me think," Balu said, stretching out his hands.

Made of blood and DNA
Skin and bones in a complicated way
I'm fragile

Phillip decided to jump in too, clearing his throat.

Give me your hands and caress my brow
Together you and I will get by somehow
Fragile

Everyone happily clapped along as Johnny, Balu, and Phillip came together to write the song on the spot. Johnny started to increase the tempo to a New Orleans type of shuffle and continued to sing.

I need more oxygen, I got to eat
I'm burning up inside, I can't take the heat
I'm fragile

The group applauded and clapped as Johnny pushed the song further and played the tempo until he found it. The song flowed. Johnny was very happy with it. It was an easy song that opened up effortlessly and was fun to sing. The song had been waiting for him for a long time. It was all there and just needed a day of tailoring to refine it and give it a bridge.

Nick ordered another bottle of the Bordeaux, and Johnny played some more of his songs. They played together all night, clapping and singing along, and taking turns with the guitar. Balu rapped and Phillip played his manouche gypsy style songs. The night passed by joyously. Carol stayed with Johnny in his room upstairs, wrapped in his arms in the hotel bed.

Chapter 27
The Bad Dream, The Weekend and The Truth

After a magical night of song and wine, Johnny and Carol went up to his room. They fell into each other's arms, stripped all their clothes off and went to bed. They kissed and caressed each other until they fell into a deep, peaceful sleep—a timeless place allotted for the human body, soul, and mind. A place of oneness where no tragedy nor trauma could find them except in a nightmare.

He caressed her smooth and soft skin, with her head nestled under his chin. His pulse dropped, he fell asleep and began to snore. Together they fit perfectly like a glove. Here it was at last, the warm and true love Johnny had dreamt about, while going through his darkest and loneliest times.

His mind drifted from any anchor of reality and into a dream state. An ample gray-blue space opened up, and a black crow flew towards him. The crow was an intense black color, a black that you could fall into. The crow came very close and then turned away, almost hitting him. He wondered where the crow went, the crow reappeared on a tree branch and started cawing. More trees appeared, and Johnny recognized the place. It was where he went camping when he lived in Detroit as a child, the same location where the militia group met. Johnny's memories understood light and shade more than actual forms.

Candy came walking into the campground and started doing abstract ballet, making up the dance as she went. She was wearing new ballet shoes and was proud of them. She kept looking at them as she danced. She threw her arms out, spinning, and then moved backward and forward. This pleased Johnny to see his little sister as she truly was, free and innocent. Her attitude slowly became angry as she built up speed. Candy stopped and disappeared, and when she returned, she was wearing her yellow gold prom dress. She was now standing outside their house in Detroit.

"What are you doing?" Johnny asked confused and stressed.

"I'm waiting," she told him, smiling. Johnny thought it was strange she was in her prom dress, she never went to prom and didn't graduate high school. He was happy to see her and went to greet her. As he approached her, she took off running down the street. Johnny called out to her yelling her name. He followed her. Candy stopped in a Super 8 motel parking lot, the same motel near their old Detroit house. Johnny was even more confused. "Candy, what are you doing?" he asked. She didn't respond.

He tried again and called out, "CANDY, WHERE ARE YOU?" still no response. Johnny entered a side door of the motel and walked down the hallway. The motel was old and dirty with thin worn orange carpet with water stains, and the paint was peeling off the walls. There were several doors to each room and a soda and ice machine at the end of the hallway. There was a man's silhouette at the machines. Johnny couldn't figure out who it was. He looked closer. It was Pete, Candy's boyfriend, Priscilla's father.

"Hey, Johnny. Good to see you!" Pete said. Grinning, wearing a Hawaiian shirt with a cocktail in his hand. He smiled to reveal the mess of a mouth he had, broken and black teeth. Pete looked worse than horrible. Greasy long dirty black hair, his face was gaunt with acne and sores and dark circles of death in his eyes. He was shing gray and black.

"Come in and party," he told Johnny in a warm and sincere tone. Even though Pete was a bit of a psychopath, he did have some likable qualities.

Then the dream shifted, and Johnny found himself in a hotel room. Baby Priscilla was on the bed, smiling and kicking her feet. There were shadows and faceless people coming in and out of the room. Johnny's heart began to beat faster and he became worried at what was going to happen. This dream was on its own and certainly not a common one.

"HELLO, JOHNNY!" Candy yelled out. She was still in her yellow gold prom dress.
Johnny tried to speak, but the words wouldn't come out; the dream was becoming too much for him. Pete threw Johnny a beer. Johnny caught it and looked up to see Candy smoking a crack pipe. She let out a big mouthful of smoke, and her eyes rolled to the back of her head. Johnny felt frightened and looked for a way out of the room but instead walked into the bathroom. The tub was filled with the guns Candy and Pete stole. Johnny looked in the mirror, and Candy appeared behind him, standing in her yellow gold prom dress with a musket rifle in her hand. She began loading the musket with a ball and gunpowder. Johnny was impressed that Candy knew how to load the gun. Priscilla came crawling into the bathroom on the dirty floor, that now had mice running around on it.

Johnny was in shock and looked up to see Stanley standing in the doorway. Johnny looked back into the mirror, to see Candy's reflection, that was now double. She then lifted the gun, pointed it at Stanley, and shot him. The weapon exploded with a big puff of smoke. The musket ball took off half of Stanley's face. Stanley fell to the ground next to Priscilla as blood came gushing out of his head. Johnny looked at Candy and she stood still, emotionless like stone, full of determination and conviction. Johnny tried to get out of the dream but couldn't. The black crow reappeared, landing on Johnny's chest, moving closer to his face. He broke free from the nightmare.

"NO, NO, NO, CANDY!" he yelled as he shook and trembled with fear and sweat.

"Wake up, Johnny. It's ok," Carol said, pulling him closer.

Johnny turned his face into her chest.

"It's ok. It's gonna be ok. You are alright. Nothing is going to hurt you," she told him. Johnny continued to cry.

"It was horrible," he told her, shaking and trembling. "My God, you wouldn't believe the dream I had. It was horrible."

"What happened?" Carol said softly, "you can tell me."

Johnny began recalling the horrible moments, piecing them back together, going through the nightmare's images and emotions. Carol continued to comfort him. Johnny realized he had to call home to check on Candy. It was too early to call right now because of the time difference. He went back to sleep drifting off in Carol's arms.

Johnny woke up three hours later. It was around 10 A.M., and it was another beautiful day in Paris, a crisp fall morning September 2002. He looked at his watch and decided to call his mother in a few more hours. He dressed quietly so he didn't wake Carol and decided to go get coffees and croissants. On the table was the paper with lyrics to the song they had written the previous night . Johnny looked at the words Carol transcribed. He turned the paper over and wrote her a note, 'Out to get coffee and croissants. Love you. Be right back'. Johnny looked at the note and wondered if he should have left out 'love you". He questioned his spelling of croissants; he had no idea how to spell the word and just gave it a guess. He realized he and Carol were moving fast but decided to go blindly into this love without reservation. He felt connected to her emotionally, spiritually, physically, and intellectually—it was more than he could have ever asked for. This was the love he was looking for he felt. True love.

Johnny went downstairs and the Indian man was back on duty. The desk clerk was a good reminder for him to slow down. Johnny said hello and exited the hotel to find a boulangerie. On every corner there was a one, with an even better pastry than the previous one.

Johnny walked to the boulevard and found Le Magique Pain de le Via. He opened the door and was greeted by the sweet fresh smell croissants coming out of the oven. Behind the bakery display case were dozens of fancy looking multicolored cakes, tartes, pastries and breads. He couldn't figure out what to order or how to proceed. He panicked. "Bonjour," Johnny politely said to the woman working. "Puis-je, s'il vous plaît deux croissant avec deux cafés...to go," He said, managing as best as he could with his thick English accent. He felt as though everyone would be looking and laughing at him. There were not, no one cared. The woman smiled at him and got him his order. He paid her and thought humanity's highest attributes were surely exemplified in its quest for better pastry.

"Hey, Johnny boy, my little American. What are you doing?" Yelled Carol from the hotel window half naked. Smiling and smoking.

Johnny looked up and smiled, went back into the hotel and quickly made his way upstairs. Together they drank their coffees, ate their croissants, laid around all morning, telling each other hidden secrets, they had waited a lifetime to share.

It was now three P.M., he decided it was a good time to call his mother. Carol went to take a bath, to give Johnny some privacy. It was nine A.M. in Boston. Johnny picked up the phone and called the front desk to get an outside line. He then dialed his mother's number. After several rings, she picked up.

"Hello?" she answered.

"Hello, mom?"

"Hello, Johnny, how are you? I am happy you called! I have been thinking about you a lot."

"I am great, really really good!"

"Shoo Cosmos off the table now! Sorry Cosmos was stepping on my new puzzle."

"Yes, it's great here Mom, I love it. I should have come here ten years ago. There is so much to see and interesting people to meet!"

"That's great, Johnny, just great. I am very happy you called." She paused and he could hear her lighting a cigarette.

"Yes, and I wanted to know how Candy is?" Silence. She began.

"Ok, there are two things I need to tell you."

"Yes, I am listening."

"Candy is in jail."

"Oh, shit…"

"Yes, she and Pete were arrested in a motel in Waltham. The police caught her with Stanley's stolen guns, cocaine, and heroin. They tried to sell the guns to an undercover cop. She's probably going to do at least five years in a woman's correctional prison. We can't afford a lawyer, and maybe it's the best thing for her. At least we will know where she is, and she will be alive."

"Oh, shit," Johnny repeated. Feelings of despair filled his body. "And what about Priscilla?"

"I have decided to take care of her. I don't know how but I am going to do it, I am. I went and saw a therapist, and I am going to continue with it. I need help and I am leaving Stanley as well. I was just like Candy when I was a young girl. It's no wonder she is the way she is."

"Wow, mom, that's incredible of you. I am really happy you are leaving Stanley. That's good!"

"Yes, it's long overdue. I should have left him many years ago. It's going to be difficult, but I can get assistance, do therapy and see Candy on the weekends. I have to be there for her. It's time for me to be honest. I am getting off the pain medication and doing yoga." She went quiet. "Now, the other thing I need to tell you. When you were here last time, just before you left, I was about to tell you something, but Stanley came home and was drunk, and you and he got into an argument. Do you remember?" she asked. He paused and remembered the argument.

"Yes, sure, I remember. Of course. What was it?"

"It's about your father. I need to tell you the truth."

"Yes, mom, you do. That would be nice."

His mother took a deep breath, "Johnny, I don't know how to say this, so I will just state it out loud. Your father is Jim Morrison."

"Stop it Mom, this is not the time for this, be real please" He stated. "I am being real, it's Jim

251

Morrison," She repeated. "WHAT? WHO ?" He shouted, becoming angry, "Are you serious? Jim fucking Morrison, the lead singer of The Doors? What the fuck, mom! I don't have the energy for this bullshit. Seriously, now is not the time to be messing around." He took another deep breath and put the phone down. What the fuck, he thought. He picked the phone back up.

"Let me get this straight. After all these years, you knew this, and you didn't tell me?"

"Yes, Johnny, I am sorry. Please forgive me."
Johnny let out a deep sigh.

"I don't believe it!" Why didn't you tell me before?"

"I was ashamed."

"ASHAMED? HOW SO?"

"I was nineteen and working as a go-go dancer at the Whiskey A GoGo club in L.A., and that's how I met him, Jim. I was living on the Sunset Strip at the time. The Doors were the house band, and we became friends. I would always see him at the clubs and parties. A few years later, we met at a record shop. He asked me if I wanted to go for a drive in his new car, and we spent the weekend together," she confessed letting out a deep breath, "we slept together."

"Why didn't you tell me! What the fuck, mom! All these years you've been hiding this?" Johnny began to get angry, "that's not right, mom!"

"I wasn't sure and was ashamed. You see, I don't know how to say this, Johnny, but I will. Jim took me to a party in Laurel Canyon and we did LSD," she paused again.

"And?"

"I was in an orgy, and there were a lot of famous people. I was young and impressed by them all, and you know it was the summer of love. People didn't have hang-ups about sex at that time."

"Continue…"

"I had sex with Steve McQueen, Dennis Hopper, Peter Fonda, and Jim, but I was in love with Jim. As the years passed by, I thought to myself, there was no way I would tell anyone this, but now I can't hold back the truth. Over time, it became more apparent to me that it was Jim. You looked more like Jim than the others, and I always felt in my heart it was Jim. I was in love with him, and we spent about five days together, so the chances of him were even greater. Then when you said you were going to Paris, I knew it was him. He died there and is buried at the Père Lachaise Cemetery. I tried to tell you last time you were here, but Stanley came and started the fight. There! Now you know! That's it," his mother said and let out a sigh of relief.

"Wow! I just don't know what to say, mom. I will start by saying, I am happy you told me. I am not angry. I understand, I do. It makes sense now."

"Really, you're not mad? You don't hate me?"

"No, mom, it makes sense. All of it."

"How so?"

"I don't know, but it does. All these songs I try to write and the fact that I am here in Paris and how I feel in my heart, I have always felt a sense of a guiding spirit and wondered that maybe it was my father. But, you say you had sex with other people? Who again did you have sex with? I want to get this straight."

"Dennis Hopper, Steven McQueen, and Peter Fonda."

"Why didn't you contact Jim?"

"I did. I told Jim I was pregnant, and he said he was going to Paris, and we would deal with it when he returned. He was going to Paris to get away from being a pop star and wanted to get serious about being a writer and a poet. He was hanging out with the wrong people as usual, and he couldn't get away from the drugs, but he was trying. He took some heroin and overdosed in a bathtub. That's how the story goes, anyhow. Then they buried him there, and just like that it was over."

"Wow, that's heavy Mom. REAL HEAVY"

"Well, there you have it. I told you, and sorry for not telling you sooner. I am going to be there for Candy and Priscilla and start being honest and make a real change for the better. You are such a beautiful son, Johnny, I love you very much."

"Oh geez, mom, I am going to start crying...stop it. Well, I need to hang up...for now. This was a lot. I will call you later and tell Candy I love her and she will get through this."

"Ok, Johnny. Thank you for understanding."

"For now, I do. I need to think about everything you told me. I will talk to you later. Love you."

"Love you too. Bye."

"Goodbye."

Johnny hung up the phone feeling exhausted and light-headed. He needed to sit down and think. Carol finished her bath and came into the room. Johnny looked at her and asked, "Who do I look like Dennis Hopper, Steve McQueen, Peter Fonda, or Jim Morrison?"

Chapter 28
Heritage

"Heritage"
Something that comes
or belongs to someone by birth

Carol looked at Johnny and smiled, amused by the question. Of course, we all want to look like someone famous, she thought.

"Hmm," she said, "let me see. For certain you don't look like Dennis Hopper or Peter Fonda because I know what they look like, I saw the film *Easy Rider*, and you don't look like either one of those guys. Steve McQueen, I don't know, I never saw his movies. In fact you do look like Jim, but even more beautiful than him." She smiled, jumped on him giving him kisses.

"Wait, you are not going to believe this," Johnny said in-between Carol's kisses. He took a deep breath and asked Carol for a cigarette. He began to explain what his mother just told him. For the next 30 minutes, Johnny shared the conversation he had with his mother. Carol listened intently and was surprised, amused and a little shocked by what Johnny was telling her. She could

256

relate and was happy for Johnny. At least he knew the truth and the truth will set you free, she told him. The shared experience of having your father taking from you, bonded them in a unique way beyond words. With Johnny, it was Jim's overdose, and with Carol, it was the communists overthrowing Vietnam; both their fathers were overthrown, overtaken, and consumed by a force greater than themselves. However, Carol's father Carl, managed to escape, but it was a mystery as to where he went. He could be out there, she believed.

"I don't know much about The Doors and never really cared for them, but it's kind of cool. My father is Jim Morrison, the lizard king. What a relief, finally, I know the truth!" Johnny said and started to sing in a crooning style, pretending to be Jim.

Come on, baby, light my fire
Trying to set the night on fire

"Ha!" Carol laughed, "you sound just like him!" She started to giggle and kissed Johnny. "That's a crazy story. Jean Yves is going to love this," she told Johnny, laughing.

"Who's gonna love what?" Johnny asked.

"My stepfather, Jean Yves, super cool guy. He's a big Doors fan. He loves Jim Morrison and has all his records."

"Really?"

"Oh yeah, if you want, we can go see him. You can meet my mother too."

"Great! I would like that. Let's go."

"Oh, and guess what?"

"I don't know. What?"

"Jean Yvesn, looks just like Claude Lelouche."

"Who is that?"

"You don't know Claude Lelouche?" Carol was surprised Johnny didn't know Claude. He was one of France's greatest comedians.

"No, I have no idea who he is."

"Oh, that's right. I guess he wouldn't be on American TV."

Carol explained who Claude was, while they got ready to go to the studio in Montparnasse to meet Carol's parents.

They arrived at the studio and parked the Vespa. On the sidewalk, in front of the studio, there stood a two-sided sign with hundreds of passport photos. The passport photos were of children from the quartier, and mostly used for student IDs. The studio advertised headshots for actors, models, and passport photos. Jean Yves was the photographer, and in his free time he pursued his passion of street photography. Carol's mother, Kim, oversaw the business aspect of the studio. Carol worked part-time there while pursuing her photography too.

Just before opening the door, Johnny turned to Carol and quietly told her, "Please don't say anything about Jim being my father." She agreed and understood his concern. Carol opened the door and they entered into a 60 square meter storefront that operated as a studio. On the walls were big photos of portraits and street scenes, and there was a big round table in the middle of the space. Carol's mother jumped up from behind a desk and came over to greet them. She was excited to see her daughter and meet Johnny, she gave them both a big hug. Kim, a middle-aged woman around 5'2 with short black hair and a big smile with inquisitive eyes. It was obvious to Johnny she came from Vietnam.

"Parle Français? Kim asked Johnny. Johnny would never have guessed Kim had survived such hardship coming from Vietnam and making her way to France. She had a glow of inner peace and walked with grace.

"Not yet no, but I will!" Johnny replied a bit sheepishly.

"Carol, you must teach him French," She ordered.

Jean Yves came walking out from the backroom and was happy to see Carol. He was wearing jean overalls with a blue sweater. He was a good-sized man with curly brown hair and round sunglasses, and he was just as content as Kim. Kim and Jean Yves made a fine example of a happy couple. This is what Claude Lelouche must look like, Johnny thought.

"Bonjour tous," said Jean Yves, he came over and kissed Carol on both cheeks. "Oh, the American is here," he continued, switching to English. "Carol already told us about you.

"Pleasure to meet you," Johnny said to Jean Yves.

"I speak English, so don't worry, you don't have to speak French. It is a good occasion for me to practice my English," He said with a smile and heavy French accent.

"Thank you,"

"Welcome to Paris," Jean Yves said to Johnny. He then jumped right into the current political happenings, "So, are we going to invade Iraq?"

"I don't know. I hope not," Johnny replied.

"This president Bush, is he mad? Does he refer to French fries as 'freedom fries' because France does not approve of invading Iraq?" Jean Yves asked looking to Johnny for the answer.

Johnny had a blank look on his face, he didn't know what to say. Kim came over with the coffees, rescuing Johnny from the question.

"Please, Jean Yves. It's not polite to discuss this at this time," She said.

"Of course, you are right. Excuse me, Johnny."

"It's crazy, and that's why I had to get out of that country. I needed a break from it all," Johnny confessed.

Carol jumped in, "Johnny is a musician, and he wants to learn about Jim Morrison and The Doors. I told him you know all about Jim Morrison and was a big fan." Carol looked at Jean Yves. Jean Yves was puzzled by the request but went with the flow.

"Yes," Johnny said, feeling the need to speak up. "I write songs and sing them in the streets. I want to do some of Jim Morrison's songs and learn about him, possibly. Carol said you're a fan?"

"Oui, je suis. I have all their records and all of Jim's writing. J'adore The Doors. I saw them in concert eight times and met Jim when he was here in Paris, just a few weeks before he died . Let's go to the backroom and we can listen to some records if you like"

Carol and Johnny followed Jean Yves behind a curtain while Kim stayed in the front of the studio. Jean Yves led the way into a decent size room cluttered with boxes, books, plants, cameras, a couch, a daybed, three shelves with vinyl records, a bicycle, a hot plate, and prints on the walls of expose, cultural events and museum shows. In the middle of the room was another big round wooden table and six chairs, just like the one in the front room. They had sacrificed all the space in the back of the studio for the front part, which was open . On the wall was a framed black and white print of the May 68' uprising in France, a man standing on a burned car throwing a rock. This caught Johnny's eye, he had heard about the revolution and was curious.

"What was May 68? Was it a real revolution?"

"Oui, exact. It was," Jean Yves answered.

"What were you protesting about?"

Jean Yves laughed at the naivety of the question. "A better life," Johnny was puzzled by the simplicity of the answer. Jean Yves continued, "Yes, we were not happy, and we wanted a better quality of life, so we protested. We were able to bring the country to a halt and talk about how to achieve a "bon vie" better life." Johnny was still quite astonished by the simplicity of what seemed logical for Jean Yves but unimaginable for him. Johnny nodded his head in agreement.

Jean Yves walked over to the shelves of records and took out The Doors' first album, *The Doors*. He slid the record out of the cover and inspected it for dust and scratches. For him, vinyl was like fine wine. He placed the record on the turntable and turned on the receiver. The record started to rotate and he placed the needle gently on the album. A warm familiar sound of pop, crackle, and hiss came out of the JBL speakers. The song "Break On Through To The Otherside" opened the record. A fast and furious tempo with bossa nova drum beat, kicking into gear right away with a powerful sound of an organ. Jim's opening line came next. It was sung with the force of a southern Baptist preacher.

> You know the day destroys the night
> Night divides the day
> Tried to run
> Tried to hide
> Break on through to the other side

Johnny's heart sped up. He was instantly swept off his feet by the energy and force of the hypnotic and magical music pouring out of the speakers. The song flowed forward like the rapids of a river, heading straight for a waterfall; you were in the song without a choice. Carol began dancing, and this amused Jean Yves. Johnny could see the love in Jean Yves's eyes; he loved her as much as his own child. Jean Yves then looked at Johnny to see his reaction to the music.

"YES!" Johnny shouted.

Jean Yves then started to explain the song, "It's fucking great! Jim is singing about a search for getting to the other side. The other side, to break free from the chains of reality, to where the freedom resides. He wasn't singing about a commercial breakthrough, that's for sure, but one of the endlessness of mortal time. Just listen." Jean Yves turned up the volume.

Made the scene
Week by week
Day to day
Hour to hour
The gate is straight
Deep and wide
break on through to the other side

"Je pense qu'il était un chaman," said Jean Yves quickly.

"What's that?" Johnny asked, not sure what Jean Yves had said.

"I think Jim was a shaman," Jean Yves repeated.

"How so?" asked Johnny, not sure what a shaman is but pretending to understand.

"He was acting as a medium between the world we can't see and the world we can see. At his concerts, he danced in a ritualistic way, connecting people to a world of possibilities. Healing the rupture of our true connection to our ancestors caused by modern life," Jean Yves told Johnny.

"Wow, you have thought about it," Johnny said, fascinated by Jean Yves' explanation. He wasn't expecting such intellectual discourse.

"Yes, I have thought about it a lot. Just listen to Jim, he knows what he is singing about. At university, I studied Arthur Rimbaud, Antonin Artaud, and Guy Debord, and when I met Jim, that's all we talked about. He was such an intelligent and soft-spoken young man,"

"Ok," Johnny agreed, feeling kinda dumb for not knowing any of the names mentioned.

The next song on the album "Soul Kitchen" began with a more powerful organ. It reminded Johnny of the organ at Saint-Sulpice. The song quickly shifted into a funky groove and a reference to time with the opening line.

"The clock says it's time to close..." Carol sang and grabbed Johnny to dance. He didn't want to dance.

"Not now, I'm trying to listen," he said to Carol as nicely as he could.

Jean Yves turned to Johnny, and said, "Jim is a poet, just listen to these lines."

Brain bruised with numb surprise
fingers weave quick minarets
speak in a secret alphabet
I light another cigarette

learn to forget, learn to forget

The third song "The Crystal Ship" began, and Johnny listened intently as Jim's sincere singing of a beautiful love ballad that suggested a world that one could easily imagine in Homer's *Iliad.* The sound went right through Johnny; he had goosebumps and his eyes began to water. Jim's voice was deep, sincere, and full of purpose with the piano, guitar, and drums following behind him. A slow love song swept through the room. Carol took Johnny's hand, and together they slowly danced. The song felt like it was just for them, made for this moment of being in love. Jean Yves took a minute to excuse himself to check on Kim in the front room. Johnny and Carol looked deeply into each other's eyes and floated to the music. Jim sang about this crystal ship taking them away.

Johnny was sure beyond any doubt that Jim was his father. There was a new feeling of happiness and security that overcame him, and he felt proud to be who he was. He feared it would soon wear off, but deep down inside him, he knew it wouldn't. Is this true happiness? he wondered. The song was full of sorrow yet was gentle and loving. Carol gave Johnny 'another kiss', like the lyrics in the song suggested.

Before I slip into unconsciousness

I'd like to have another kiss

Johnny felt like this was a sacred moment for him and Carol. Jean Yves came back into the room, and the record started to skip just as Jim went into the lyric. The skip repeated the lyric five or six times. Jean Yves promptly picked up the needle from the record and placed it on the fourth song, "Twentieth Century Fox". This song was fun, upbeat and retained The Doors' danger element. Whimsical, melodic, sporadic drumming, the signature organ sound, and of course Jim's poetic lyrics and crooning. The song was about a fashionable beauty queen from Hollywood, the kind of girl all the guys wanted to have but couldn't get. It made Johnny think about his own mother. Who knows maybe it was about her, he wondered. It would have been around the same time as well. He thought about the photos he had seen of her from that period, in her mini skirt with white go-go boots and a big hairdo.

Johnny stopped dancing and sat down to listen closely. Imagining the song was about his mother. He could see her dancing with her go-go boots and long brown hair flowing across her breasts, dressed in a mini skirt on top of a platform. He thought about what she told him on the phone about the party and the orgy with LSD. The more he thought about it, the more uneasy he felt. Who wants to think about that? he asked himself and dismissed the thoughts. The song ended with Jim's crooning.

"Got the world locked in a plastic box
She's a Twentieth Century Fox"

Kim joined them with a bottle of wine and four glasses. She handed the bottle to Jean Yves, who found a corkscrew and swiftly opened it. Jean Yves poured everyone a drink. The next song began with a pumping waltz organ and Jim belting out the words, "Oh, show me the way to the next whiskey bar".

"The Alabama Song," Jean Yves told them as he raised his glass to toast. They all then raised their glasses and toasted. "This is a fine drinking song. However, they didn't write," Jean Yves continued. "It was written by the German playwright Bertolt Brecht. It's a perfect cover song for The Doors as it's theatrical and wrecked in despair with clowning around in the atmosphere."

"Il est trés gentil," Kim said with a smile, looking at Carol and Johnny.

"What's that?" Johnny asked.

"My mother says you are very nice,"

Kim looked closer at Johnny, and in broken English said to him, "All your souls are together with you. You are a good man."

Johnny, slightly confused asked, "All my souls?"

"Yes, in Vietnam we believe we all have three souls. They are immortal and can travel in or out of the body. When the souls are in the body, they give it life. Some people have two souls outside the body and are not aware of their life. When all three are in the body, you are fully awake. You have all three in the body,"

"Really?" Johnny replied, surprised and delighted. "Ok, I can deal with that. Thank you."

"It's nothing. Welcome to our home, Johnny. We can see that Carol likes you. You must stay for dinner."

"I would love to."

Jean Yves smiled. He was joyful to share this moment with everyone. Side A of the album came to an end and Jean Yves went to the record player, "Shall I play the other side?"

Carol and Johnny screamed out "OUI!"

The next song came on and blasted from the speakers. It was "Light My Fire". There were more keyboards, hard drums, and lean guitar riffs with moody references to a wild romance.

Girl, we couldn't get much higher
Come on baby, light my fire

"They sold over a million copies the first year this song came out, and they were offered $100,000

269

for it to be used in a Buick car commercial," Jean Yves informed them.

"What?" asked Johnny, making sure he heard correctly. "To be used in a car commercial?"

"Yes," answered Jean Yves, and continued, "Of course Jim said no, they would never in a million years sell out. If there was one thing Jim stood for, it was that he did not compromise at all. Integrity was everything to him."

Johnny instantly felt guilty for selling his song to the prosthetic company. "SELL-OUT!" Shouted a voice within him. He downed his glass of wine, hoping the effect would wash away his conscience. He asked for another. SELL-OUT shouted the voice again. Jean Yves poured him another glass of wine.

"Are you ok?" Jean Yves asked Johnny.

"Yes, I am fine," Smiling and shaking off the voice in his head. For the next five minutes Johnny let himself get lost in the song's electrifying guitar solo.

Jean Yves cut in, "'Light My Fire' was a seven-minute song, quite rare for a radio hit song to be so long." The song ended and there was a pause before the next song. Everyone caught a moment of silence and realized how loud the music was. Carol was thrilled to be sharing this moment with Johnny. She looked at him and smiled. It was clear to see they were in love.

A thumping bass line came blasting from the speakers, with sharp and precise drum beats, accompanied by a loud church organ. The hip seductive song filled the room. "Back Door Man". A Willie Dixon blues song, 5th on the album. Carol continued to dance, and Kim excused herself to make dinner. Jean Yves continued to talk as if he was teaching a class on The Doors. He was happy to have a good listener like Johnny. Jean Yves took a big sip of wine and continued.

"What was so unique about The Doors is they were inspired by the blues, jazz, pop, and funk and maybe even the polka. Each musician came from a different perspective; Jim, a natural born singer with a baritone voice, who could reach a tenor range and also sing a soothing ballad. His love for philosophy, poetry, and mysticism added to the ideas and intensity to his singing.

Ray Manzarek the keyboardist, was classical trained who could play any style and improvise to Jim's antics and lyrics. Also appeared to be the adult in the band, looking at the others in a fatherly way, creating a safe environment.

The drummer, John Densmore, a jazz drummer at heart with a gift for simplicity, syncopation and meaningful dynamics. He knew just how to hit them, when , where and not. Never over playing.

Robby Krieger a gifted guitarist who understood the silence and spaces of the songs. Playing melodic riffs with rich tones, textures, slide techniques and Spanish Flamenco style combined with the blues. This mix came from the psychedelic music scene in L.A. It was the perfect mix, a perfect mix. Un chef-doevre" Jean Yves stated.

The next song that came on was "I Look At You". It was a catchy little rock-pop love song. Johnny put his glass down on the table and asked Carol to dance. The song reminded him that being in love was supposed to be fun, free, and innocent. They looked deeply into one another's eyes, held hands and spun around like little children. Jean Yves was happy to see Carol in love, it brought back memories of when he met her mother, Kim. She was taking courses at Sorbonne University, when they met and fell in love. They went out every weekend enjoying evening walks through Paris and spending hours in the Tuileries Gardens together. Jean Yves raised his glass and shouted, "PARIS, LA VILLE DE L'AMOUR."

The next song was, "Take It As It Comes". A straight-forward fast beat with heavy organ and Jim's preacher's voice. The song was about how to be in love, how to accept things as they are and to not get in the way of the process. Johnny felt the presence of Jim's spirit in his fatherly toned voice, as if giving him advice. At one point in the song Jim shouted and screamed, Johnny was now surely convinced he was singing directly to him.

> Time to live, time to lie
> Time to laugh, time to die
> Take it easy, baby
> take it as it comes
> Don't move too fast
> If you want our love to last

Jim's deep rich and hearty voice filled the room. Carol and Johnny stopped dancing to have a break and cigarette.

"I hope I could help you learn about The Doors," Jean Yves said to Johnny.

"Yes, you have. Thank you!" Johnny replied.

Johnny excused himself and went to the bathroom. When he came back, the song "The End" was starting. Carol had lit some incense, and Jean Yves was reading the liner notes on the album cover. They both looked up at Johnny as he took a seat at the round table. At once, the song's mood took Johnny hostage; he couldn't figure out what he was hearing and experiencing. He listened closely to the sound of the exotic guitar chords that mimicked a middle eastern guitar. The shaking of a tambourine gave the effect of a rattlesnake coiled and ready to strike. The song had a strong presence of something holy, sacred, alien or far out—it was ritualistic and uncompromising. The song proved that The Doors were most certainly living up to their name. If there was a door to pass through to the other side, it was through this song. This song was not like anything else that came from the flower pop and summer of love of the 60s movement. Johnny listened closely to Jim's voice permeating the foreign landscape of sound that the band created for him to sing in.

This is the end, beautiful friend
This is the end, my only friend
This end of our elaborate plans
The end of ev'rything that stands
The end
No safety or surprise
The end
I'll never look into your eyes again

The song made Johnny think of his childhood friend Teddy. Coming to Paris had stirred up many memories and one was how much Teddy had meant to him. Johnny had dismissed it all these years, as no big deal. It wouldn't stay buried any longer. He then thought about how cool his mother must have been to hang out with a guy like Jim. Johnny reflected on what Kim had told him earlier, about having three souls. Maybe my third soul is coming home now that I know who my father is? He wondered. Johnny picked up the album and looked at the cover. He saw Jim's face staring straight at him. No wonder I have been trying to write songs all my life, it's in my DNA. It was the only time Johnny felt the presence of his ancestry or real roots. It was strange, he could never pinpoint these feelings and fleeting vision, there was always a connection to something, almost like a mirage. He felt love from the spirit of his father.

The song continued and entered into a state of manic madness. Jim repeated the line "a friend" Like chaotic fragments of the subconscious and dream world-like scenes, and situations, all colored the song. The song made Johnny think about the statue outside of the opera, the dancing Bacchus "The Dance" with the tambourine, with naked angels holding hands. Jim continued singing in the background, "Driver, where are you taking us?" Johnny listened, as the music flowed with punctuating guitar chords. The song began to weave together a tapping sound of cymbals, and the organ's chords were drawn out, giving the sound a drone effect. It got weirder and weirder, and then Jim began to narrate about a killer getting up before dawn and putting on his boots.

"This for me is real surrealism," Jean Yves said, "we are in the dream of unconsciousness, freed from the control of reason, free from the normal values. It's art in the finest sense, but audio or performance art, like painting with music. It makes me think of Artaud and his sound work."

Johnny listened to Jean Yves and nodded yes. He was paying more attention to the song than Jean Yves. Jim continued narrating the song to what sounded like a murder scene.

The killer awoke before dawn
He put his boots on

Jim was retelling the events of a killer visiting his brother and sister, and then killing his father. You couldn't make out what Jim was saying about the killer approaching his mother, Jim's voice became muffled and screamed with agony.

Jean Yves interjected, "This is the Oedipus complex. Jim must have been reading Freud when he wrote this."

Johnny was surprised. He thought he was the only person who would dare sing about murder. His song "Electric Chair" had the same theme. Johnny felt proud and began to develop more respect and a deeper connection to Jim.

The song began to get chaotic and crazy, building to a crescendo. Kim entered the room, and Jean Yves jumped to the record player and pulled the needle off the vinyl ending the song abruptly. It was almost as if he wasn't allowed to be playing the song. What's that all about? Johnny wondered, confused by Jean Yves' reaction.

Jean looked at Johnny and whispered, "I'll explain later."

Kim told everyone dinner was almost ready and went back to the front room.

Jean Yves looked at Johnny and began to tell him what had just happened. "You see that song was used in a film about Vietnam, and every time she hears it, it brings back bad memories."

"Ok, I understand," Johnny said.

Jean Yves took the album off the turntable and placed it back into the sleeve and back on the shelf. He then thumbed through the albums and pulled out The Doors second album, *Strange Days*.

"You'll love this one," Jean Yves told Johnny. He put the record on the turntable. Kim returned.

"Ok, dinner is ready. Turn down that crazy music and let's eat," Kim said as she carried a tray with large bowls towards them. The bowls looked like they were filled with salad. The tray also had rolls and a big bowl of rice. Kim placed one bowl in front of each person and smiled. Jean Yves quickly came to help take the rice and put it on the table. He then got four glasses and a pitcher of water, and four sets of chopsticks. Carol was excited to see her favorite dish, Cao Lau, a pork noodle dish.

"You like that crazy music, Johnny?" Kim asked. "Not me. I think it's drug music." She started to laugh and continued, "You are skinny, you need to eat."

Johnny took the chopsticks and tried to use them; he fumbled, he didn't know how. Carol offered to help Johnny and showed him how to use chopsticks. Jean Yves offered to get Johnny a fork, but Johnny insisted on learning how to use the chopsticks and continued along until he got it enough to enjoy the dinner. Kim shared rice wine with everyone, and Johnny took a sip, and to everyone's surprise, he liked it very much.

The Doors played in the background as they ate their dinner. It was hard for Johnny to focus while the music played. He wanted to devote this time to listening to his father. He saw everyone talking but he didn't know what they were saying. He felt beholden to the voice and music coming out of the speakers, he would have preferred to lay back and listen.

"So, tell us, Johnny, where are you from?" Kim asked.

"I was born in San Francisco, then moved to Detroit and lived in Boston for most of my life," he told her.

"And now you want to live in Paris and marry Carol?" Kim said and laughed.

"MOM!" Carol shouted at her.

Johnny smiled and laughed along and said, "ok." Everyone took their time eating and feeling no pressure.

Carol asked Jean Yves if it was possible for her to borrow The Doors records to take with her to her flat so Johnny could listen and relax. Jean-Yves said yes. Johnny needed to know more about Jim. This new knowledge of Jim being his father came in waves, and it was hard to process. Is this really happening? Johnny thought.

"You said you met Jim?" Johnny asked Jean Yves.

"Yes, we hung out. We had a friend in common, Leo, we all hung out at the Café Rose. I met Jim when he was trying to lay low and clean up. It was the same for the Rolling Stones too, they would come to Paris when things got too intense for them back home. The life of a pop star was becoming too demanding for Jim and he was much too creative and authentic for mainstream culture. Plus he was upsetting the apple cart with his concerts, calling his audiences slaves and causing riots at his shows. He was starting to be a real threat to the status quo. From what I understood, he needed to get back to his real creative self, like the beat poets, so he came to Paris to work. Like Oscar Wilde, Jim was here in exile and faced prison time for some charges against him in Miami. There was even talk about him making a film. Still, he couldn't shake all the leeches who wanted to hang out with him for the money and drugs because he was very generous."

"I heard he overdosed, is that true?" Johnny asked.

"It's a bit of a mystery. There was no autopsy, and it was a closed coffin burial. He was dead and buried in three days. The story was he was out drinking at The Rock Roll Circus nightclub with his girlfriend, snorted some heroin, went home, took a bath, and died," Jean Yves told Johnny.

"He is buried here in Paris, right?" Johnny asked.

"Yes, he is at the Père Lachaise Cemetery on the other side of Paris. Some people believe he may have faked his death.

"Do you think he did?"

"I don't know. I do know he was crazy enough to and he had the money and the motive as well. He was most likely going to jail in Miami."

"Why was he going to go to jail?"

"They say he exposed himself on stage at a concert," Jean Yves said with a look of disbelief.

"Wow, they were really after him," Johnny concluded.

The music continued as everyone ate. It became apparent that Johnny was tired, and Carol suggested they get going. Jean Yves loaned ten Doors records to Johnny. He would be able to listen to them at Carol's on her turntable. Johnny and Carol thanked Jean Yves and Kim for a wonderful visit, gave them a big kiss and hug. They gathered up their belongings, and were on their way back to Carol's apartment.

Johnny and Carol quickly zipped back to her place. Johnny was happy to be back at the apartment where he could give his full attention to listening to the records and allow himself to feel closer to his father. Carol had an old RCA record player, she set up, and Johnny felt more at home than he had ever felt. They decided they would visit the Père Lachaise Cemetery the next morning. Johnny needed to see where his father was buried.

Johnny studied himself in the mirror with the album covers. He looked at the photo of Jim, and inspected his reflection, trying to see if there was any resemblance. Carol suggested they look at the reflection of him by candlelight. She believed the spirit of the person would be visible, by this method. She retrieved a candle and lit it. Johnny looked intently at the dim lit reflection. Taking a hard look at the photos, he had to admit that he looked more like his mother than he did Jim. At times he could see the essence of Jim in his eyes and then thought maybe he had Jim's mouth. One thing was for sure, Carol agreed he looked more like Jim than Dennis Hopper, Steve McQueen or Peter Fonda.

Carol placed Zeus the turtle on the table and started making drawings of him. Johnny rested on the bed and listened to the music; he was listening for hidden messages in the songs. He went back to the mirror and by candlelight observed the reflection. "Maggie M'Gill", a slow blues song. Johnny almost jumped out of his skin when he heard the third verse.

Illegitimate son of a Rock n' Roll star
Illegitimate son of a Rock n' Roll star
Mom met dad in the back of a Rock n' Roll car

Well, I'm an old blues man and I think that you understand
I've been singing the blues ever since the world began

Johnny couldn't believe what he was hearing. Jumping out of bed he ran to the record player and picked the needle to replay the verse. He dropped the needle in the same spot and yelled to Carol, "DID

YOU HEAR THAT?" Carol heard it as well and was just as surprised. They played the verse over several times. Johnny felt restless, and the song evoked emotions in him that he couldn't process. He felt confused, angry, and began to question his mother's sanity. He needed to call her and go over the details one more time.

Johnny called his mother and promised Carol to keep the call short, because of long-distance charges. Johnny's mother went over the details again. She stressed that she had told Jim she was pregnant. She had recognized that he was the father, and they had planned to do a test. He was very nice, she said. Johnny felt much better after the conversation. He hung up and told his mother he loved her. In the past, they never said 'I love you'. This was new. Things were getting better.

Carol put Zeus to sleep in his flowerpot, and she and Johnny crawled into bed and fell fast asleep in each other's arms. Johnny was anxious to get up early and visit Pere Lachaise.

Chapter 29
Picnic at Père Lachaise

Carol made crab salad sandwiches with cut carrots, grapefruit juice, and her favorite homemade brownies. She put everything neatly into a knapsack.

"What's all that for?" Johnny asked.

"We're gonna have a picnic at your father's grave,"

"Ok great!" He had never heard those words spoken 'your father' and he had never been on a picnic either. "You're the boss." he said.

"And you're bringing your guitar too. It's a beautiful sunny day,"

"You think so?" he asked.

"For sure, it's a good chance to write a new song. You came here to write songs, didn't you?"

"Of course I did, you're right."

Johnny was learning more about her and her instructive nature. It made him happy to be feeling what it's like to be in a relationship. She was showing him the way to make this world right. I need to write a song about her? he wondered. He thought of a title for the song 'the woman on the red scooter".

Maybe this would be his chance to finally write a love song. He hoped, but had no time for that now, he needed to get ready. Soon they were out the door on the vespa en route for the cemetery.

Carol pulled up to the curve, to the circular driveway in front of the cemetery's main entrance. Johnny surveyed the big thick stonewall. It was around 20 feet high and a few 100 feet long. He thought it looked like a fortress or something from the middle ages.

"Over 70,000 people are buried here, many artists including my favorite painter Modigliani," Carol told Johnny as she took off her helmet. "Come on, follow me."

She took Johnny's hand and together they entered through the enormous copper and wooden doors. Inside was an ancient village for the dead, with small groups of people wandering around. Hard to tell if they were sightseers or family members of the deceased. Overcrowded with decorated tombs, shrines, monuments, gravesites, dolmens, fresh and dead flowers. If there wasn't a tomb, there was a tree. The placement of the graves seemed to have no order, other than "a free spot". Maybe at one time it had neat rows, but over time, nature and government had changed that. "Pere Lachaise is overcrowded, everyone wants to be buried here." Remarked Johnny.

Little streets and pathways with twists and turns that followed the course of time. The sunlight was bright and there was much shade from the many green trees.

"I am surprised at how peaceful it is." Johnny remarked.

They walk aimlessly following the guidance of their intuition. Johnny asked the spirit world to guide him and to give him a sign, some kind of message of being close to his father. He wasn't sure what to expect, but he felt content and confident. They passed by Marcel Proust's tomb, Frederic Chopin, Balzac, and Eugene Delacroix. Johnny had heard all their names before but did not know exactly what they did. Carol shared little stories about each person as they passed.

They reached Modigliani's grave and stopped to rest. Carol took out her sketchpad and drawing pencils. She began to sketch Johnny in the style of Modigliani . She took her time with the lines. "Stay still and keep your head up, with hands on your knees," she instructed.

She was confident in her drawing skills. After 20 minutes of sketching and eyeing Johnny, she finished it with a captioned ; 'Johnny in Paris , with love, for you my dear Modigliani'.

"Let me see," He asked. She held up the simple drawing. "Wow that's really good!"

She signed and dated Carol Lam, September 27, 2002, and placed it on the tomb with a small rock on top of it. They held hands, sat in silence for a few minutes, then got up and continued the walk.

The next grave they came across was Edith Piaf. It was in pristine shape, polished marble and covered in fresh flowers. A small stone crucifix took up the top half . Edith was born in 1915 and died in 1963. Inscribed on the vase were the initials E.P., it reminded Johnny about Dotty and the conversation they had about dying.

"Do you think we die?" Johnny asked Carol.

"No, I don't. I think we transcend and move to another dimension,"

"But do you think we have our memories with us?" He asked.

Carol thought for a few seconds. Her nose flared more than usual, and then she said, "Yes, we do. I believe that. How about you?"

"I do now, why not? It's a nice thought, I have no fear of death when I think of it like that. So, yes, we take our memories with us. That is what believing is." He guessed.

Johnny picked up his guitar, Carol grabbed her knapsack, and they moved on. They could hear the sound of crows but couldn't see them. They were soon walking past Frédéric François Chopin and then spent a moment at Oscar Wilde's tomb. From there, they walked for another ten minutes and came to a bend in the road. They saw a group of people gathered around a tomb, as they got closer, they noticed it was young people. It looked like a hippie gathering. Judging by the eight or ten people hanging around, they assumed it was Jim's resting place.

"It's not as bad as the Mona Lisa," Carol remarked.

"Ha, what?" Johnny asked, confused.

"It's a joke. The Mona Lisa is in the Louvre, it's impossible to see because there are so many tourists in front of it."

They approached Jim's tomb, it was angled between four or five other tombs, almost hidden from the little street. It had the appearance of a teenager's bedroom. It needed to be cleaned, littered with tokens, trinkets, beer bottles, drawings, flower's and graffiti on the stone. Even the tombs next to it had markings of graffiti. Carol and Johnny squeezed into a little spot close to the head stone.

With them, sat four Italian kids, three boys and a girl, with mobile phones and cameras, talking and taking pictures, also an American couple sharing a hash pipe and an old hippie hanging about. The old hippie appeared to be a traveler. He could be American, but Johnny wasn't sure.

Johnny felt peaceful and calm, he wasn't seeing through his eyes but with his heart. The sun became brighter and brighter. Objects became more defined, and he began to feel a magic glow sweep through his body. His eyes glazed over with light tears and a smile appeared on his face. He felt a calm oneness and acceptance with all around him.. He suspected it was just his mind playing tricks on him, "So what he thought, let my mind do what it will do. I am here and this is where the journey has brought me".

"Thank you." He whispered to Carol.

She looked at him affectionately and smiled.

Johnny ran his hand along the marble stone. Reading the scrawled graffiti on it.; *Break on through, The End, I love you, Jim and moi, progress is a suicide, kill kill, I get high, make love not war, born to lose, god is dead and fuck the system.*

Someone had spray painted 'lizard king' in red. Underneath it two different messages had collided together to form one message, *Johnny what have they done to your sister? Ravaged and plundered and ripped her and bit her, stuck her with knives in the side of the dawn.* It was the lyrics to The Doors song "When The Music Is Over". Johnny didn't know the song and somehow his name was attached to it. Is this the sign he prayed for? He wondered. Is the spirit of Jim telling him to look out for Candy? he asked himself.

The Journey of Johnny Vincent

"This is a good time to write a song," Johnny said aloud. "Good idea" Agreed the hippie. Johnny pulled out his guitar and started strumming. The Americans offered their hash pipe to Johnny and Carol, but they declined. Carol made a seat on the ledge of the tomb and took out the sandwiches, carrots, and brownies.

"Hey, sing us a Doors song," one of the Americans asked.

"I would love to, but I don't know the chords yet. I prefer to make up a song here and now." Johnny replied.

"Go for it, dude," the old hippie added.

Johnny strummed an E minor chord. Returning to the song he had been trying to write before coming to Paris "World Gone Bad" inspired by "I Put A Spell On You" by Screaming Jay Hawkins. The song had been following him for months, maybe this was the right moment to finish it. He purposely began to sing in a low, slow voice like Jim's, pretending to be him. He focused on Candy, thinking about how the beat poets followed their stream of consciousness.

She grew up in the tall grass down by the river
After they took out all the gold and silver
Sleeping a floor cause she doesn't have a bed
Drinking water poisoned with led
My city is dying   and Candy is she is crying

She heard the news they're bombing Afghanistan
She doesn't know why, she doesn't understand
She needs ballet shoes and a doctor's note
Fever gets high without a raincoat
My cities dying, Candy she is crying

Carol started writing down the words as Johnny sang. The old hippie clapped. Everyone else ignored Johnny.

"I like it, keep playing. It's really good," offered the hippie.

Johnny continued to play and searched for more lyrics. Carol put the sandwiches and carrots on the stone and invited the hippie to help himself. Carol and the hippie began talking in French while eating . The hippie must have been around 65, was in good shape and his face lit up with every smile he made, which was about every 30 seconds. He had rosy cheeks and blue eyes with long silver hair, a red bandana for a headband and a big gold earring in his right ear. It looked like he was dressed for the 'summer of love' with a tie-dyed t-shirt and camping jacket and sandals.

He told them he was from Holland but now lived in Paris. His name was Steven and in the sixties and seventies, he was a folk singer in Europe. Johnny listened to them talk and continued to search for more words and chords. The other people in the group said goodby and were on their way. That left the three of them to enjoy the serenity of Jim's grave.

After 20 minutes, Johnny decided to go for a little walk, to finish the song and have a moment alone. He excused himself and took a pencil and piece of paper. He started to reflect on all that had happened in just the last 10 days. He thought about Boston, and how useless he felt there, without friends or happiness. He was starting to feel a new sense of gratitude, for the value and meaning he was discovering. It was beyond what he could have imagined. When he came back to the tomb, Carol and Stephen were talking about Jim.

"Jim's alive," the old hippie said.

Johnny looked surprised at Steven's remark. "Alive? What do you mean, alive?"

"Well, I don't know for a fact if he is buried here or not, cause like, dig it, it's a mystery man. But knowing the way Jim lived, he probably is buried here cause he pushed the limits. If anyone wanted to know what was on the other side and pass through the biggest door facing us all, IT WAS JIM MAN. The guy certainly had a death wish with the lifestyle he lived. But he lives on in his music and the cats he sang against ? Man, those cats were dead you know, the walking dead. So, if Jim's body is here, he still lives. Through the music man, through the music.

You dig what I'm saying?" Johnny and Carol both nodded in in agreement and the old hippie continued, "I wouldn't be surprised if Jim were in the south of France or the States. The music of The Doors was making it obvious for his listeners to see through the lies of society, but in a much deeper way than the Beatles or Stones. With The Doors it wasn't about a haircut, a style or trend. Reality has consequences and operates in other dimensions. Jim knew the freaks and madmen who run the world. He knew, they had no regard for humanity."

"How did Jim know all that?" Johnny asked.

"His father was a Navy Admiral for Christ sakes, in charge of the U.S. naval forces in the Gulf of Tonkin Incident, which sparked the Vietnam War." Carol looked at the old hippie and gave her full attention to what he was saying. The old hippie noticed Carol's increased interest. He continued, "Looks like Jim's dad helped start the Vietnam war. So Jim saw things on a higher level for sure. I am sure of this, dig it. I think his father was also in charge of the relief efforts for Vietnamese refugees after the fall of Saigon."

"Refugees?" Carol asked.

"Yes, in 1975 the Vietnamese refugee crises," Johnny and Carol looked at each other surprised at what the hippie was sharing. He continued, "So, yeah, Jim knew how the system worked and how it could only operate through the guise and reward of freedom. His music exposed that and he was gaining power. He had to get out. They were going to do away with him if he didn't."

"Did you know him?" Johnny asked.

"Not personally just through his music,"
They all looked at the big black letters JIM MORRISON written on the tomb. The hippie decided to leave and wished Johnny and Carol well. He picked up his bag and went on his way. Carol and Johnny were confused and excited about what he had shared with them.

"So, my grandfather created the events for you to be here? Is that correct? Did I hear him correctly?" Johnny asked Carol.

"I guess so, but he may have been smoking too much hash. We need to look further into it".
They packed up their things and headed on back to Carol's flat.

Chapter 30
Grave Digger

Johnny and Carol arrived back at her flat and fell onto the bed. Johnny held her close and she felt safe in his arms.

"Johnny, can I ask you something?" she whispered.

"Yes," he said.

"Do you love me?"

"Yes, I do and had been not knowing how to say it." He moved his body so he was facing her and looked into her eyes, "Carol I am in love with you. I have never felt so much for anyone ever in my life."

Carol looked at him closely and smiled and tears came to her eyes. She kissed him. "Oh Johnny I love you so much", she shrieked out in joy.

"Being in love is beautiful," he said to her. "You know what I love about you the most?"

"No, please tell me."

"I can't because if I tell you, it may go away. You will become conscious of it, and then it will lose its innocence."

There were many things Johnny loved about Carol. He loved the in-depth sincere look in her eyes that suggested another galaxy outside of this one. He loved her top lip, her eyebrows, her ears, her hair, and hands. He loved that she had a warm glowing spirit that surrounded her; it was like another world to her, and he couldn't explain it no matter how hard he tried. He truly loved all of Carol. He understood why Dotty didn't approve of love stories, to share it verbally would be giving it away. It had to be shared through actions. He feared if he told her all the little things he loved about her would evaporate. She may analyze it and that might kill it.

"The mystery of love. It's all we have, the only thing that matters. Let me look at you. You know you are beautiful," Carol said to him. She looked into his eyes, and they began to kiss while she caressed his face. He unbuttoned her shirt, and together they undressed and went under the bed sheets. Kissing and running their hands over each other's bodies all night, making love and staying in bed until the next day. Eighteen hours passed between their dreaming and love making. The only time they got up was when Carol woke to make veggie burgers, which they ate in bed.

Throughout the night Carol kept thinking about what the old hippie Steven had said about Jim's father being a Navy Admiral.

"Today at the cemetery, there was something that the old hippie told us," she said.

"Yes, he had a lot to say," he replied.

There was a pause, and she continued, "I came to France when I was one-year-old. When the communist took over the south, we had to leave right away. We were a part of Operation BabyLift, a mass evacuation of children. It was really close for us, my mother and I had to hide, and finally, we made it out. My mother was able to stay with me through the evacuation; many children were separated from their parents and went to orphanages. We were unable to get on one of the planes leaving, because there was such a demand all at once. An American businessman had chartered some 747 Boeing airplanes to get us out. It was very nice of this person ,who I have never met. I think one day I will find out who he was and visit him, to thank him in person. My father had to leave right away, and all documents of him were lost or destroyed. I just know his name is Carl Surgeon, and he was from Texas." She looked at him with a look he'd never seen before, a look of peace, confidence and timeless wonder. Everything was perfect and mature to her; her eyes were wide open and her posture was firm.

"Would you like to find your father?" he asked her.

"I don't know. Well, maybe." she said.

"You don't know?"

"He could try and find me, right?"

"I don't know. Maybe he has."

"You are right, yes. I want to meet him, for sure."

"I could help you if you want." He offered.

"Yes, maybe someday, that would be very nice. Could you take me to Texas?"

"Why not? I would love to. There are organizations that can help you find him. I am sure of it, especially now, with the use of the internet and the world wide web, it's the information highway. The information highway is supposed to link us all together. For sure you will be able to find him with the new technology," he assumed.

"Well then yes I guess, of course I want to know. Do you know how to use computers?"

"No I don't but I have seen people with them more and more, they are making them easy to use. Soon they will be everywhere". He said.

Carol got up and went to the window to smoke a cigarette and look at the stars.

"Come see the stars. It's beautiful, look!"
Johnny rose from bed, and together they sat at the window , looking up into the starlit night.

"Look, it's the Big Dipper," She said, pointing to the star formation in the sky. "See?"

"No, I don't. To be honest, I have never been able to make sense of star constellations. I just can't find them," He confessed. "I never admitted that to

anyone, I always pretended I could see them, but honestly, I can't. It makes no sense to me at all."
Carol laughed and pointed her finger to the different star formations, explaining which was which.

"I just don't see it, and I pretended when I was in school. I was always pretending. I didn't understand the math equations either," He told her, getting it off his chest.

"What do you mean? You didn't understand math?" she asked him.

"No, I didn't. I didn't understand English class or science. I am dyslexic, so things didn't really connect for me. I had to pretend I understood the lessons. It was a nightmare and incredibly boring. But even when it was explained to me, I just wasn't able to grasp what was being taught. It was a constant frustration, it left me feeling like a failure; I felt punished for it all the time. It's like trying to use a glue that doesn't stick, no matter how much you use it still doesn't stick. The only bright spot for me was writing songs and playing the guitar."

"That's horrible, Johnny. Didn't the teachers know?"

"Yes, but it was too late, they just didn't know what to do with me. My writing songs and playing guitar saved me, even if I wasn't good at it, it didn't matter. It was the only time I felt complete and whole."

"What? You are good at it, Johnny!"

"That's ok, Carol. I don't care if I am or not at this point. I only do it because it saves me, and it's what my soul calls me to do. I know this now, it's not about being good or bad."

"You're an amazing person. You are really special."

"I am really lucky to have met you, Carol."

"Thanks to Jack, the roller skater!"

They smiled at each other.

"Let's go back to bed," Carol offered, putting out her cigarette in the ashtray.

She turned toward the bed to see the flowerpot and check on her Turtle Zeus. She looked closely at him. He wasn't moving.

"Zeus, are you ok, my baby?" Carol asked and picked him up. He didn't move.

"Zeus! Are you ok? Oh no, he is dead. He is not moving, oh shit."

"Wait a minute. He may just be getting ready to hibernate for the winter. Sometimes turtles can appear dead but are alive," Johnny reassured her and continued. "Let's place him back in the pot and check on him in the morning. We should know by then."

"Ok, I hope so," She said and looked at Zeus closely, calling out his name. "Zeus, wake up!"

"Let's go to sleep," He suggested.

Together they returned to bed and fell asleep wrapped in each other's arms.

They woke up several hours later in the same position. It was a healthy deep sleep. Carol woke first around eight-thirty A.M. She got up from bed and went straight to see Zeus. He was in the same position as he was the night before and didn't move at all. "Johnny, wake up. I am sure he is dead," she called out. Johnny rolled over and slowly got out of bed to inspect Zeus.

"Oh no, he is dead. I am sorry, Carol. There is nothing we can do," He said, comforting her with a hug.

"Poor Zeus. He was such a good turtle. What did I do wrong Johnny?" she said, weeping softly. Johnny was without an explanation, he gave her a soft kiss. She dug a little hole in the flowerpot and placed Zeus in it and covered dirt over him. "Rest in peace, Zeus. May your spirit move on and travel through the universe. I was happy to know you. Thank you for sharing your time with us. Sorry if I did something wrong I did my best to give you love and a home."

Carol turned away from the flowerpot and went to make her and Johnny coffees and tartines with butter and jam. Johnny sat at the table thinking about Zeus, she returned five minutes later.

"I have to go to work soon," she said. "If you want, you can hang out. I will be back around five P.M."

"Yes, I would like that. I want to relax and listen to The Doors records and try to learn some of their songs,"

Carol paused and then said, "Why don't you move in? You can't stay at the hotel all the time. It's going to cost too much. Stay with me, ok?"

"Are you sure?" Johnny replied with a smile.

"Yes, why not?" she said with a bigger smile.

"That sounds great. I would love to. Only if you think it's ok. I will go get my things and return the keys and see Nick."

"Yes, it's ok. I want you with me." She stated. They kissed for a few minutes more, she got ready for work and left Johnny to himself.

Johnny took a quick shower, got dressed, and headed out to the hotel. Walking down the street, out of nowhere, Johnny heard, "President Bush shot dead!" The words echoed through the streets. Johnny knew the deal. No not this time, you're not fooling me. He said to himself. I'm not taking the bait and buying your paper. Soon Johnny was face to face with the seller, waving newspapers and shouting, "PRESIDENT BUSH SHOT DEAD!" His sales pitch was a gold mine, bating customers with bogus headlines. Johnny had since learned he had paid tuition for his two children to go to American Universities by selling newspapers. Johnny smiled at him as he walked by not taking the bait.

Johnny arrived at the hotel, and Vita was working at the front desk.

"Hey Johnny, how are you?" she asked, happy to see him.

"Hello, Vita. I am really good. Nice to see you too. I am going to check out today, so I came to get my things and return the keys."

"That's too bad you can't stay longer, but I understand you must move on," she said.

"I am going to stay with Carol,"

"That's good. I am happy for you, but you know you can see us anytime. We are always here," she assured him.

"Thank you. I will."

Johnny went up to his room and packed his suitcase with what little he had. He then closed the door and walked downstairs to find Nick, who was sitting in the lobby reading Shakespeare.

"Hello, Johnny! Have you heard? Something is rotten in the state of Denmark!" Nick recited loudly.

"No, I haven't. What's wrong with Denmark?" Johnny said amused.

"Nothing, it's just a quote from Shakespeare. You look good my boy! How are things since yesterday?"

"Getting better and better all the time. You wouldn't believe it! Knock on wood," Johnny answered, and bent over to knock on the table and took a seat.

"Ok. Please tell me my boy."

"You were right about asking the universe a question and the divine law stuff that you told me about. I know who my father is. I called my mother, and she finally told me."

"Johnny, that's great. I am very happy for you."

"Yes, you are not going to believe who it is."

"Really, why?"

"Are you ready for this?"

"Yes I am, please tell me."

"It's Jim Morrison. My mother had an affair with him in 1971, the year I was born. She didn't know how to tell me about it, but I won't go into all of that. Yes, Jim Morrison is my father." Johnny smiled and waited for Nick's reaction.

"Wow! That's incredible, Johnny. We never know how things work out. Life is stranger than fiction. I am happy for you because, well, I can see you are happy, and that's good."

"Thanks, Nick."

"That's Jim Morrison from The Doors, right? *The* Jim Morrison?".

"Yes, that's right."

"You know, you do look like him. Seriously, you do."

Johnny nodded in agreement and continued, "Jim is buried right here in Paris. Imagine that? Right here. It's sad he came to Paris to be left alone and work on his poetry. My mother told me that he was going to return to the states and most likely would have recognized me as his son, but he died."

Nick nodded and added. "That's right, I remember now. He was really big back then in the late sixties. We lost Janis Joplin and Jimi Hendrix, they both died that year too. Joplin overdosed on heroin and Hendrix of asphyxia while intoxicated with barbiturates. They called it the 27 Club. There was another rock and roller who died, but I can't remember his name. With Jim, there was a mystery around his death. Some people thought he might have faked his death to avoid prison."

"You think so?"

"I don't know, Johnny, but it is strange how an American can get quickly buried into the most famous cemetery in the world." Nick picked up his Shakespeare book and recalled, "It's written on Shakespeare's tombstone: Good friend for Jesus sake forebear, to dig the dust enclosed here, blessed be the man who spears these stones, and curse the man who moves my bones."

"Why does it say that?" Johnny asked.

"I guess Shakespeare was worried that someone would dig up his grave. His way of making sure no one would, I guess. In those days people would rob the graves. I think it's empty, just my feelings." Nick continued, " But I am happy for you that you finally know who your father is."

"Thanks Nick! And I am moving in with Carol. I came to say goodbye."

Nick eased his shoulders back, lifted his head and straightened his glasses on the ridge of his nose, and spoke in a firm and sincere tone, "It has been really nice to meet you, Johnny, and I do hope to see you again. I should be around for at least another week. Then it's back to New York." Nick reached for his wallet, searched for a business card, and handed one to Johnny. "Please feel free to call anytime if you are in New York City."

"I will, and it has been a real pleasure meeting Nick. Good luck with the film and thank you for your guidance. I will call you if I am ever in New York."

Nick leaned towards Johnny, reached out and gave him a good solid hug and smile. "Remember: Open your eyes and ears, solve the case in days, not years."

Johnny smiled and stopped himself before crying, picked up his suitcase and was out the door.

Back at Carol's, Johnny hunkered down for a good week concentrating on learning The Doors songs. It was nice to be in a real home with love and comfort. He played his guitar 15 hours a day and worked on his new song "Candy's Crying." He was convinced the song was going to be a hit, and more importantly, it dealt with current issues he felt were lacking in contemporary music. This was the song he was searching for and it could open doors into the music business and make him a lot of money. He told all this to Carol and she was excited for him. The question was how to get the song to the right people. In between working on his own music, Johnny learned several Doors songs, "Light My Fire", "Soul Kitchen", "Riders On The Storm", "L.A. Woman", "Crystal Ship", "People Are Strange", and his favorite, "Love Her Madly".

His connection to the spirit of his father ran through his blood. This is my true heritage, he thought. He began to sing with new vigor and sincerity, which he wasn't used to. His teeth-chattering had also disappeared. He felt important like he was somebody and didn't need to hide from the world anymore. He would catch glimpses of himself in a mirror or window and would be surprised at who he saw. The person he saw now looked like another person, a person he admired. He worried these new feelings would end because they felt too good to be true.

Johnny put his guitar down and looked at the little burial Carol had made for Zeus in the flowerpot. She had decorated the grave with a little wooden stick umbrella, the kind used for a cocktail. Johnny thought about Jim's tomb and the mystery around his death. He questioned his mother's sanity. Maybe she was mad, he thought. She had always been a little strange or just silly. Could I dig up the grave for a DNA sample? he wondered. That would be impossible and ridiculous; there is no way he could do that because some fan claimed to have had sex with Jim and had a baby. There were probably many other people who also thought Jim was their father, he said to himself. Johnny dismissed these negative thoughts of doubt and despair.

Chapter 31
Back Out on the Street

It was the first week of October. The leaves were beginning to fall, and the days becoming shorter and cooler. Johnny saw his first rainy day in Paris. He noticed people were beginning to bundle up for the fall temperature. The summer aura was gone. Life was getting back to its regular groove. People wore faces of discontentment as they sped around the city 'get out of my way' was now the Parisian vibe.

Johnny knew he would have to make some money to buy warmer clothes and prepare for the winter. The everyday reality of being a Parisian was becoming more visible to him. He was able to muscle his way through the streets, to find the good busking spots. He was doing good playing his new songs and plus The Doors songs. He couldn't believe how well The Doors songs suited him; they matched his singing style and he marveled at the mystery and pathos each song carried. He had never felt this way about cover songs before. Since learning them, it opened a pathway to his own songs, allowing him a command and objectivity that he didn't have before. This new dimension gave him room to breathe and he was able to explore his vocal range and playing technique. The street audience seemed to like his originals as well, and he had no problem making 500 francs a day, about 80 American dollars.

Johnny started helping Carol with the rent, and this allowed her to take time off work to pursue her photos. She would sell her photos while Johnny sang his songs in the street. Placing them against walls or Johnny's guitar case, it made for a good backdrop and scenery. Black and white photos of the Moulin Rouge dancers and Paris street scenes. She usually sold a few a day from 50 to 100 francs. Together they complimented each other. The ideal artist couple, her photos and his music. They rotated locations making sure to not outlive any welcome, keeping it fresh. They were having fun and it was working really well. Johnny couldn't help thinking that maybe Jim was coming to Paris seeking the same simplicity. Even though Johnny wanted fame and fortune, he knew in his heart that it couldn't get any better than this.

A few days later while playing at the Saint-Michel fountain , they were approached by the crazy vagabond Michael Jackson fan. It was the young man Johnny had met in the park during his first day. Johnny noticed him at once and hoped he wouldn't recognize him. The man, still dressed in the same clothes he was wearing when Johnny first met him, stood by waiting for Johnny to finish his song.

"Hey, I know you," the young man interrupted as Johnny finished singing. "You're the American. How are you?"

"I am good, how about you?" Johnny replied politely.

"Just amazing. I am amazing. I love this word, 'amazing'. In America, everything is amazing," the young man babbled.

This caught Carol's attention and she came over to him and smiled.

"Hello, I am Alex," He said to her. Smiling, revealing a missing tooth.

"Bonjour, je m'appelle Carol,"

"Oui! Je parle Francais. Je suis de France. Moi, je m'appelle Alex."

Johnny began to look uncomfortable with all the French being spoken as Alex and Carol noticed and switched back to English.

"I met this guy in the park," Alex confessed to Carol. Alex then pulled out a pint of Southern Comfort from his back pocket and raised it in the air. "To Michael Jackson, the best singer in the world. Billie Jean is not my lover!" He then took a swig and offered some to Johnny and Carol.

"No thanks," Johnny said with a deadpan expression.

"I'm all set too," Carol added.

Johnny went back to focusing on his guitar and hoped Alex would leave. Instead, he chimed in, bringing up the Billie Jean song again.

"Play Billie Jean, the best song ever to exist," said Alex as he started to sing the song and moon dance like Michael Jackson. "She was more than a beauty queen from a movie screen…"

Johnny sighed and again hoped Alex would leave, but he understood this was the way it was sometimes when you played on the streets; you have put up with people and situations you don't really want. Alex continued to sing.

> Billie Jean is not my lover
> She's just a girl who claims
> that I am the one
> But the kid is not my son

All of a sudden, the words grabbed Johnny by the throat, and he became irritated.

"What is that? What did you just sing?" Johnny demanded.

Alex went on to sing the verse once again. Johnny didn't like what he was hearing or feeling; he felt like a fool and his blood ran cold. He felt like he could faint. A voice fumed in his head, a voice that didn't belong to him, a voice that only he could hear. "My mother is a Billie Jean type. "My mother is a Billie Jean type" Screamed the voice in his head.

"My mother is a Billie Jean type!" Johnny announced as his face melted in disgust. He felt as though a thousand fingernails were being scratched on a blackboard as Alex the madman sang. "Billie Jeans not my lover".

"Stop! Stop! Stop!" demand Johnny, ordering him to leave.

"Just get out of here, please!" Johnny shouted. Carol could see Johnny was getting upset and was trying to understand what was going on.

"Easy," Carol comforted him.

"Ok, hey, I am sorry, You Americans really get mad for nothing, don't shoot" Alex gasped as he took another swig from his Southern Comfort .

"Let's drink to Janis Joplin," Alex drawled and continued, "she loved Southern Comfort. To the great Jimi Hendrix and the eternal Jim Morrison too. The 27 club. Cheers."
Johnny became even angrier.

"Come on, let's go,! " Shouted Johnny. "I have had enough for today."

"Hey, alright. I'll leave you guys alone," Alex huffed.

"Sorry," Johnny mumbled. "It's not your fault. I am just having a bad day."

"Sure...sure, pas de problem," Alex replied.

Johnny and Carol packed their belongings and found a nearby park. Johnny needed a quiet place to tell Carol what was happening and why he was so upset. They sat down on a bench under a cherry blossom tree. Johnny put his head in his hands in disbelief.

"Oh no, Carol. Why? Why?" he cried.

Carol ran her fingers through his hair and caressed his brow. "What Johnny? What is it?"

"The song the guy was singing is about a woman who claims she had an affair with Michael Jackson AND had a baby with him! You see now?" She thought for a minute.

"Ok, yes, and you think your situation is similar to your mother and Jim Morrison?"

"Yeah, it could be. My mother is kinda crazy, and maybe it would have been better if she didn't tell me. I feel like some kinda offspring from a fantasy of a madwoman. She was probably a crazy fan. All famous people have someone claiming to be the child of them"

Carol countered quickly, trying to make Johnny feel better, "But your mother told you the truth. She wouldn't make something like that up. Seriously, Johnny, would she?"

"Who knows, but maybe I was better, not knowing. Do you know how many women have fantasized about being with Jim? Probably millions. I am going to need some proof."

Johnny's teeth started to chatter.

"Are you cold?"

"No, it's something I do when I get nervous. It's an old bad habit. It's nothing."

Johnny began to feel better after a 20 minute time-out. They left the park and walked for 10 minutes. They found themselves in front of the famous Shakespeare bookstore. Built in 1919 it had seen lots of important writers, Ezra Pound, James Joyce, and Hemingway just to name a few. Above the sign it was written, "Be not inhospitable to strangers lest they be angels in disguise". The bookstore was built a 100 meters or so from Quai De Seine. It was a four-story building alongside a few gothic-style buildings with stained glass windows, and weeds growing up the walls. Benches and flower boxes with a shrubbery created the setting to feel and look like a country medieval cottage. It looked like a place where Shakespeare himself would have visited. Together they sat quietly on the bench, taking in the surroundings, feeling the October day, trying to forget the Billie Jean song. The moment of silence they created, was enough to permit the synchronicity of life to do its part.

"JOHNNY! How are you, my brother?" a voice called out from behind the shrubbery.

Johnny and Carol turned to see Balu in his usual rap street clothes. With him, another man who looked to be about the same age, about 6'4 and could have been a bodybuilder, wearing jeans and a black leather jacket.

"It's good to see you. This is a tre bon surprise, ooh la la. This is my cousin Bazuba." Balu yelled out. Balu introduced everyone and continued. "He's the guy I was telling you about."

"Pleased to meet you," Bazuba said, and shook Johnny's hand and gave Carol the customary two cheek kisses. "My cousin Balu speaks very highly of you. He said you're like a brother,"

"Thank you, Balu, is like a brother to me too." Johnny stated.

"You look upset," Balu observed, taking a closer look at Johnny.

"Maybe we can go get a drink and I can explain if you have the time," Suggested Johnny .

"Sounds good. I know a place close by. I have some bad news too," Balu confessed.
The four of them left the park and headed towards The Hundred Dreams Café.

The café bar was quiet and looked like a British pub. With stone walls and no windows a hangout for Sorbonne students. They sat at a table and ordered a pitcher of sangria. Carol excused herself and went to play some music on the jukebox. She put a few franks in and the music started. "Les Rita Mitsouko" came over the cheap speaker.

"What is the bad news?" Johnny asked Balu.

"My brother is dead…" Balu said and began to weep.

Johnny offered condolences. Balu thanked him.

"It was a shock, I got the news this morning. That's why Bazuba is here. We still don't know what happened. We're waiting for more news. It's related to the elections for sure,"

"That's horrible," Johnny said. "What was his name?"

"Mosi. He was much older than me, one of my father's first sons with his first wife. I didn't know him very well, but we had met two times,"

"I knew him very well," Bazuba added.

Bazuba looked at his portable phone, anticipating it to ring with the details of Mosi's death.

"Bazuba is a bodyguard," Balu confessed.

"Yes, that's right, for many famous American actors. If they come for the Cannes Film Festival, I might work for them," Bazuba divulged.

Carol smiled and asked, "Which ones?"

"Woody Allen, Brad Pitt...but don't tell anyone, I am not supposed to share these details."

The pitcher of sangria arrived. Carol poured everyone a glass and they made a toast to Balus' brother. " To Mosi" Balu expressed.

Balu then turned back to Johnny, and asked, "So, what is bothering you? My brother?"

Johnny took a deep breath, gulped down some sweet punch and said, "I found out who my father is."

"That's great! Yes? Is it not good?"

"Well, yes, but I can't be certain. I just can't be one hundred percent sure if it's him. My mother claims it's Jim Morrison, but I am not so sure."

"Just ask Jim," Balu sputtered, not knowing who Jim Morrison was.

"Yeah," Bazuba added, trying to feel involved in the conversation.

"Well, that's not so easy, you see...Jim is dead," Johnny told them.

Johnny proceeded to explain who Jim Morrison was. How he died and was buried at the Père Lachaise cemetery in Paris. He told them the exact details of what his mother told him. They both looked at Johnny, bewildered.

"You must get a bone from his grave so you can do a DNA test and find out!" Bazuba blurted out. Balu broke out laughing and ordered another pitcher of sangria. He knew when his cousin said something like this, he meant business. Balu knew what digging up a grave entailed and laughed as he drank.

The drinks were tasting good, they were getting a nice buzz, feeling relaxed. Even though Balu had lost a brother, a brother he hardly knew, he was still in good spirits. "It's simple. Let's go to the cemetery, dig up the grave and just take a bone, then you can do a DNA test," Balu declared .

Balu had adventure in his eyes. He was the kind of person who was passionate about the search for the truth. The truth in itself was the object. The situation is not so much. Truth for the sake of the truth, was his perspective. He operated in another dimension and welcomed a situation such as this. It meant action and tangible results. He continued, "There is a special meaning for me meeting you. I have never met anyone like you, and I must do something to help you on your journey. I think my God wants me to. If I can help you find your father, then I must. It's no problem for my cousin and me to get a bone from a grave. I can call another cousin of mine, Udo. You will like him. He is a real peaceful guy. He has a construction company, and he can get us in his truck and take us to the cemetery". Balu had a plan.

"Do you think it's bad luck?" Johnny asked.

Balu thought for a second, and responded in a confident tone, "If it's your father, how can it be bad? You just need a bone to get a sample. Your motives are honest and sincere. We can ask the spirit of your father when we get there."

"The cemetery has a big wall surrounding it," Johnny said scratching his head.

Balu laughed and added, "You don't know my cousin." Bazuba smiled and gave Balu his phone. Balu dialed his cousin. "Hello, Udo, ça va? C'est moi, Balu...oui, très biens. Je suis au Café de Cent Rêves avec mes bon amis et aussi Bazuba. J'ai besoin de ton aide. Apportez votre camion et venez nous chercher. Merci mon frère. Ok vingt minutes. A toute l'heure." Balu hung up the phone and handed it back to Bazuba with a smile. "Hang tight, lets enjoy the moment. It's all we have. Udo is on the way."

Carol went for another pitcher of sangria. When she came back, she took out her camera and photographed everyone. Johnny posed with Balu and Bazuba, they clowned around together and Carol clicked away capturing the fun moments. Johnny thought of the photos of the Beat Poets he had seen at the Hotel. Would these photos be hanging on a wall somewhere in the future, he wondered. After 15 minutes, Johnny paid for the four pitchers of sangria, and they all left to go outside to wait for Udo to arrive.

Udo arrived ten minutes later in a mid-size white truck. He pulled up to the curb and stepped out from the truck. Medium build without an ounce of fat, wearing jean overalls, a t-shirt, wild dreadlocks and a big smile with a gap between his two front teeth. He gave Balu and Bazuba bear hugs. Udo then placed his right hand on his heart and nodded towards Johnny and Carol, expressing a greeting. "Good to meet you," he said to them. Udo seemed to be filled with gratitude or high on something; he had a sparkle in his eyes that was ready for anything. "Let's go," he insisted and Carol took some more photos of Johnny and his new friends.

Everyone agreed to meet at the cemetery. Carol and Johnny decided to go on the Vespa. Johnny put his guitar in the back of Udo's truck and noticed a toolbox, shovels, pickaxe, and ladder.

Johnny and Carol arrived first at the cemetery and parked by the front gate. It was 11 P.M. dark and quiet. Johnny looked around and at the wall, it was way too high to climb and plus there were too many lights. They could easily get caught, he thought. A few minutes passed, and then Udo arrived and parked at the end of the wall. Johnny and Carol walked over to meet them.

"We must look for a side entrance, a door where the workers enter. Let's go this way," Balu instructed everyone.

Bazuba and Udo reached into the back of the truck and pulled out the two shovels and a pickaxe. Together they walked for about a 100 meters alongside the wall, then took a sharp left turn for approximately another 50 meters. There they came to a 15 foot chain-link fence with barbed wire at the top. This is going to be impossible to get over, Johnny thought. They all continued to walk, and finally, they came to the side door, the service entrance. It was a normal-sized wooden door, but it was locked and needed a code. Udo looked at it closely and then looked at everyone and gave a big smile showing the gap in his teeth. His eyes lit up with assurance and confidence. He gave the door a straight push with his foot, and to everyone's surprise, it opened without a problem. "How did he know that"? Thought Johnny. This was easier than what anyone had anticipated.

They entered and closed the door softly behind them. Shadows from the trees and gravestones gave it a feeling of being in a forest. In a single file they followed each other closely. Walking as quiet as they could, like children sneaking out of the house after dark. The pitch-black night made it difficult to see. Trees rustled in the wind and the city noise was far off in the distance. To Johnny's surprise it was more peaceful than imagined. The ghosts were asleep and everything was in its place.

A path led them to a driveway in front of a barn and a house. The lights were on in the house. "There's a security guard," whispered Bazuba, pointing at the house window. Johnny motioned for them to follow him. He took the lead, trying his best to remember exactly where it was. Carol pulled Johnny's arm, and they followed her instead. She remembered where it was.

"Right over there," Carol said, pointing to Jim's grave.

Johnny recognized the grave site and made his way between the 2 other tombs. They arrived at Jim's tomb. Balu turned on the flashlight and pointed it at the grave, to see 2 empty Jack Daniel bottles with sun flowers sticking out of them, the casing with dirt, littered with fan letters and memorabilia and the head stone;

JIM MORRISON

DECEMBER 18, 1943 - JULY 3, 1971

Bazuba cracked his knuckles ready to do some digging.

"Want me to start ?" Udo asked.

"Ready when you are," Balu asked, looking to Johnny for direction.

Udo held out his hand and motioned everyone to stop and listen. In the dark, they could see he was feeling fearful. Something wasn't right.

"I can feel his spirit. He is with us," Udo warned.

Johnny looked into Udos dark face and lit up eyes, for confirmation. "It's ok, you can do it" Udo advised. Johnny grabbed the shovel.

He thrusted it into the soil. Scooping up a big full scoop of dirt. He dropped to his knees, tossed the shovel to the side and plunged both hands into the dirt. At the foot of the grave, he kept digging with hands, clawing and scooping. Everyone was surprised that Johnny was going to dig it by hand. He soon tired out and imagined the rest. On his knees with fingernails sore with dirt, he imagined.

Opening the coffin and facing his father's skeleton, wearing leather pants and snake skin boots, like he dressed on the album covers. He imagined taking the boots, and a rib bone for the DNA test, the boots would be for compensation for his absence. He continued the scenario in his imagination. What if the coffin was empty? he would be the only one to know Jim faked his death. If that was so, he vowed to keep the secret to himself.

Everyone watched and anticipated what Johnny was going to do next. Johnny looked up to the dark night and spoke.

"The bones of my father are of me. I am the bones of my father," He repeated.

Johnny was becoming more intense and seemed stuck to the ground with his hands in the dirt.

"Are you ok?" Balu asked.

"Yes, I am," Johnny mumbled. He started to sober up, speaking slowly and quietly. "We cannot do this. This is crazy! We must respect Jim's resting place. Let it be as it is."

Carol placed her hand on Johnny's shoulder. "It's going to be ok, Johnny, don't worry. I know how you feel"

"I can't walk in my father's shoes," Johnny put his head in his dirty hands and started to weep.

"My brother, you are not alone. I knew you wouldn't dig up the grave, but you needed to make this choice. We will leave you and Carol to be alone. Have this time together with the spirit of the father." Balu said.

"Thank you, Balu, Udo and Bazubi," Johnny said quietly.

The two men looked at Johnny and put their hands to their hearts, and then disappeared into the darkness.

"Talk to you tomorrow," Balu said to Johnny and then followed his cousins.

Johnny and Carol sat at the foot of the grave, staring at the tombstone. Carol rested her head on his shoulder. They sat together quietly in the darkness of the night.

"Maybe we should go to Spain for a month. I can play in the street, you can sell your photos, sound good?" Johnny whispered.

"Sounds good, my love. Je suis avec toi mon amour."

THE END